Falling for a ROCKSTAR

Falling for a ROCKSTAR

MICHELLE MANKIN

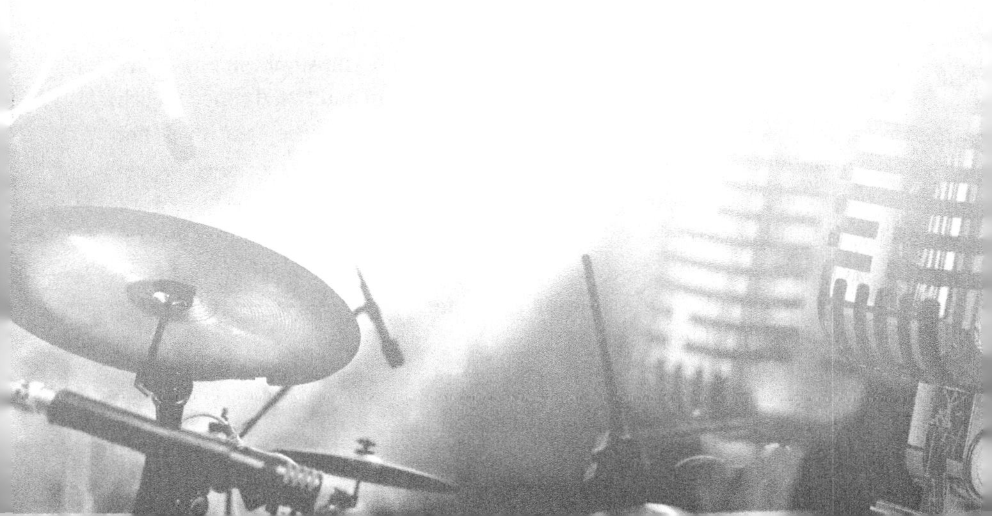

Falling for a Rockstar

Formatting: Elaine York, Allusion Publishing
www.allusionpublishing.com
Cover Photo by: Wander Aguiar Photography

Falling for a Rockstar: 7 rockstar romances

In the mood for a rockstar romance? How about seven rockstar romance books? This new collection by New York Times bestselling author Michelle Mankin features seven bestselling rockstar romance samples. 298 condensed pages from each of the hot, romantic, and full length rockstar romances featured in the eBook. This sampler of Michelle Mankin's most popular books begins with a rockstar prince who is tired of wearing his crown and ends with a very sexy rock club that everyone is talking about.

The novel samples included in this collection are:

The Right Man
Southside High
Hot Summer School Night
Oceanside
Find Me
Strange Magic
Rock F*ck Club

The RIGHT MAN

About the Book

Rush McMahon is one of the biggest rockstars on the planet. Handsome, talented, and famous, he has his choice of pretty women. After finishing another successful tour, he should be on top of the world. He pretends to be, but he's not. How can he be anything but miserable when his brother just married the woman he once loved?

Jewel Anderson is desperate and all alone in the world, except for her impulsive roommate Camaro Moltepulciano. She's hungry. The rent for her tiny apartment is overdue, and Cam just gave the last of their money away to someone less fortunate. Jewel has a heart of gold like her best friend Cam, but hearts can't be traded to pay for rent. Since both refuse to return to the homeless shelter where Jewel was almost assaulted, what can two nearly destitute women do?

Rush is a bad boy lead singer living a lie.

Jewel is a good girl at the end of her rope.

He is her last option.

She might be his only hope.

What happens when Rush and Jewel meet on a dark street corner in LA?

Can a chance encounter between two people from opposite worlds lead to happily ever after?

The Right Man is a modern-day retelling of Cinderella by New York Times bestselling author Michelle Mankin.

"Think Cinderella meets Pretty Woman. It just made my heart sing." Lexxie Lin, Un Conventional Bookworms.

"Blew me away. Loved it." Carly Phillips, New York Times Bestselling Author. Do you believe in fairy tales? In happily ever after? In love?

PROLOGUE

"Tell me about Cinderella again, Gran," the little girl asked Alice as she reached to switch off the lamp.

"It's time for bed, sweetheart."

"Just one more time. Please." Jewel blinked her big golden eyes. "I'll go right to sleep afterward. Promise."

"All right." Alice's expression softened. Her granddaughter was the apple of her eye, and she could hardly refuse the child anything. Carefully, she tucked the ruffled pink comforter she had sewn for Jewel around her. "But how about a different love story this time?"

"Another fairy tale?" Jewel lisped through her two missing front teeth. She was about to start second grade, not yet ready to set aside the happily-ever-after endings of her favorite childhood stories.

"Much better than that." Alice smiled, and nostalgia warmed her heart. "A real love story. The story about how your grandfather and I met."

"Oh, goody." Eagerness bloomed in the seven-year-old's peaches-and-cream complexion.

"All right. Once upon a time—"

"That's how all good stories start," Jewel said with a knowing nod.

"Yes, you're right, and this is a good one. The very best." Smiling, Alice stroked her granddaughter's silky hair. This nightly ritual was her favorite part of the day. "Once upon a time, there was a fall celebration in our little town, and everyone received an invitation. I just had to go. You see, there was a handsome boy who had caught my eye."

"Granddad?"

"Yes, precious one." She patted the girl's small hand. "My best friend, Pauline, told me he and his friends were planning to attend. But there was one problem. I had nothing to wear."

"What did you do?" The little girl's auburn brows knitted together. "Did you wish for a gown from your fairy godmother?"

"Wishes are the seeds of desire within your heart. Sometimes to make them come true, you have to plan and take action. I knew Pauline's sister was my size, so I borrowed a dress from her."

"And you went to the dance in an enchanted carriage?"

"Nothing quite so fancy." Alice chuckled. "I went in a rusty old farm truck."

"Oh." Jewel frowned, and her bottom lip jutted out.

Drawing her granddaughter back into the tale, Alice waved a hand in the air as if to sprinkle stardust. "Nevertheless, the night had plenty of magic. Excitement buzzed in the air. Fireflies twinkled in the field like fallen stars. Streamers fluttered from the barn's rafters. The tables were laden with delicacies fit for any princess. I brought my mother's famous peach pie."

"That's my favorite!"

"I know, sweetheart. When I set the plate down, I looked up and immediately found him. Your grandfather stood so tall, head and shoulders above the rest of the crowd. So handsome in his crisp white shirt and pressed jeans, he marched straight to me. People cleared out of his way as if he had given them some silent command."

"And then what happened?" Jewel asked.

"He stopped in front of me and said, 'I'm Eli. I've seen you around town.' And I told him, 'I'm Alice. I've seen you around too. I like your blue eyes.' Then he said, 'I like your honesty, Alice,' and smiled at me, a smile so big and bright, it melted my heart."

"Did it hurt when your heart melted?" Jewel asked, her button nose scrunched.

Alice laughed. "No, dear. It means it felt warm and happy. So then your grandfather said, 'I have to confess something. I only came to the party tonight to see you. You're pretty and sweet, and I've been watching you and hoping to meet you for some time now.' Then he held out his hand, and I took it without hesitation. When his fingers closed around mine, I knew."

"What did you know?" the little girl whispered, her eyes as big and round as a harvest moon.

"That he was mine. That I was his. That he was gentle, kind, and everything I needed."

"How could you tell?" Jewel asked.

"Because his steady gaze was true, and his grip was sure. Because he was considerate. Because while we danced, he told me his plans for the future, and how he wanted me to be part of it. And then he asked me to marry him."

"After one dance?" The little girl's expression turned wistful. "Just like Prince Charming in Cinderella."

Alice nodded. "Your grandfather was a simple farmer, just like his father and his grandfather before him. The passing of the tobacco farm from one generation to the next was the only part of his life that resembled royalty. He worked hard from sunup to sundown every day to provide the necessities we currently enjoy: food, clothing, and shelter. But the very best thing he gave me was his love."

Cupping Jewel's cheek, Alice said, "Through that love came your mother, and then you. Carriages, castles, and crowns are fun to dream about, my darling, but having all that finery won't make you genuinely happy. Only real love will. Real love will stay by your side, through thick and thin. Real love will make the good times better and the bad times bearable. Use your head to find love like that, Jewel, and trust your heart to do what's right to keep it."

Jewel nodded. "I know."

Surprised, Alice chuckled. "Is that so?"

"Yes, Gran." The girl studied her grandmother for a moment. "I know because you've shown me."

"I hope so, sweet girl. I hope you don't forget, and that my example is enough. I hope you never have to learn the hard way about how difficult life can be."

"Like my mother?" Jewel's lip trembled.

Alice studied her granddaughter, surprised by the clarity of the child's perception. She'd mistakenly believed Jewel had been too young to remember the circumstances of her life before her grandmother had adopted her.

"Beauty is reflected in honorable actions, not pretty promises, not in what a person has or how they look on the outside." She took and squeezed her granddaughter's hand. "And the right man—a good man—is one who will look at you with love in his eyes. He'll listen. He'll be gentle. He will show he cares by the changes he makes in his life for you."

Alice smiled bravely, blinking back the tears that threatened at the memory of her Eli, and gave her granddaughter the best advice she could.

"A good man's arms, not a castle, will be the most perfect home you will ever find."

Chapter ONE

RUSH

Naked and on my side, I was being worked over by three curvaceous women in the middle of my hotel bed. I weighed the supersize tits of the babe in front of me, not sure if they were fake or real, while the chick who pressed into me from behind ran her manicured nails around my nipples.

Guys who tell you that isn't a turn-on? They're fuckin' lying.

Tension built inside me as the third woman worked my cock. She knew what she was doing. Determined, she kept at me as I lengthened in her hand, not stopping even when I was distracted by a phone call from my drummer, Jack Howard, about another argument between him and my bassist, Benton Kennedy. My bandmates had been at each other's throats the entire week, ever since Ben had been busted having phone sex with Jack's wife.

I didn't get the constant competition between them. Maybe the rivalry arose from their different backgrounds. Jack had been raised in an abusive low-income home, while Ben had a privileged upbringing where his physical needs were indulged but his emotional needs were ignored.

But why poach another guy's woman? There was plenty of unencumbered snatch on the road.

Groupies at the venues. Groupies on the bus. Groupies at the pre-show hotel parties like this one. A never-ending surplus of them. They threw themselves at us constantly. The last stop on the tour tonight? No exception.

Apparently noting my inattention, the groupie behind me pinched my nipples at the same time the one down low fisted my rod like a super-tight cunt.

Refocused, I felt a tingle begin at the base of my spine. The chick crouched beside me shoved one of her basketball-sized globes into my mouth, and my body drew taut. Fake or real, tits were tits. I had a pair of fantasies to suck on, two pressed into my back, and two more shadowing my cock.

I swirled my tongue around the globe in my mouth and sucked its elongated nipple between my lips, then bit down. Fantasy Chick liked that a hell of a lot. She moaned, and the hand working my steel-hard cock sped up.

Finally, inevitably, it happened. Three bodacious babes, naked and writhing on my hotel bed with me? Yeah, that setup had the desired effect.

Despite a bump of coke and too much whiskey, I groaned low in my throat and let go. My spine stiffened as I released my load. Spurts of hot cum coated the pumping hand fastened around my cock.

"All right, darlin'," I said as I sat up.

Over and done, from the heights of make-believe to the depths of reality I crashed. Disappointment awaited me on the other side.

"That's enough. Hands off my junk."

As my dissatisfaction came roaring back, I didn't bother pretending I was interested anymore. Because I was an asshole. But also because I knew what this was, and so did they. I got a reprieve from the hubris of my own headspace, and they got bragging rights that they had done it with Rush McMahon, Black Cat Records' biggest rock star. An even exchange.

And now I wanted them gone. Their clashing fragrances filled the air, searing my nasal passages and making my eyes burn.

"Nothing personal," I said as I carefully swept Fantasy Chick out of my way.

The down-low chick was already on the floor retrieving her clothes. The ringleader of the trio, she seemed well versed with the *fuck 'em and leave 'em* drill.

"Pick up your cell phones in the other room on your way out," I said gruffly.

"What about our VIP passes?" the ringleader asked, her voice shrill and her calculating eyes narrowed.

"Those too." I whipped the rumpled sheet off the bed and tucked it around my waist. "My manager will see that you're taken care of. Go on. Move along." Shuffling them toward the door without allowing them time to finish dressing, I explained. "I gotta get ready for the show."

I clicked the door closed behind them and turned to press my back against it, squeezing my eyes shut as the weariness of the nine-month-long tour slammed down on me. I was so fucking sick of it. Night after night, day after day, it was always the same. Show, long bus ride, hotel, chicks, booze, more chicks, more booze.

"Be careful what you wish for, my boy." My father's words of advice rattled around inside my skull as clearly as the day he'd spoken them. *"Dreams are great things—unless they're misguided ones."*

He'd thought mine were misguided. The way I felt today, I certainly couldn't argue with his assessment.

Don't, I warned myself. *Don't you fucking feel sorry for yourself. You're Rush McMahon, on top of the world. Top of the charts. You busted your ass, and you made it. And now you have everything you ever wanted.*

Yet, as I opened my eyes and glanced around the opulent suite, I knew I had nothing I really needed. Nothing that mattered. And no one in my life anymore who truly understood how I felt.

I raked my hand through my hair. *Bullshit!* Introspection like this was a waste of time. It didn't change anything.

No, what was called for here was self-medication. At the proper dosage, it would suppress the brain's tendency toward focusing on unproductive matters while keeping it coherent enough to be functional.

With that goal in mind, I tugged the sheet tighter around me and pushed away from the door just in time to escape the rising sound of the irritated voices on the other side. Groupies never responded favorably to being forced to sign nondisclosure agreements.

No signature? No cell phone.

Yeah, I might feel like a loser at the moment, but I wasn't a fool. No way in hell was I going to let some random chicks I'd just fucked screw me over with a viral video.

Returning to the center of the room, I paused at the glossy mahogany table and grabbed the half-full bottle of Jameson I'd abandoned earlier. I lifted it into the air in a toast.

"Here's to you on your wedding day, darlin'. And here's to me, myself, and I—and the fuckin' success I am without you."

Fuck, that sounded lame. Apparently, banging groupies hadn't gotten my mind off anything.

Exchanging one rock star's vice for another, I brought the bottle to my lips and knocked back an unhealthy swallow. My throat warmed, and the chill inside my chest receded.

A pleasant numbness settled into my limbs as I snagged my cell from the charging cradle. I loaded some of my music and hit PLAY, needing some fucking sound to drown out the silence.

Whiskey in hand, I headed toward the balcony on a mission for some perfume-free air. I threw open one of the French doors and slipped through the gap.

The outside speakers crackled as they picked up the first track. My guitar chords streaked like a blazing comet through the darkness. It was some kickass ax work, if I did say so myself. And I did. Hearing it brightened my gloom.

I set the bottle on a cushioned lounger—not that I wouldn't hit it again or tag another chick later. I just had a better option for now.

With my own voice serenading me, I moved to the edge of the balcony to take in the view. Elbows propped on the iron railing, I surveyed the twinkling lights of LA from fifteen stories above.

Jack's drums pounded the melancholy from my chest. Ben's snaky bass groove further improved my mood. A breeze gently lifted the layers of hair at my brow, soothing me.

My lips curved. My twisted guts unraveled.

Liquor and drugs were only temporary fixes. Music was my preferred therapy. The lifeblood of my soul. The rhythm of my heart. My unshakable foundation.

Brenda had never fully understood that . . . or me. Like my dad, she'd thought my career was some post-adolescent phase. Even if I hadn't screwed up with her, she and I would have never worked.

On that depressing note of clarity, I finally noticed the cold of the stamped concrete seeping into the soles of my bare feet. The chill spread throughout my body, raising goose bumps on my skin.

Sighing, I turned away from the view. At the lounger, I bent and snagged my bottle before reentering the suite. On my way to the shower, I shook my head as an unmistakable ringtone stopped me in my tracks.

Shit. I walked back to my phone. My manager's disapproving image lit up the screen.

"Hello?" My gut tightened again as I braced for the inevitable lecture.

"You're not dressed yet, are you?" Bradley Marshall asked, sounding as stick-up-his-ass irritated as he usually did lately.

"No, man."

"Pre-show meet and greets are in ten minutes."

"I know. Gotta shower first."

"I'll bet you do. Hell, Rush, you probably need a hazmat unit to get clean after rolling around with that unholy trinity. The blonde had some video of you snorting coke off her tits. Must have taken it before we confiscated their phones."

"Uh, well . . ."

"I deleted it."

"Thanks."

"Not smart."

"I know, it's just—"

Brad sighed. "Yeah, I know. Today's been rough for you. But you didn't really think she was going to wait around forever, did you?"

"No, man. I lost her. I know the score."

A beautiful, caring woman like Brenda? I'd known it would only be a matter of time before some other guy came along who could give her what she wanted. Things I couldn't or wouldn't offer.

Fidelity. Reliability. A permanent home.

"You send her the flowers?" I asked. Red roses. Her favorite.

"Yeah, but I don't think it was such a great idea. Those aren't the kind of flowers you send somebody on their wedding day."

"I had to do something."

"You shoulda just called. Told her you're sorry you screwed up with her. Wished her well. If Randy sees 'em and figures out who they're from, it'll just piss him off."

"Too bad. My brother's marrying my ex-fiancée." I had been prepared for her to move on. It was who she'd moved on with that had blindsided me. "Doesn't anyone get that I'm the injured party?"

Brad snorted. "You stepped out on her."

"We were on a break! And she'd withdrawn from me emotionally long before that."

So did everyone else back home when I dropped the bomb that I was leaving college to pursue a career in the music business. Everyone except for Brad.

"Not an excuse," he said.

Brad didn't bullshit, just spewed the facts as he saw them. He always gave it to me straight, which was one of his best qualities. He had a lot of them—intelligence, loyalty, honesty. There were a lot of reasons he was my best friend, my only one these days. My bandmates didn't count. We enabled one another's dysfunctions.

"I know. I get it. I came clean with her and accepted the blame."

I raked a hand through my hair, and my agitated movement stirred up more noxious perfume. The fragrance stung my eyes again, making them tear up. It sure as shit wasn't the sharp shards of regret.

I had made my bed. Gotten laid in it before I ended it with her. But I was good now. Things were better. I'd moved on.

So, why did every step I'd taken since then feel like the biggest lie of all?

Chapter TWO

JEWEL

"Shit," I muttered, waking to my alarm blaring. Rolling over, I fumbled for my cell. After swiping off the clock function, I frowned into the grainy gray twilight. I couldn't believe it was sundown already.

"Get a move on, Jewel, my precious gem. Nothing's worse than time that's wasted."

Gran's age-warbled voice was only in my mind nowadays, but hearing it echo in the lonely hallways of the past made tears prick my eyes.

"I miss you," I whispered to the painting of her that hung on the wall opposite my bed. Eyes a golden shade nearly identical to mine, though infinitely wiser, seemed to gaze back sympathetically. If only I'd heeded her wisdom. "I'm sorry, Gran."

Her serene expression radiated forgiveness because that was the way I wanted to read it. But there would never be any absolution. All that remained was the portrait. An amateur one. After all, it had been my hand that had painted it. The lessons to improve my craft that I'd hoped to take when I moved to LA had never come to pass. More practical concerns like food and shelter had quickly taken precedence over art and dreams.

Reminded of those pressing needs, I tossed aside my threadbare covers, bolted upright in bed, and threw my legs over the side. I needed to get ready. No one was going to wave a magic wand and make money appear.

Swallowing hard, I grounded myself by gripping the edge of the bed—the cot that functioned as one—in my apartment that was barely larger than a broom closet. A translucent scarf thrown over a light bulb didn't soften the harsh reality.

My current accommodations were a far cry from the comforts I'd once enjoyed inside my grandmother's foursquare home. Here, cardboard boxes served as tables. Plastic cartons stacked as shelves. Foil over the lone window curtained the light during the day.

My already sagging spirits sank lower when I noted the other cot beside me was unoccupied. The rumpled sheets provided no clue as to where my roommate had gone. She was probably gallivanting around doing who-knew-what as usual. Camaro Montepulciano had a kind heart, taking me in when I had nowhere else to go. She'd shown me the ropes. But she rode on the winds of her everchanging moods.

I let out a disappointed sigh, but I didn't fault her. Cam had her flights of indulgence; I had mine. Painting, mainly, though I only had the dregs of a few basic colors left to work with and no more canvases. No escaping through the strokes of an imagined reality today.

Feet on the floor, I firmed my frown into a determined line and got out of bed. I stood, my fingers curled into my palms. The embers of a once-bright hope flickered uncertainly inside my chest. Wishes couldn't fan them to a healthy glow, not when blanketed by so many suffocating regrets.

I closed my eyes, allowing myself a moment in the meadow in my imagination. A crown of common daisies on my head and a handful of them in my tiny grip. My grandmother beside me, her strong fingers wrapped around mine.

Gran had been my firm foundation when the world around me was shaken. It had been eighteen months since she passed, but her loss hadn't gotten any easier. For me, grief wasn't just a burden, it was a razor-sharp knife that had carved out a permanent cavity inside me.

Opening my eyes, I blinked through the sting of tears and ineffectively rubbed my hand over my aching heart before I shuffled to the shower.

Predictably, the hot water ran out halfway through, and I had to rinse my hair in a cold stream. Sliding the plastic curtain back, I stepped over the rim of the tub and placed my feet on the old towel that stood in for a bathmat. Ribbons of russet against my slim shoulders wept rivers that rushed downward over the slopes of my breasts. I grabbed a towel from the rack and draped it around my slender frame. It absorbed the excess moisture from my body, but it couldn't wipe away the pain.

At the cracked pedestal sink, I picked up the comb from the glass shelf and began the time-consuming process of running it through the long strands to untangle my hair. My empty stomach grumbled. I ignored it and the reflection of myself in the rusted mirror. I preferred not to acknowledge the hard-learned lessons reflected in my eyes.

Finished with my hair, I set aside the comb and returned to the adjoining room. Maybe I had a leftover packet of crackers in the bottom of my bag.

Crouching beside my cot, I removed the slouchy handbag I stored under it. I rummaged through the contents, looking for money and food, but discovered it was as empty as my stomach. Setting it aside, I pulled out the box that contained my clothes. Not the ones I was most comfortable in. The other ones.

My work clothes.

I laid out the lace and the silk on the bed. Seductive undergarments on one side. All the pieces to the costume that made up my outward persona on the other. It helped to compartmentalize the two aspects of my life. What happened to her, my alter ego, didn't happen to me. It was a lie, but sometimes I believed it.

Lingerie and outfit on, nail polish and makeup applied. I tucked my hair under a wig and arranged its platinum-blond pigtails around my face, avoiding looking at my heavily mascaraed eyes rimmed in kohl as I took a quick glance at my reflection.

The white oxford shirt had been too tame before I took a pair of shears to it, cutting off the sleeves and baring the midriff all the way to my bra. The red-and-black-sequined skirt I'd salvaged from the dumpster at Goodwill was so short, it revealed the racy crimson-and-black garters that held up my fishnet stockings. Black sky-high stilettos completed the look.

The whole effect was my artistic bent put to practical use. When I was done, my persona was part naughty Catholic schoolgirl and part comic-book villainess.

I tugged on a hooded jacket against the night chill and stuck out my tongue at my reflection before I left the bathroom. *This chick doesn't take anything seriously. She doesn't put up with shit, and she does what needs to be done.*

Shoulders back, spine straight, invisible armor against reality in place, I left the apartment. The musty corridor was deserted, thankfully, except for a half-naked man lying on the hallway floor. I stepped over him, and he grunted.

"Sorry, Terrance."

"It's okay, Jules." His wizened face riddled with pockmarks, he peered up at me through his good eye. "You going out?" The idea of that seemed to make him sad. He wasn't alone in that sentiment.

"Yeah." My gaze slid away. I had no food. The rent was overdue. I had no choice.

"There's always a choice." Gran's voice echoed inside my head again. Only she was gone, her bright, shining ideals carried off with her, leaving me alone with no one but myself to rely on.

"Watch out for Wanda," I told Terrance.

"She on the warpath?"

"If you mean is she on a mission to clear out the nonpaying residents who like to nap for free in the hall, then yeah, that's what she's on for sure."

"Shit." He sat up and reached for the oversized garbage bag that contained all his belongings. "Don't have no place else to go," he muttered.

"And there but for the grace of God go you." Gran's voice. And that small-town upbringing I'd run away from.

I sighed. I couldn't let him inside the apartment. But the shelter on Peach? I had a token for a bed. I'd gotten one just in case I had nowhere else to go.

Bracelets jangling on my wrist, I dove my hand into the pocket of my skirt. "Here." I offered the token to Terrance.

"You sure?" he asked, even as he stretched out his thin arm to take it.

"I'm sure."

I fought back the wave of trepidation and got my feet moving again. Traversing the remaining length of the narrow hallway, I pushed open the door to the stairwell. I glanced around inside it to make sure it was clear before I started down.

At the bottom, I pressed the bar to open the heavy steel door but jumped back when a diminutive black woman with an attitude as huge as the Hulk appeared inside the circle of light from the overhead motion sensor.

"Wanda," I said.

Shit. Shit. Triple shit.

I wobbled on my stilettos. My retreat was cut off as the door to return inside the building snapped closed behind me.

"Jewel Anderson, I thought I might find you here." In a business suit, her glasses sliding to the tip of her nose, Wanda raked her gaze over me. "Going somewhere?"

"Um, yes. I—"

"You conveniently forget that your rent is due?" She arched a brow.

"No, I'm just—"

"Sneaking around. Three days late." She clucked her tongue. "You'll pay the late penalty. I'm not floating you a zero-interest loan."

"I know you won't. I didn't expect you to. It's just that we're a little short this month."

"You two are always a little short. I should've kicked your sorry asses out the first time. Girls like you—"

"Not a single person is on a waiting list to move into your apartments," I said, my spine stiffening. "Tiny rooms. A/C and heat that's always fritzing out. No blinds on the windows. Hot water that barely works." I put a hand on my hip and lifted my chin. "And you don't know me or the type of girl I am."

Wanda scoffed. "Girl, I know everything I need to know about you. Cheap-ass hooker, blaming everyone but yourself for the predicament you find yourself in." She looked down her nose at me, and even though I stood a half foot taller than her in my stilettos, I was the one who felt small.

I didn't like her. I didn't like her at all. Even when the rent wasn't due, I avoided her.

"I'll have your money after tonight," I said, though my stomach churned on nothing but my bravado.

"You will, or I'll be evicting you first thing tomorrow morning."

Once she hit me with that ultimatum, she spun around. Her sensible heels clicked on the concrete as she marched the length of the alley. Probably off to her office to roll around on her stacks of cash and polish her broomstick.

Mean. Evil. Spiteful woman.

My eyes burned from within their kohl frame as I watched her go.

Don't cry, I told myself, curling my hands into fists and focusing on the bite in my skin from my nails rather than on my fear that my roommate and I would likely be on the streets soon.

I squeezed my eyes shut. I couldn't give up before I even tried. It wasn't just me. There was Cam to consider.

Reopening my eyes, I forced my body into motion, navigating the trash strewn in the alley. Crushed aluminum cans. Broken liquor bottles. I stepped gingerly between them, feeling as used up and empty as the abandoned items around me.

At the sidewalk, I slowed my pace and ducked into the shadows beneath the awning of an adult-clothing shop. I glanced over my shoulder. No sign of Wanda or anyone else watching me.

I let out a sigh and caught a glimpse of my reflection in the plate glass.

My eyes were wide pools of gold beneath dark auburn brows. If only they were an actual physical commodity I could pawn.

I slammed them closed. Fool's gold. They gave away too much. It was unwise to appear vulnerable outside the apartment.

Opening my eyes again, I narrowed my gaze and gulped in a deep, determined breath. Then I reached for the hood on my jacket and pulled it over my wig.

Be brave, I told myself, remembering another of Gran's sayings. *"Bravery isn't the absence of fear; it's the ability to keep going despite insurmountable obstacles."*

Bravery was my choice. One foot in front of the other.

My night was only starting; I still had to get on the bus. It would take me two transfers to get to the better-paying side of town. Further, I had to hope that I looked more tempting than the girls who had already set up shop over there.

If I didn't, I was fucked, and not in the way that would get me the money I needed to pay the rent.

Chapter THREE

RUSH

"Rush. Rush. Rush."

The chanting of my name echoed in the cinder-block corridor after I left the stage.

"They want a second encore," Brad told me, as if I didn't already know.

"They can't always get what they want." I snagged the white towel a stagehand offered me and swiped it across my brow.

Narrowing my eyes at my manager, I noticed the chicks we swept past vied for his attention as much as they did for mine. Blond, blue-eyed, barely older than me, Brad was the manager of the ten-million-dollar-a-year Rush machine. He was also catnip to the backstage pussy that went for his Armani brand of boring boardroom predictability.

"Life sucks and then you die, right?"

"Rush." His tone was warning as he glanced up from his phone and the glow of platinum profits from tonight's sold-out show. "Not here." He lifted his chin to remind me of our audience. "Put a lid on the negativity."

He might have a point about the crowd. My PR rep, the stylist, and the visiting record-label VP had signed nondisclosure agreements, same as the groupies. While my staff was paid handsomely to keep their mouths shut whenever I shot off mine, I held no such sway with the ticket-holding masses.

"I'm not making apologies for how I am."

Brad frowned as we entered the dressing room. "You weren't always this difficult."

I brushed past him on the way to the bar. Out of deference to my company, I poured a tumbler of whiskey. Alone, I would have chugged it straight from the bottle. I threw back the socially acceptable portion, but the fire the amber elixir ignited barely registered. Ditto for the lingering adrenaline rush from the roar of the Staples Center crowd.

Get a grip, I told myself, staring at my reflection. The guy within the rectangular frame of bulbs surrounding the mirror looked a little too needy and wrung out. His brown hair was plastered to his skull, and so saturated with sweat, it appeared black. The eyes were the real giveaway. Twin portals whirled with a vortex of negative emotions.

"No more drinking." Brad snatched the bottle of Jameson from my grasp. "You know what happened last time you got trashed."

"I remember. No need to rub my nose in it." Sales had gone in the shitter after someone posted a video of me going nuclear on an overly aggressive paparazzo.

I had zero regrets. Asswipe had it coming for shoving his camera in my mother's face at the funeral. If my father had been the pillar of strength in our family, she was the pedestal. Only she had crumpled completely when they lowered his casket into the ground. Remembering that day and all that had been lost, the ground rumbled at a Richter-scale magnitude beneath my feet.

The betrayal of my ex-fiancée marrying my brother was a minor temblor in comparison.

It wasn't only that my father was gone, or that Brenda had moved on, it was that so much had been left unresolved with each of them. I knew my failure as a man was the common factor with each.

As the specter of that truth rose within me, my mouth went dry and my hands twitched. I needed another drink. No, I wanted to drain that entire fucking bottle of whiskey dry. And I knew what that meant. The narrow line I'd been walking with my drinking had gone well beyond a casual thing.

I ripped my gaze away from my reflection and glared at Brad. "Is my car washed and gassed up?"

I could see no other cure for what ailed me. I needed to get away before I did something ill-advised. Paparazzi were like a plague of locusts, ready to devour my mistakes, and talking heads were on standby to regurgitate the lurid stories for mass consumption.

He scowled at me. "Yeah, but do you really think you're in any condition to drive?"

"I need some fresh air."

"Rush, you've got interviews and the VIP meet and greets."

"You said we were through with all the bullshit after tonight."

"After tonight's *obligations*. It's not all about you. Your fans are what keeps the Rush machine cranking out the cash, and you know it."

"Yeah. All right. I get it."

I closed my fingers into tight fists, wishing they were gripping the leather-wrapped steering wheel of my Porsche instead.

"They get an hour." I could do sixty more minutes for him and for my bandmates who worked as hard as I did. But that was it. I was as sick of myself and the arrogant rock-star act as everyone else was. "After that, I'm gone."

"Everyone out." Brad barked the order to the media reps who had followed us into the dressing room. "Rush needs a shower." He cast his authoritative gaze around the throng within the claustrophobic ten-by-fourteen-foot space.

As usual, when he spoke, people listened. It was an innate ability he'd been honing since I met him in grade school and he convinced our headmaster that after-school suspensions were inhumane.

"Interviews will run according to the order on the sign-up sheet," Brad said, and the already rapidly emptying room cleared out even faster. Everyone hoped to be first in line.

When only my entourage remained, he addressed our small crew. "Thanks for all your hard work tonight. I'll meet you in the green room. For now, I need you to give us some privacy."

They filed out, and as soon as the door shut behind them and we were alone, Brad narrowed his gaze on me.

"Been on tour for nine months without a fuckin' break," I said quickly, recognizing the impending lecture gleaming in his eyes. "I gotta go off the grid before I go completely insane, man."

"I hear you."

He studied me a long beat. Whatever he saw turned his light blue eyes storm-cloud dark.

"I've got your back. You know I do. But you aren't the only one who's dead tired. If you go underground this time, I need you to stay underground, all right? I've been at the center of this whirlwind with you, and I'd like a breather from the chaos too. So, no aspiring actresses during the break. No models. And no more Rock Fuck Club chicks."

"You expect me to be celibate?" I raised my brows.

"As a priest."

"After the stunts we pulled in Catholic school, I don't think they'd allow either of us to become men of the cloth."

"Real wine swapped out for grape juice." His flattened lips twitched.

"Frogs and garden snakes in the sisters' lockers." I grinned. "They were prophylactic measures. Our stunts served a purpose."

"Kept those rulers off our knuckles after that, didn't they?"

I nodded, missing those days when we'd not only had each other's backs, but also confided everything to each other. Simpler days. Simpler lives.

Brad's expression turned serious again. "So, you headed to your condo in Santa Monica?"

"Yeah, after I drive around a bit. Clear my head."

"You mean go to a bar, pick up a chick, and get laid again."

"Probably."

"Your standards are appallingly low." He shook his head. "I'm going back home. I'll be reachable on my personal number if you need me."

"Bree giving you another chance?" I asked. He'd been practically domesticated by her.

Shit, I'd given up on that gig after my one and only failed attempt. Why settle for one woman when I could have however many I wanted each night?

"I hope she does." Brad's brow creased, and suddenly, he seemed less like the confident business manager and more like my geeky grade-school friend. He knew my issues as well as I knew his. The past year had been tough on both of us. But this girl mattered to him.

Giving me a serious look, he said, "Make this break count, Rush. I plan to. Get your head together. We've got from now through New Year's off, then we're back out on the road."

• • •

Stuck at a stoplight an hour later, I impatiently drummed my fingers on the steering wheel. The street sign seemed to mock me, probably because I'd seen it before. At least three times.

How the fuck did I end up circling back to the same corner on Wilshire?

I glared at my navigation display. Unreliable piece of shit. This wasn't anywhere near the hotel where my next hookup was waiting.

I zoomed in on the map. Maybe I could take Hollywood Boulevard around and then just cut back in at . . . *Fuck.* That route for whatever reason was all red. A parking-lot standstill. And I didn't know this part of town well enough to come up with an alternative.

My phone rang. The display switched off the map to reveal it was my mother calling.

My heart stuttered. Our communication was irregular, especially sparse since the funeral. Her phoning at this time of night led me to immediately anticipate a crisis.

"Hey, Mom," I said. "Is everything okay?"

"No, not really."

"Are you sick?" My voice lowered to a strained rasp. An out-of-the-blue phone call similar to this one had broken the bad news about my father. A massive heart attack. Gone within a matter of hours, before I could even say good-bye.

Had I come to terms with it? Had she?

Hardly.

"No, Rush." Mom's voice sounded a little strange, as if I'd caught her off guard. "I just had my yearly routine checkup."

"Okay. Good." Shaky, I steered the Porsche to a nearby curb. Since I was using the Bluetooth connection, I hadn't taken my hands off the wheel, but it was too distracting to drive while talking to her. "So, what's up?"

A quick glance out the windows confirmed I wasn't in the best part of town. Porn shop. A couple of skeezy-looking bars. A by-the-hour motel. I clicked the locks.

"I'm lonely. Sad. I rarely hear from you anymore. You're my boy, and I miss you."

Her voice hitched, and my stomach bottomed out as if it had been dropped from a height.

"Mom, I'm sorry. It's just been crazy busy . . ." I pulled in a breath, not knowing what the fuck to say. Even before the rift between us, I hadn't been any good at the emotional stuff. It wasn't the way I'd been raised.

Life had been rough growing up in the heartland. Dad had been a farmer and rancher, the family livelihood largely dependent on the Indiana weather. Our lives revolved around pragmatism and planning.

There wasn't any thought of getting in touch with our feelings, no understanding for a son who preferred to express his creativity through music. And certainly no neutral ground for reconciliation after I left them and chased after my unlikely dreams.

And now the man who had modeled the values of strength and silent stoicism was gone. Far beyond my reach. The chance for us to explore those feelings was taken with him.

"It's my first Christmas without your father," she said, and the reminder stole my breath. "The house is too quiet. Like a tomb with your brother and Brenda away on their honeymoon."

Randy had never moved away from home. The ever-dutiful son, he'd taken over the management of the farm after Dad died. But with my brother out of town, it wasn't surprising that Mom had reached out to me in a low moment.

I didn't much like the idea of her being all alone in the big empty farmhouse, miles away from the nearest neighbor. Worry and guilt wrapped a tight band around my chest. I hadn't been out to visit her in months, not since the funeral.

"I was going through my old photo albums after the Johnsons stopped by to check on me," she said. "Do you remember the year Thunder climbed up the Christmas tree?"

"Yeah, Mom," I said, fighting back a smile. I'd forgotten about that cat. "He was just a kitten. He was so small, he looked like one of the ornaments."

"Yes, that was before he got fat and mean."

"He slept in my room at night. But he used to bring you mice whenever he caught 'em. He left them on the front doorstep so you couldn't miss them. I think he wanted your approval."

The cat. Me. I got the ironic parallel, but did she? Would she ever see value in the choices I made?

"Yes, I think you're right. He also used to lie in wait to pounce on anyone who walked by. Those claws of his were sharp." She sighed, her breath heavy with remembrance. "You were so attached to him. You got attached to all the animals, wanted to name them all. It's hard to send them to the slaughterhouse when you think of them as pets. I guess your father and I should've seen the writing on the wall."

Was she trying to say she understood why I left? Why I went my own way? Maybe even that she was sorry? Or was I just wishfully reading between the lines?

"Why are you really calling, Mom?" I said, putting it out there. "I haven't heard from you in months. I don't understand. You're going to have to tell me straight out what you need from me."

She sighed, and the line fell silent for a moment. "Just that I don't want there to be long stretches without us talking to each other anymore. That's all."

Chapter FOUR

JEWEL

"You look hot." My roommate clattered toward me at a precarious pace in her skyscraper heels.

"Thanks, Cam." I stamped a hand to my hip and posed for her as the bus door closed behind me, and she stopped and twirled to show me her backless dress. Her long black hair swished the exposed skin above her ass. "You're not so bad yourself."

"Digging the cartoon-character-slash-schoolgirl vibe." Her dark red lipstick framed an approving smile.

"Thought it might sell well with the older guys on this side of town."

"Sick bastards acting out their underage-girl fantasies. You're probably right." She unwrapped a piece of gum, split it, popped half in her mouth, and offered me the other.

"Appreciate it," I said as I took it.

"You're late." She narrowed her olive-green eyes at me. "You stop to take a client on the way over?"

"Nah." I shook my head. "Just another run-in with Wanda."

"Bitch."

"Yeah." I agreed readily, my empty stomach twisting. "You made your half of the rent yet?"

"Nope." She shook her head. Glossy ebony hair spilled over her delicate shoulders.

"But I thought you had most of it saved already."

"*Had* most of it." She slowly blinked her pretty eyes at me.

"What do you mean, had?" My stomach didn't just twist, it knotted.

"I gave it to Lori."

"Oh no." I squeezed my eyes closed for a second, but there was no shutting out the shitty reality.

"I had to." My roomie donned a pleading expression. "She was sick. She had the shakes and was puking her guts out."

"She's a heroin addict, Cam, and needs to go to rehab. She'll just use that money for another fix."

Bright pink neon lights advertising a triple-X show blasted my gaze. A reminder, not that I needed one, that the harsh world we lived in couldn't be remedied with kindness.

"You don't have your part either?" she asked.

I shook my head.

"We're fucked." Frowning, she touched my arm. "I'm sorry, Jewel."

"It's okay." Kindness might not change much, but I couldn't blame Cam for it.

I covered her fingers with mine. Even through the worn cotton of my jacket, I could tell her skin was freezing cold.

"Two softies is what we are." I gave her a warm smile. "I probably would've done the same thing. What are the odds we'd end up rooming together, huh?"

"You regret moving in with me?" Her crimson lips trembled uncertainly.

"No. And anyway, it was your apartment to begin with. Lucky for me, you took me in. I had no job. Barely any money after my boyfriend screwed me over. You took a chance on me. Rescued me." I squeezed her hand and frowned. "You're freezing."

I removed her fingers, unzipped my jacket, and shrugged out of it. Goose bumps erupted on my exposed flesh, and there was a lot of it, more than Cam revealed in her slinky slip. A guy in a passing car let out a piercing whistle and gave me a leering look, and then he was gone.

"Put this on," I said.

"I'm okay. It's seventy degrees outside. I'm hardly freezing."

"It's damp. There's a chill in the air. Take it." I shook the jacket at her. "I was just going to tie it around my waist, but it messes with my look."

"All right." She frowned at me, but put it on.

"You make *any* money tonight?"

I held my breath for her answer as we moved into our usual position by the streetlight closest to the curb. Best to flaunt our attributes in the light while we could. The longer we kept on making our living like this, the sooner we would wind up falling back into the shadows to hide the toll it took on us.

"Fifty bucks."

"That's something. Good for you."

"One blow job." Her brow creased. "That's hardly rent."

"It's a start." I bit down on my plump, often-abused bottom lip. "Maybe we can convince Wanda to let us pay what we owe in installments."

"Maybe," she said, but we both knew there was zero chance. No excuses. No exceptions. Wanda was a total hard-ass.

"Hey." Cam lifted her chin to point at a sleek sports car idling at the curb. "Would you look at that."

"What?" I swiveled to glance in the same direction.

"It's a Porsche 911 GT2 RS."

"I know what kind of car it is."

She raised a disbelieving brow.

"Okay. No, I didn't. You're the car expert, Camaro Montepulciano."

"Not an expert. Not like my dad."

"Yeah," I said softly. "But you have nearly every make, model, and spec memorized like he does."

A love for all things automotive was his one and only legacy to her. After she'd lost her job as a cashier in the auto parts store and her father discovered what she'd taken up as a second career, he completely shut her out. Yet she religiously read *Car and Driver* magazine every morning as though it were a devotional, just on the off chance that he might one day change his mind and welcome her back.

"Special silver-metallic finish," she said almost reverently as she drank in the sight of the expensive car. "Rear-wheel drive. Six cylinders. Three-point-eight-liter twin-turbo engine. Seven hundred horsepower. That baby can do zero to sixty in two point seven seconds."

"Sounds super sexy." I snorted, not as impressed by cars. "So, go get him."

"Nah." She shook her head. "You look way hotter than I do."

"Not true, but all right. I'll go over and take a shot, if you're sure. Though I better move fast, since I've probably only got two-point-something seconds to snag him if he stomps on the gas." I straightened my shoulders.

She shook her head at me as I took my first step. "Work your approach faster, roomie. He just put his blinker on. He's gonna get away. And that's $293,000 worth of sports car, before options."

In other words, if I played it right, I might make rent.

I picked up the pace, jogging inelegantly to the vehicle, and bent over to tap on the passenger window.

When the driver slowly turned his head, my heart that was hammering from my dash to the curb slammed to a complete halt as his gaze hit mine. I'd never seen eyes like his before, so gray, the shiny platinum finish of his Porsche seemed tawdry in comparison.

A long moment passed as I took in his features. Tousled brown hair a little long in the front, strong jaw, chiseled lips, straight nose. He looked me over in return.

"Hey, handsome," I said when he lowered the window.

I feigned confidence, though anyone who really knew me would have noticed that my voice was pitched a higher octave than usual. The potential for rejection with the initial approach always made me nervous. This one more than most. He was way too cute to be trolling the streets for a paid fuck.

"Want a date for the night?"

"You even legal, little girl?" he asked, his sable brows arching higher above his heart-stopping eyes.

Okay, maybe I had taken the schoolgirl thing a bit too far.

"Twenty-one last March."

Most guys didn't care about legalities. Was he a cop? I dismissed the idea immediately. Not likely. Not in a $300,000 car. Just cautious, probably. Another factor that made me wonder why he was cruising for sex.

I batted my eyelashes at him. "You wanna see my driver's license, honey?"

The guy gave me a bored look. "No, not really. Just wanted to acknowledge your tap on my window." Lifting a hand, he made a shooing motion. "You can step away from the car now. I'm not interested. Just pulled over to have a conversation on my phone. I mean, do I look like I need to pay a fucking prostitute to have sex with me?"

His rejection stung, making my temper flare.

I glared at him, spitting out my response without thinking. "With manners like that, you couldn't possibly pay me enough to put up with you."

"Get your filthy little hands off my car, Harley Quinn." His gray eyes flashed fiery silver.

I planted my fists on my hips. "I'm not going anywhere."

Those eyes of his were second-place silver to my defiant gold. I wasn't an exotic half-Italian beauty like Cam, but his dismissal triggered my attitude. Attitude I couldn't afford, but I let it rip anyway.

"Get your statusy piece-of-shit car off *my* corner. I was here first." Holding my head high, I flicked a pigtail over my shoulder. My bracelets jingled my irritation as I strolled away.

Take that, rich guy.

He didn't immediately leave, and I didn't turn to see what he was doing, even though I could feel his gaze on me. Swaying my hips provocatively, I moved to the car that had pulled in front of his Porsche.

Locks suddenly popped behind me. "Hey, Harley! Wait up."

I spun around and froze.

He stood next to his vehicle, the streetlight bathing his sculpted form. The breadth of his wide shoulders split open the lapels of his black leather jacket. He wore no shirt beneath it to hide the view of his chiseled pecs and abs. His smooth, golden-tanned skin glistened in the light as he casually propped his elbow on the roof of his car. Narrow hips and long legs in low-slung jeans completed the compelling portrait.

A shiver that had nothing to do with the chill in the air rolled through me as I withstood a heavily hooded leisurely scan from him.

His verdict? I couldn't tell.

Mine? He was great—if you went for an incredibly handsome guy with arrogance stamped into every single cell of his flawless body.

"What do you want?" Not giving an inch, I narrowed my gaze, shooting haughty daggers at him.

"How much?"

My mouth went dry. There was no mistaking what he wanted.

Me. For a price.

My mind blanking, I licked my lips to moisten them. Sex with him? I shook my head, but the thought of it only increased the heat that had combusted within me.

Pulling in a deep breath, I forced myself to take a mental step back. Methodically, I sized him up like Cam had taught me to do, and discounted his looks and his body. It was the car and the value of his clothing that mattered.

"Two hundred," I said. "Cash."

"You're joking."

"I never joke about money."

At an impasse, we stared at each other. One heartbeat became one too many.

"You're wasting my time," I said, deciding for him, and moved toward the other car.

"All right, Harley."

I stopped and turned to give him a big smile, and he went completely still. When his smoldering gaze dropped to my mouth, my lips tingled from its intensity.

He whistled under his breath. "You should've led with the smile. I would've agreed to twice that."

Chapter FIVE

RUSH

My gaze was drawn to her pretty mouth as it gaped at my admission. It was wide, glossed in red, with a Cupid's bow at the top and a plush bottom lip. *Perfect.* I imagined tracing the lines of her mouth with my tongue, then I would lick the gloss off. Make a feast of her.

Her mouth was made for making love to as much as it was for expressing her mood. That amazing smile took her from beautiful to blinding. As surely if she'd flipped an internal switch, she went from intriguing to irresistible. That smile alone changed her from a possibility to a certainty in my mind.

My previous rendezvous was easy to dismiss. I had no interest in her at all anymore.

No, I wanted *this girl.*

I'd take those ruby-red lips wrapped around my shaft to start. Then I would peel away her clothes and explore every inch of her sexy body.

Taste it.

Feel it.

Take her, again and again.

In my mind, I traded the fire of our opposing wills for the heat of our mutual passion. I'd been imagining how hot it would be to fuck her from the moment she shot me down and turned her back on me.

As I hurried to open the passenger door, my already eager cock jumped when my arm brushed against hers, and my grip tightened on the metal handle. My pulse raced as fast as my imagination, and my nostrils flared as I watched her slip into the seat.

"Thank you," she murmured softly, glancing up at me through sooty lashes.

Her voice was low and throaty. I wanted to hear it and feel it when I had my cock buried deep inside her.

I noted that she seemed surprised when I opened the door for her. Yeah, well, I guess most of her clients just popped the locks and ordered her to get in.

Why the hell I was treating her like a date instead of a hooker, I didn't really know. Maybe it was my Midwest upbringing. Maybe it was my guilt for the flinch she hadn't been quick enough to hide after I insulted her earlier. Maybe it was her million-dollar smile.

Whatever. I didn't plan to fully analyze it. *Hell fucking no.*

"You're welcome," I said politely while taking a self-serving moment to fully enjoy the view. She was a looker, for sure. Long shapely legs, round ass, full breasts. She had an hourglass shape any guy would lust over, though she seemed a little undernourished.

Pressing her legs together and crossing them at the ankles, she settled in. Her demure behavior only added to my confusion as I shut the door.

Time to move things along. To get out of this neighborhood. To get *us* out of this neighborhood. It wasn't safe. Plus, I needed to get her alone to have my way with her. Anything I wanted with her, I could have. I was a paying customer, after all.

Her gaze followed me as I quickly rounded the hood. What was she thinking? She seemed genuinely into me. I wasn't totally clueless with chicks. I recognized the signs. Darkened eyes. Parted lips. But then again, maybe she was just really good at her job.

I yanked open my door with more force than necessary.

“Smiles cost extra,” she said, her tone sassy as she flipped her platinum pigtails over the black leather headrest.

I lowered myself into the seat and glanced at her, noting the remnants of one playing on her lips. The stinging retort I had ready to deliver evaporated from my tongue.

She was damn cute. The supple red suede of her seat seemed to conform to her. More confusing than her behavior was the proprietary rush I felt looking at her beside me in my car.

I reached for my seat belt and snapped it into place.

“What? No comeback?” She let out a low, sultry laugh that affected me as strongly as if she’d wrapped her slender fingers around my cock.

“I’ll keep that in mind,” I said, then mentally cursed myself for sounding like a dumbass.

“You do that.” Her small smile widened into a full-blown one that lit up her eyes.

Suddenly, she became the only thing I saw. Gone was the interior of the car. The rounded aviation-style dials. The polished chrome. The gold-and-red crest on the center of the steering wheel. Everything receded but her.

I ripped my gaze away from her. “You have a usual place?” My voice was overly loud, my grip tightening on the wheel.

She was staring at me again; I could sense it. What could possibly inspire such unnerving scrutiny? I desperately wanted to know.

“What?” she asked, and I couldn’t resist.

I turned my head to take her in.

Her golden eyes widened, and she blinked at me in return. At a distance, they were striking, but up close, her eyes were fucking phenomenal.

Suddenly, I couldn’t think straight. My cock twitched, so tight and uncomfortable that I had to make a conscious effort not to adjust myself.

I pulled in a deep breath. A necessary one, but a mistake that flooded my senses with her fresh peachy scent, a light fragrance that took me home, reminding me of the peach pies my mom used to bake.

Fuck me.

I cleared my throat, and when I spoke, my voice was gruff. "Where do you want me to do you, babe?"

"Oh. Yes. Um." She wet her lips, seeming caught off guard by my abruptness. "Don't you mean *me* doing *you*?"

"Yeah, darlin'." Oh, hell fucking yes. Now we had things refocused. "For sure."

Her gaze dipped to my lap as if to gauge the magnitude of that task. My already steely-hard cock hardened even more. Her gaze pinned to my lap, she made a low appreciative sound. My spine tingled as if she'd actually traced my sizable length.

"Where?" I asked, trying to focus and remind her of the issue of logistics. "This ain't happening here."

"There's a park nearby," she said.

"I'm not having you blow me in a public place. You want us both to get arrested?"

"No." She shook her head. Her expression clearing, she no longer appeared dazed. "But if you want to go to a motel, that's a different price structure. I have to consider travel time. Hookups like that tend to go over an hour. Plus, they . . ." She trailed off, seeming nervous.

For the first time since she'd gotten into the car, she glanced away from me. Her brow creasing, she stared out the windshield. Her focus seemed to be on the car in front of us, where a hooker with long black hair was bent over with her face near the open window, propositioning the driver.

I glanced at my passenger. Was the other hooker someone she knew? Or maybe the other driver was a potential customer she thought might pay better? Or had her attention wandered because of something else?

She licked her lips. Swallowed.

Was she scared to be alone with me? Given the direction of my thoughts, she probably should have been.

I cleared my throat. "I'm not doing a by-the-hour shithole place either." Motels like that were often a roach-infested health-code violation. I hadn't stayed in one since my first tour.

"Okay." She turned to face me, tilting her head as if she didn't fully get me.

I found it cute. She was more than cute, but I ignored that and all the other conflicting feelings I had regarding her. I needed to take charge and get the situation back on track to get what I wanted.

"The Chamberlain's close." I typed the hotel's name into my GPS.

Avoiding my eyes, she said, "I can't go in there."

"Why the fuck not?" My lips flattened.

"I just can't."

She frowned as if I'd insulted her again and crossed her arms over her chest. The movement lifted her tits. I bit back a groan as I imagined her holding them for me so I could suck on them.

"Well, we gotta go somewhere, darlin'." As a concession to the possibility that she might be frightened, I left off the *and fast.*

"*I* don't have to do anything," she said, her tone defensive. "Sorry to waste your time." She reached for her door handle.

Oh. Hell. No. I clicked the locks.

"What are you doing?" She glanced back at me, her eyes wide.

"You stay."

"Open the damn door." Her voice rose as if she were panicked. "That's my friend at the car right in front of us."

Ah. Realization dawned.

"I'll scream." She rooted around in the bag in her lap and pulled out a small cell phone. A cheap burner, for sure, but it would still work. A shadow passed through her eyes as she added, "I don't like being trapped."

Had she been trapped before? Had someone hurt her? That thought made me see red, and I reconsidered the way I'd handled the situation.

"It's okay, Harley." I clicked open the locks and raised my hands in a conciliatory gesture. "You can go if you want to."

Disappointment rose as she swiveled to the door and grasped the handle.

"But I'd like you to stay." I let out a breath. "Please stay."

When she froze, I realized it was the politeness that she'd responded to. I filed that away as something to remember.

She turned to glance back at me, her brows raised. Surprised, maybe? Apparently, she'd noted that I was a little arrogant.

"You're right. I don't use that word often. I rarely have to anymore," I muttered, and she tilted her head at me again. "Listen, I've had a particularly shitty day. One of the worst I can remember in a long while. I'm dead tired, but wired too. You ever feel like that?"

Slowly, she nodded.

"Then you know how it sucks. But I know one guaranteed way to feel better. You offered to have sex with me, and I'm willing to pay. If we can agree on a new price and a place, can we proceed?"

"I guess," she said hesitantly.

"So, will four hundred cover the extra commute time?"

Her nostrils flared as she stared at me. Seconds ticked by before she said, "Eight hundred."

My eyes widened. "That's a lot of money, Harley."

The chick had balls to ask for that amount, but I already knew I was willing to pay it.

"Done." I wasn't wasting fucking time on haggling. "So, we're agreed on price. Now on to location. Is it the Chamberlain in particular you object to?"

"No. Not really." Her gaze straight ahead, she narrowed her eyes as she watched her friend climb into the car in front of us.

"Hmm. Well, the rooms are nice, and I'm familiar with the staff. If I call them, they'll do everything they can to make sure my stay . . . our stay . . . is comfortable." I grabbed my phone from the center console. "Is there any special request you might have? Something I can have them do that might change your mind about going there?"

I hit her with my most sincere expression, and she stared back at me as if I were an enigma to her. Well, that went both ways. I couldn't for the life of me figure her out either . . . a girl who looked like a hooker but acted like an ingenue and smelled like a juicy peach.

"Could you ask them for a room near the entrance?" she asked softly.

"I could do that. Sure."

"Maybe one on the first floor?" She bit down on her lip as if uncertain of my reaction. "With a patio, if they have that?"

"All right."

The silver ring on my middle finger glinted in the light. A gothic cross, an homage to my upbringing. I spun the cross around to my palm so I didn't have to see it. I'd remove it before we got started.

It wasn't that the things I planned to do with her were anything I hadn't done before. Just that the way I felt right now—afraid to get busted, afraid she might throw on the brakes—it reminded me of my awkward teens and fooling around in the back seat of a car with a girl I really liked.

My hair fell into my eyes as I completed my task and returned my phone to the console. The call connected and rang over the car's speakers before someone answered.

"Chamberlain Hotel, West Hollywood," a woman said in a chirpy voice. "Manager Mindy Johnson speaking. Can I help you?"

"Yes, Mindy. This is Rush McMahon." I paused to glance at my companion. Did she recognize my name? She was studying me as closely as I was studying her. But there was no recognition in her gaze.

"Mr. McMahon. Yes, we haven't seen you since your last launch party. How are you?"

"I'm fine. A little tired from traveling. I've got someone with me, and we could use a room."

"Absolutely. The usual amenities?"

"Yes. Only I have a few additional requests. Is there a first-floor suite available? One near the front entrance? With a patio?"

"Let me check." A keyboard clacked in the background. "Yes. Only it's just a regular suite."

"Does it have a separate shower? A garden tub? A seating area? A fully stocked bar?" Basically, easy alcohol access and plenty of places to fuck her.

"Yes, all of that."

"Then that'll be fine. We should arrive shortly."

"We'll be ready for you."

"Your name is Rush?" the girl asked after I ended the call.

I nodded.

"Should I know you?" Her gaze narrowed.

"Most would." I assessed her. "However, you don't seem to."

"No, I'm sorry. We don't have a TV, and I'm not big on movies and all that stuff."

"Why not?"

"I'm not from around here."

"Obviously." I'd noticed an unfamiliar accent in some of her phrasing. "Most everyone in LA is obsessed with the whole entertainment industry. Are you against that kind of thing?" I asked. "Even music?"

"Not really against. Just not interested, I guess."

My lips curved. No built-in expectations or biases. I liked that she didn't know me.

"Gran wasn't keen on those things," she said.

"Gran?"

"My grandmother."

The girl's expression changed, closed off. There was something more, but she wasn't going to share it with me.

"So, the one hour? At the hotel?" Her lips moved for a few seconds as if she were doing some internal calculations, then she said, "I only take cash. You have it on you?"

"No."

"Cash up front. No exceptions."

"Pretty steep up front." I slid my gaze over her. "How do I know you're gonna be worth it?"

"I'm worth it." She blazed a confident smile at me.

"I'll be the judge of that. Soon."

Anticipation coursed through me. For the first time in a long time, I found myself not only engaged, but looking forward to something.

"You, sir, are getting a bargain since I'm not charging you for the first couple of smiles. From now on, the tack-on fee for those is a hundred each."

Her grin widened, and my brain short-circuited on the brilliance of it.

"I'm sure you know," she said softly, "that nothing worth having is ever free."

You can read the rest of the story on Amazon.
Free in kindleunlimited. The Right Man is book 1 in the Once Upon A Rockstar series. It is a completed series.

The Right Man
The Right Wish
The Right Wrong
The Right Song

Southside
HIGH

About the Book

• • •Complete Series Now Available• • •

My best friend and I want the same girl. But Lace Lowell is mine. She was mine first. She'll be mine forever. Sure, she was his friend when they were kids, long before I ever met her. But that's in the past. This is now. I'm Warren Jinkins. War. My name is my battle cry. I take what I want. I don't ask, and I want her.

I'm in love with two men. Bryan Jackson is the guitarist in our band, and War is the lead singer. They're sexy bad boys, the most dangerous guys in our school. All the girls at Southside High want them. But loving two guys is a problem—especially when those two guys also love each other.

Chapter ONE

WAR

"He got arrested."

"Again?"

"Yeah. They threw him in that alternative school for troubled teens for a while."

The murmurings of fellow students followed me as I confidently strode onto school property like I owned it, which I practically did.

The first bell was about to ring, and the patchy lawn in front of the school swarmed with disaffected youth. Irritated by the buzz my return had stirred, I considered shoving my fist in someone's face, agitate the hornets in the nest while letting off a little steam of my own, but I decided against it.

Arrogantly cool was always the way to go, so I kept my sunglass-shaded gaze trained straight ahead. I knew how to play the game. At Southside High, having a bad attitude was everything.

"Fucking shit, War," my wingman said. "Why didn't you tell me you were coming back to school today?"

Lifting his sunglasses onto his head, Bryan Jackson tossed his cigarette aside and broke away from a group of smokers by the front steps. His expression as chill as mine, he fell into pace at his rightful position beside me. We hadn't seen each other in months, but he didn't mention it. He knew the drill. We'd come a long way from our middle-school days when we'd had our asses handed to us.

"Got shit to do, Bry." Beneath the shadow of the two-story brick building, I veered to my left, following the sidewalk that led around it. "You up for dishing out a potential ass-kicking this morning?"

"I'm up for whatever." Bryan huffed beside me. "But slow down." His chin held high, he let his gray-green gaze pass through other students like they were just background noise, same as mine did.

"Been gone a while." I slowed my steps. "Back now. Wanna get the usual bullshit over with. Reestablish my cred." I glanced at him. "Who's taken advantage, I mean, taken over in my absence?"

"Kyle." His strong jaw tightening, Bryan shook his head, unleashing long layers of his brown hair. "He's been acting all high and mighty, hinting that you were never coming back."

"Fucking bastard."

"You know how it is. Only one can rule." Bryan shrugged one thickly muscled shoulder.

We both worked out. Pounding the weights had been my gym credit at the alternative school, but even so, I remained middleweight boxing class to Bryan's heavyweight.

"Getting ready to fix that shit right the fuck now," I said firmly. I might be a middleweight, but I had heavyweight power behind my punches.

We turned the corner together. Without the building to buffer it, a strong gust of wind whipped at both of us. Bryan's shorter hair blasted back from his face. My medium-length hair escaped the red bandanna I wore around my head to contain it, preferring to be unrestrained like I did.

With that wind, it was bite-ass cold. I wanted this done so we could go inside.

Kyle was right where I expected to find him, in my spot next to the scraggly hedges behind the building. An unlit cigarette dangled from his lips. His head was down, his riotous black hair casting sinister shadows into his greedy gray eyes. Unsurprisingly, he wasn't alone. He had a client with him and a protector.

Kyle was a dealer. I'd known him since middle school. He was always dealing.

"Kyle, *psst*," his protection hissed, his red-rimmed blue eyes narrowed on me. "Look-it. War's here."

I didn't recognize the hulk-sized dude who was his new sentry. His previous one had been shipped off to the alternative school along with me, but unlike me, he hadn't returned.

"Hey, asshole," I said, curling my ringed fingers into fists and peering past the hulk to Kyle. "Your new sentry sucks."

"Now wait a minute," Hulk said, but I cut him off.

"Out of my face, asshole. I don't have time for you." I stared him down, pulling into play the couple of inches of height I had on him.

Asshole's job as a sentry wasn't watching for teachers. Knowing what was good for them, they didn't patrol this corner. It belonged to lowlifes like me, though the staff had their territory to defend like we all did. Classrooms, hallways, and the cafeteria were their domain. Coaches and jocks had the right of way in the gym and around the football field. The Latino gang La Rasa Prima had the entire south portion of the school.

"When'd you get out?" Kyle asked, acting all cool and shit as he looked at me.

I glared at him. "Earlier than you expected, apparently."

"Don't get your boxers in a twist." Kyle passed the ziplock bag containing an assortment of pills to his client, then turned and strutted to me. As his client slinked away, Kyle jerked his chin up, a respectful greeting to me.

"Don't play around, man." I marched straight to him, ignoring the bag of muscle who lumbered into action to stand beside him. Physically, I might not be the biggest badass here, but my reputation was. "You know why I'm pissed."

"Give 'im his cut, Randy," Kyle said. He not only knew my reputation, he'd experienced it.

"Okay." Randy uncrossed his arms and started to reach his hand into his letterman jacket, but that start was all he got.

My forearm to his throat, I slammed him back into the brick wall and poked the pointy end of my newly acquired switchblade under his chin.

"Be real still, motherfucker," I said low as he blinked his no longer bleary blue eyes at me.

"Settle down, War," Kyle said, sounding strangled behind me.

"You got Kyle, Bry?"

"Oh yeah," Bryan said. "I got him on the ground. He doesn't look so good."

"Fuck, War." Kyle wheezed, and I knew without taking my eyes from Randy that Kyle was in a fetal position, his hands cupped over his shriveled junk. "Randy was just gonna give you some cash. I kept your corner for you while you were gone. I ain't gonna try to keep it. You want it back, all you had to do was ask."

"I take what I want." I dug my forearm into Randy's windpipe one more time just for fun. "I don't ask anyone for anything, ever."

I stepped back, away from Randy. He eyed the blade and me with the right amount of trepidation now, remaining where I'd pinned him.

I clicked my blade closed and turned to Kyle, jerking my chin toward the building. "Get your worthless sentry and your sorry ass out of here."

"But, War—"

"Stay off my corner. Go. Now," I snarled the words at Kyle, my lips pulling back from my teeth.

Wisely, Kyle and Randy decided to do as told. I kept my gaze on them until they disappeared into the building.

"Why'd you wanna give Kyle such a hard time?" Bryan asked.

"He had my corner," I said. It was as fucking simple as that.

"He had it because you told him to keep it until you returned."

"Yeah, so I'm back now." I shrugged. Bryan didn't always see things the same way as me.

"Why didn't you take his money?"

"Not opposed to free samples, or the other occasional perks that come my way from having a friend who deals." Focusing on Bryan, I lifted a brow. His naiveté sometimes surprised me. "But I'm not taking drug money from him and getting my ass thrown back into the alternative school. Or worse, jail."

"Sorry, man." He winced from the dig. "It should've been me who went to juvie, not you."

"Not gonna lie, Bry. That shit sucked."

Worse than I'd ever let on, though I'd do it again if necessary, but only for him. Bryan was my brother in all the ways that counted. But I wasn't sure I'd survive a second time. The shit that happened inside juvie made Southside High seem like a fucking garden party.

"I owe you big." He clenched his teeth together so tightly, a muscle spasmed in his jaw. "Never going to be able to repay you for that."

Yeah, he probably had some idea what happened in lockdown. I nodded to acknowledge his statement, but I wasn't going to rub it in. If it were anyone else, fuck yeah. But that wasn't how Bryan and I operated.

"Never going back inside that shithole again." I pocketed the blade and clapped my best friend on the shoulder. "It's good to be back. Let's go find some bitches. I need to get laid."

Chapter TWO

LACE

The office secretary kept droning on about school rules and policy long after the bell for first period rang. Already nervous about being the new girl, I nodded but shifted impatiently.

"Did you get all that?" She glanced over the rims of her purple glasses at me as she handed over my class schedule.

"Yes." I nodded again, making my blond ponytail sway.

She'd spewed a ton of information, so fast that I didn't really get everything. But what I didn't get, I'd figure out somehow.

I'd come from an accelerated program at a charter high school. Even though I wasn't quite sixteen yet, I was entering Southside High as a sophomore. I was smart, and not just academically. My brother, Dizzy, and I had been through a lot that had forced us to grow up fast.

"Okay then, let's get you to class." The secretary crooked her finger at a pretty Latina who was dressed nearly identical to me in a sweater set, jeans, and ballet flats.

I wondered if her outfit was purposefully chosen to project an image like mine was. Clothes did make the person, or so I tried to convince myself. Often.

"Sabrina," the secretary said. "Please escort Miss Lowell to her first-period class and show her where the important things are along the way."

"Yes, Mrs. Hodges," Sabrina said dutifully. She abandoned the graffiti-emblazoned plastic chair she'd been sitting on and beckoned to me from the glass office door. "Ready?" she asked, finally making eye contact.

"Yeah," I said hoarsely, and swallowed to moisten and loosen my throat. It felt thin like a straw, and tight like it had a tennis ball stuck inside it. Clasping my class schedule to my chest, I hurried to join her.

As soon as the door closed behind us, Sabrina said, "You're in a bunch of honors classes." She spoke with a slight Spanish accent. "Are you really that smart?"

Shrugging, I said, "I make good grades." I had to make them. A scholarship was my only real chance to get out of Southside Seattle.

"That's cool. Well, c'mon." Sabrina turned and practically sprinted through the empty hallway. The soles of her flats were loud as they snapped across the cracked linoleum.

I jogged to keep pace with her. It was an inelegant jog. Without a locker yet, my backpack was heavy with textbooks I'd just been given.

"I'm not saying this to be judgmental or anything . . ." Withdrawing a navy bandanna from her sweater pocket, Sabrina tied it around her loose ebony hair. "But being smart around here makes you a target. Being pretty will too. Before the end of the day, you're probably gonna get jumped."

Fear clutched my stomach, but not because of the novelty of the experience. I'd been beaten before. By my own mother, a few of her boyfriends, and at school by other students.

"You'll need to pick a group to join for your own protection." Sabrina gave me a sidelong glance. "You into sports?"

"No, not really." I shook my head, the fire-engine-red lockers on either side of me blurring. I felt a little dizzy and sick.

"In a gang?" she asked, looking hopeful.

"No." I shook my head.

"I'm in La Rasa Prima. I can put in a good word for you with Jorge if you want."

"No, that's okay." I was born and raised in Southside. I knew how that gang worked. They might keep me safe, but the cost was too high.

"It's your ass." She shrugged.

I straightened my shoulders. *I can hold my own.*

Most of the time that was true. On those occasions when it wasn't, my big brother intervened.

Dizzy and I were the only family each other had. Our mother didn't count, and the uncle we lived with only nominally. Food, clothing, shelter, he provided those, but he didn't do it out of affection. Constantly, he reminded us how us living with him put him out. But since we'd moved in with him, Dizzy didn't hover over me as much as he once did.

"Here's your locker." Sabrina stopped and banged on the metal door of locker number 303. The paint on it was scratched with the words DON'T GROW UP, IT'S A TRAP.

I almost smiled. That was my brother's philosophy, for sure.

Unfolding my schedule, I glanced down at the combination code Mrs. Hodges had written on it. While I opened my locker, Sabrina pulled a pack of gum from her pocket. I unzipped my backpack and stacked most of my books inside. The metal door clattered as I closed it and then spun the dial.

"Don't ever put anything valuable in there." Sabrina gave me a pointed look before turning away. Crooking her finger, she said, "C'mon."

"Okay." Once again, I jogged to keep up with her.

"Freshmen and sophomores have classes on this hall. This is the north side. North is for unaffiliated types." She gave me a pointed look. "In other words, losers. South side belongs to La Rasa Prima. Your first class is there. Without protection, a white girl like you isn't going to go unnoticed. Do you have a weapon?"

"No." Suddenly, I was sure I was going to hurl. Spotting a restroom, I pointed. "Can we stop? I don't feel so good."

"Sure, but don't—"

Trembling, I pushed open the door, shocked to find a guy—a handsome guy—was inside, leaning against the bathroom counter. He turned his head.

A bolt like lightning struck me as his warm brown eyes connected to mine. I forgot everything. The electrical current surging through me was so strong, my mind totally blanked.

That alone would have been enough on its own to shock me into statue stillness. So would the fact that there was a boy inside the girls' restroom.

But there was more.

Both brunette.

Both working over Mr. Brown Eyes and Shirtless.

One wearing only her jeans and bra kissed and licked his sculpted chest. The other one was dressed—*un*dressed—much like the other, but she was on her jean-clad knees in front of him, very enthusiastically giving him a blow job.

Neither took notice of me. Apparently, he had powers to mind-blank women and tasted really good. The kissing, licking, and sucking sounds bounced off the colorful graffiti-splashed tile walls, transforming the bathroom into an XXX-rated concert hall.

"Hey, beautiful." Brown Eyes' full lips slowly curved and my stomach flipped. His perfectly pitched voice was as good as his eyes. "Wanna join us?"

I shook my head, noting as I backed away that there was an additional pair of black boots inside one of the bathroom stalls. The walls of the stall rattled, accompanied by fleshy slaps and heavy breathing.

My cheeks burning, I exited the way I'd entered. In other words, just as shakily. I turned around as the door closed behind me.

Sabrina waited outside, her arms crossed, and rolled her eyes at me. "I tried to warn you."

"Who *was* that?" I asked, glancing at the bathroom door again, my heart racing.

"Warren Jinkins. The king of the losers."

"He's . . ." I envisioned him again in my mind's eye, with his long sun-streaked brown hair, warm brown eyes, and lean muscular body. Chill bumps coated my skin, and I hugged my arms around myself. "He's kinda handsome."

I undersold it, knowing not to overstate my interest in any guy. Sabrina might not be a mean girl, but I knew to keep my thoughts and feelings to myself, or mean girls would trample them.

"Jinkins is all right. A good lay. Not that I've gone there, but I see chicks throwing themselves at him all the time. But he only fucks seniors." Sabrina hooked her arm with mine. "Avoid that restroom in the mornings unless you wanna get an eyeful."

Numbly, I nodded.

"If you think Warren's good-looking, wait till you see his best friend. Bryan Jackson is super-fine."

Chapter THREE

WAR

"Blond, smoking curves, amazing amber eyes . . . she was fucking gorgeous." I strutted down the hallway, *my* hallway, spray-painted with the warning IF KARMA DOESN'T GET YOU, WAR FUCKING WILL. Bryan strolled alongside me while I tried to shake off the spell the blonde had put me under.

"Sure you've never seen her before?" Bryan asked, giving me a funny look.

Yeah, so I'd never asked about a chick before. They came *to* me. They came *for* me. And repeat. It was boring.

But not this girl. She was different. I knew it.

"She must be a new student." I stopped in front of the door to Mr. Yurelli's classroom. "Stop by the office later, and see if that chick who has the hots for you can find out who she is. Get the new girl's schedule. Yeah?"

"Yeah." Bryan nodded. "I hear you."

I yanked on the metal handle to open the classroom door, and we sauntered in side by side. The dudes clapped and muttered approvingly as we returned to our seats. Everyone knew where we'd been and what we'd been doing.

I got a couple of glances from chicks who wanted to be next, and a few glares from jealous jocks wearing varsity jackets like Randy's. I didn't get what it was about them that made some of the chicks automatically drop their panties.

After settling into my seat in the back row, I stretched my long legs out into the aisle. My wallet chain swayed on my hip. Bryan settled into a seat on my right side. He wore the same basic shit—worn T-shirt, faded jeans, even the chain.

"Comfortable, Warren?" Mr. Yurelli looked back at me, the chalk in his hand poised over some stupid-ass equation on the blackboard.

"For the moment." My lips curved as some girls giggled and a few guys guffawed.

Shaking his head at me, Mr. Yurelli returned to teaching.

Bryan opened his notebook and started writing shit down. He had a mom who cared about him and how he did in school. Mine didn't give a shit. Besides, what fucking use would I ever have for algebra?

I was going to be the lead singer in a band . . . a world-famous rock band. Bryan would be my guitar player. We just needed a few additional members to round out a group. Some good tunes under our belt, and we'd be out of Southside fast.

Fame. Money. Chicks. Booze. We'd have all we wanted, in that order. My old lady wouldn't be able to ignore me when I was on the cover of *Rolling Stone*.

After a lot of boring stuff, the bell rang. From the back of the room, Bryan and I ambled out last.

"War?" Mr. Yurelli extended his arm into the aisle, stopping me.

"Yeah? What's up?" I jerked my chin high, giving him respect. I didn't understand the stuff he taught. But since he basically let me do whatever I wanted in his class, I liked him.

"Mr. Garrett wants to see you in his office."

"Fuck," Bryan said. "What do you think he wants?"

"Dunno." I hadn't done anything wrong. But the principal summoning me to his office on my first day back, within the first hour or so of my return, was good for my bad reputation.

"I'll head there now, Mr. Yurelli."

"Thank you, Warren."

"No problem, Mr. Y."

I headed through the doorway and stopped just outside it. The corridor was crowded with Latinos, blacks, and whites, all mixed together and shuffling along apathetically. Why study? Why care about anything? We all knew we'd end up going nowhere, just like our parents.

"Catch up to you in history class?" Bryan asked.

"Yeah. Probably. I might skip, pick up another bitch." *And fuck her while thinking about the new girl,* I added silently. That had worked to make the finish spectacular with the brunettes. "If not history, then lunch. Grab us some chips from the caf and a couple of sodas. I'll meet you outside on the corner."

"Okay." Bryan lifted a finger in the air and dove into the flow.

I turned left and went upstream against the traffic. Holding my chin high and my shoulders back, I slid on my shades. People jumped out of my way. No one wanted to mess with a six-foot-one badass with an attitude.

Plus, word of what had gone down with Kyle had probably already made the rounds. My reputation remained intact. I might not be a rich piece of shit like my old man, but here on my end of Southside High, I ruled.

With the fluorescent overhead lighting shining down on me like the spotlights on a stage would someday soon, I confidently strode through the rapidly emptying hallways on my way to the office.

"Mr. Jinkins." The secretary rolled her eyes behind purple-framed glasses when I entered the office. "You've returned from the great unknown."

"Had to, Mrs. Hodges." I leaned over her desk and lowered my voice, dropping my shades a second to give her a low-lidded scan. "You're here, aren't you?"

"Oh, well." Looking flattered and uncomfortable, she shifted in her chair.

"Warren," Mr. Garrett barked from behind her. "Quit flirting with my secretary." He hooked his thumb toward his glass-enclosed space. "My office. Now."

"Later, Mrs. H." I tapped her desk with my knuckles, and I swore she sniffed the air as I strolled past. Her reflection in the glass revealed she was fanning her face with a paper file.

The alternative school had been shit, but I still had my touch with the ladies.

"Hey, Mr. G." I entered his office and folded my frame into the red plastic chair on the right. It was my preferred roost.

"Mr. Garrett," he said predictably, correcting me as always. "And remove the sunglasses, young man."

"Yeah, okay." I put my shades on my head, watching him round his desk and take a seat to narrow his brown eyes on me. "You summoned. I came. Whatcha need, Mr. Garrett?"

"For starters, I'll take that switchblade you brought with you onto my campus." He tapped his desk with his large black hand. "Now, Mr. Jinkins. I really don't think you want to violate the terms of your parole. Or do you?"

After a short stare-down while I wondered how he knew, I shook my head.

"The weapon, if you please." He tapped his desk again.

I leaned back in my chair, shoved my hand into the front pocket of my jeans, and withdrew the switchblade. When I placed it on his desk, the metal glinted, reflecting the overhead light.

"Oh, Warren." Mr. Garrett shook his head, looking resigned. "What am I going to do with you?"

"Dunno." I tensed, my gut tightening, though I actually liked him. He didn't just let me do what I wanted like Mr. Yurelli. Mr. Garrett seemed to really give a shit about me.

"Not going to turn you in, though I should," he said, and I exhaled a sigh of relief. Too fast, apparently, because he put on his dead-serious face. "But if you *ever* bring a weapon into *my* school again, I'll send you back to juvenile detention so fast, your head will spin."

"Noted," I said grimly.

"Good. Glad to hear that. You don't seem to note much of anything I've said to you over the years."

He leaned forward, picked up the switchblade, and moved it beside a thick manila folder with my name scribbled on it. Opening it, he skimmed a page, flipped it over, then skimmed another and yet another.

As I waited, I squirmed in my seat. But I stilled when he lifted his gaze.

"Been doing this a long time, Warren." He no longer looked resigned, only sad. "I know a lost cause when I see one."

My gut churned. I'd been a lost cause my entire life. Rejected by my old lady from the day she popped me out, and my old man too. He'd been married to someone else when he fucked around with my mother.

I'd only recently discovered his identity, but I shouldn't have bothered. He refused to acknowledge me when I tracked him down and confronted him, but he did say a few words to the judge on my behalf before my sentencing. Otherwise, I never would have gotten off as lightly as I did for Bryan stealing and wrecking his precious car. The asshole cared more about his Beemer than he did about me, his own son.

"You aren't a lost cause, Warren," Mr. Garrett said, and that surprised me so much, I almost fell out of my chair. "Not yet, anyway."

Shocked, I didn't know what to say, so I just stared at him.

He pointed to a page in my file. "Says here you have an interest in music."

"Fucking social worker." They'd forced me to talk to a counselor after the last fight I got into. I sat back in my chair and shrugged.

"Hmm." Mr. Garrett tilted his head and studied me. "Tell you what. I'll make a deal with you."

"What kind of deal?" I narrowed my eyes.

"I won't tell anyone about the weapons violation if you meet with Mrs. Floyd twice a week after school."

"The choir teacher?" I asked.

"Yeah. Isn't singing an ambition of yours?"

"Maybe. But I ain't interested in that sunshiny shit she teaches."

"It's up to her what she wants to do with you. Where she wants to start. What songs she wants you to practice. But it's up to you what you do with what she teaches. Are you hearing me?"

"I got any say in this?" I glanced at the blade, then up at him.

"Actually, you do. You have all the say, really. Sure, life dealt you a shitty hand, but that's the same story for nearly every single one of my students."

Mr. Garrett sighed, leaning back in his chair.

"I'm giving you a new card, Warren. You can take it and use it to improve your odds, or you can toss it aside and continue playing the shit hand you have. The choice is up to you."

Chapter FOUR

LACE

Bryan Jackson is here. At Southside High.

I was so surprised by the information that I didn't even recall Sabrina leaving, nor did I care. At least, not as much as I usually did as I stepped inside the classroom and everyone stared at me.

I hated being the new girl.

"Miss Lowell," the teacher said, and I turned to look at him. Mostly bald, he was overdressed in an outdated suit and tie, but had friendly eyes behind his gold wire-rimmed glasses. "I'm Mr. Schubert. We're studying Shakespeare's *Tempest*. If you'll introduce yourself to the class, we'll continue our discussion."

One of the reasons I really hated being the new girl was this part. I never understood why teachers always insisted on doing it.

"I'm Lace Lowell. I transferred to Southside from Alliance Prep."

Some kids gasped. I'd gasped too when Uncle Bruce had told us that he was changing jobs and we'd have to move again, during the middle of my sophomore-credited year and Dizzy's junior one. Going from a great school to a not-so-great one would make it even harder for me to get the scholarship I wanted so I could study fashion.

"Well, hello, Lace." A blond guy in a red-and-black football letterman jacket whistled low and scanned my entire body with his dark blue eyes.

I lifted my chin and marched down the aisle, pausing at his desk and kicking one of his neon-green Nike sneakers. Locating an empty seat on the back row, I took it, feeling his gaze and more than a few others on me. Ignoring them, I unzipped my backpack and withdrew paper and a pen.

Luckily, Mr. Schubert returned to teaching, and heads swiveled around to pay attention.

I listened and took notes. He had an engaging style, asking interesting questions that involved the students. I'd studied *Tempest* at Alliance, but his analysis of the material was fresh.

The class went by fast, and the bell rang again. I packed up my supplies, not surprised when the blond guy made his way back to me through the line of students exiting.

"Hey, Lace. Sorry if I pissed you off somehow." He raked a hand through his short hair. "It's just that you're pretty."

"So?" I wasn't opposed to using my looks to get what I wanted. But I knew what this guy really wanted, and I wasn't willing to give it to him.

"So I'm Randy Rhodes."

My brow lifted. His name didn't mean shit to me, but he dropped it like it should.

"I'd like to get to know you." He reached out and touched my arm, and it was all I could do not to recoil. I didn't like people, especially guys like him, touching me without permission. "Can I walk you to your next class?"

"No, that's okay. I want to stay and talk to the teacher. You go on ahead."

"But—"

"But nothing, Randy," I said quickly, cutting him off. "Listen, I'm not interested. Not today. Not tomorrow. Not ever."

His eyes narrowed. "Got it." He turned and stomped away, muttering *bitch* under his breath.

Fuck him for not taking a polite decline. Fuck his expensive clothes. And fuck his rich, popular-boy, entitled attitude.

I zipped my backpack and walked up the aisle, hitching the strap higher on my shoulder and clearing my throat at the teacher's desk to get his attention. "Mr. Schubert? Can I speak to you?"

"Yes, of course." He set his glasses on his desk and pinched the bridge of his nose. "How can I help you, Miss Lowell?"

"I enjoyed your class."

His eyes brightened. "I'm glad. That's high praise. I'm sure you had great teachers at Alliance."

"I had a few. I'm looking forward to taking your class. Can I possibly get your notes for the lectures I missed?"

"Absolutely." Looking equal parts surprised and impressed, he glanced down, and I saw he'd been reading my academic report. "Send it to your Lowell email?"

"Yes. Thank you."

"You're welcome." He tipped his chin toward the door. "Better move on to your next class. It's best not to be stranded in the hall on this side of the building when the students clear out."

Shit. Sabrina had warned me.

I stepped out into the hallway and glanced both ways. Only a few students remained, and all were wearing navy and black colors. They gave me long looks that didn't feel friendly. I didn't know where my next class was, but I figured that at this point, returning the way I'd come was my best option.

Turning, I walked fast, the fine hairs on the back of my neck standing on end as rapid footsteps approached me from behind.

"Hey, *güera*." A short Latina suddenly appeared and moved right in front of me.

I came to a screeching stop, glancing nervously at a taller girl who joined the girl who'd called me *blondie*. The taller girl had a cruel glint in her eyes.

"*Qué es*?" I asked them. *What's up?*

The shorter one narrowed her eyes. "You speak the superior race's language, *chica*?" *Girl.*

I shrugged. "*Un poquito*." *A little.* Only enough to get an A minus in conversational Spanish.

"I don't like white chicks." The taller girl reached out and fingered a lock of my hair.

My eyes widened when I heard a click and a switchblade appeared in the girl's hand.

"You afraid?" The tall girl's brown eyes glistened as brightly as the metal of her blade.

I nodded. Of course I was afraid. I wasn't a coward, but I saw no need to lie. Not when faced with someone wielding a blade.

"You're in our neighborhood. South side of the school belongs to us," the shorter girl said. "You need to pay a tribute. *Entenderme*?"

Yeah, I understood, or at least I thought I did. But before I could blink, the taller girl yanked my hair hard and sliced off a two-inch piece.

"You bitch!" Turning on her, I put my palms on her chest and shoved her backward, reacting without thinking. The locker clanged as her body slammed into it.

"*Puta*!" Her face mottled with anger, she called me a bitch as she pushed away from the metal and came at me. Her blade slashed through the air, and I jumped back to avoid it. She stalked me, her lips twisting into a cruel grimace.

Scared shitless, I backed away more, but stopped when I ran into a wall of flesh. My heart hammering, I turned my head and saw a big Latino guy standing behind me.

I started to scream, but the guy clamped his big hand over my mouth. I was so scared now; it was all I could do to keep from pissing myself.

"What's going on, Belinda?" he asked the tall girl, his voice deeply accented like hers, while I trembled.

"That *puta* pushed me." Belinda jabbed at me with her blade.

"You cut off her hair, Lindy." He made a low rumbly sound. Was he laughing? "Did you think she was going to thank you for that?"

"This doesn't involve you, King." Belinda tossed a long lock of her black hair over her shoulder, using the hand that held the knife.

"It does, 'cause you're pissing me off and making me late for my poetry class."

"*Stupido*, that rap shit of yours."

"Not stupid to me. This *gringa's* hair's not stupid to her. You need to learn to consider others. Find a better outlet for your anger. Make friends instead of enemies all the time, *entenderme*?"

"Fuck you, King," Belinda said, though her expression relaxed and she closed the blade. Jerking her chin to the shorter girl, she said, "Ándale, Yolanda." *Let's go.*

"Stay away from this one," King said low to them, an undercurrent of steel in his tone as he gestured to me. Belinda might have the blade, but he had the upper hand. "She's under my protection. Pass the word on."

"Órale." *Okay*. Belinda turned away, thrusting her arm in the air with my blond hair in her grip, her middle finger extended.

"I'm gonna remove my hand from your mouth." My rescuer's warm breath tickled the skin at my nape. "Don't scream, or teachers will come. I don't need more detention, *ese*?"

I bobbed my head, and he released me. I spun around, my eyes narrowed.

He hadn't gotten any smaller. If anything, my first glance hadn't properly assessed his size. Tree-trunk thighs, barrel chest, stomach with a couple of folds hanging over his belt. He had to be near six feet tall and well over two hundred pounds.

"I'm Juaquin Acenado. But everyone just calls me King on account of my size."

"Why'd you help me?" I asked, the suspicion in my tone obvious. I took care of myself, with the help of my brother. I didn't want to owe anybody anything.

"I like Belinda. I didn't want her getting into trouble."

A scoffing sound escaped me.

"She lost someone like I did." His expression darkened. "But that's not an excuse to terrorize people."

King studied me a long beat, and I studied him back. He had eyes nearly the same tawny gold hue as mine, but the color was more striking on him with his ink-black hair and bronze skin. He was also more handsome than I'd realized at first glance.

"What's your name?" he asked.

"Lace."

"Nice name." His eyes sparkled with sincerity. He was handsome, and apparently spoke and acted from his heart.

I decided right then and there that I liked King. A lot. "Nice of you to help me. Thank you, by the way."

He smiled. "*Que tienas agallas,* Lace."

"What's that mean?" I asked.

"You've got a lot of guts to push someone holding a blade."

"I don't think when I get angry." I made a face. "Gets me into trouble."

"Join the fucking club."

"Really. You have a temper problem?" I arched a disbelieving brow. He seemed pretty controlled.

"Oh yeah." He nodded. "Why do you think I get all the detention? Detention's where I met Belinda."

"Detention's a bad scene here?" I asked.

"Yep." He cringed. "So's walking the halls when no one's around."

"I'm becoming aware." I hitched my backpack into a better position. "I'd better get going."

"Where's your next class?" he asked.

"Don't know, really."

"How about I walk you there?"

"I'd like that. I mean, órale."

"Cool." He bumped my shoulder, and when I skidded a few steps, he chuckled. "Sorry."

"I'm not. Glad I met you today, King."

"Glad I met you, Lace."

I smiled. I didn't do that a lot because I didn't have much of a reason to before. Didn't see the point. But I felt lighter walking beside King.

Alliance might have been a nicer school, but Southside didn't seem all that bad anymore.

Chapter FIVE

LACE

At my locker, on one side of me was a girl in basketball gear fixing her lipstick, using a mirror on the inside of her door. On the other side of me was an interracial couple seriously making out. I grabbed the history book I needed to take home with me and closed the door.

"Have a nice afternoon," I murmured.

After the incident with Belinda, I figured it was prudent to be on somewhat friendly terms with as many students as I could, locker mates especially. Who knew when I might need someone to come to my aid again?

"Hey, sis. How's it going?" My brother approached with an easy saunter. With an even easier grin, he asked, "Guess who I just saw?"

"Who?" I asked, clutching my heavy textbook to my chest.

"Bryan Jackson."

My eyes widened. I'd been on the lookout for our childhood friend all day.

"I invited him over to our place tonight, and a bunch of other people too. Someone's bringing a keg. We'll play some tunes," Dizzy said, and my heart started to race as he raked a hand through his spiked platinum-and-black hair. "This school is super cliquish. I think it's important to establish from the get-go with as many people as possible what type we are."

"Which is what, exactly?" I asked.

"Not any type. Unless there's one for kicking back, having fun, and making music."

That was my brother, a rock 'n' roller to the core. He did his own thing, his own damn way. Dizzy didn't let much faze him.

"You gonna zip that book up in your bag?" He dipped his gaze. "You're hugging it like a lover. You look like a total nerd."

"Hey, don't stereotype me just because I'm trying to make good grades."

"Never. Even if it's not my thing, I'm proud of you." He pulled me close, the leather of his favorite jacket cool against my skin.

My brother didn't often hug me, but he was one of the few who did. Our drugged-out mother, who we never saw anymore, rarely had. It was her fault I was uncomfortable being touched without permission. Dizzy knew why. He'd been there when it happened. Bryan and his mom were too.

Almost raped.

The "almost" part was supposed to make it not such a big deal, but it had been the reason why Child Protective Services had gotten involved, and the reason we'd moved in with our uncle. Also, the reason why I suspected that Bryan had never spoken another word to me.

That hurt. Dizzy, Bryan, and I had been best friends. I'd wanted—dreamed—that one day, Bryan and I would . . .

Well, I didn't indulge in girlish fantasies anymore. I kept my head out of the clouds these days, and my mind on achievable goals.

"Did he say yes? I mean, is Bryan coming over?" I asked, avoiding my brother's knowing gaze as I put the book in my backpack.

"Yeah, he's bringing his best friend. A guy who's supposed to sing pretty well." Slinging an arm around my shoulders, Dizzy steered me down the hall. "I mentioned the Fender. Amps. Bry asked about you."

My heart rate didn't just speed up at that, it skyrocketed. "What'd you tell him?"

"Just that you have an even bigger ego now than you did then," Dizzy said with a grin.

At the end of the hall, he pushed the metal bar to open the door to go outside, and held it open for me. I stepped through, and cold air blasted me as we descended the front steps.

"You should've worn a jacket, Lace." Stopping me on the side-walk, he unzipped his and draped it around my shoulders.

"I didn't want to drag a heavy coat around all day," I mum-bled, wanting to get us back to the subject of our old friend. "Is that all you said to Bry about me?"

My brother's eyes suddenly twinkled. "I told him that you're a center-stage hog."

"Diz." I narrowed my eyes. "That's not true."

"Lace." He shook his head. "Anytime we're messing around with music, you showboat. Just like you did the Britney Spears stuff when we were kids."

"Rockers are supposed to put on a show."

"Not serious rockers."

"Hmm." I raised a brow. "So James Hetfield, Robert Plant, and Ozzy Osbourne don't showboat and aren't serious rockers?"

"Those are all *dudes*." My brother rolled his eyes.

"Diz—" I put my hands on my hips.

He snorted. "Don't get testy and go off on a tirade about em-powerment for women."

I was so caught up in our debate, I barely registered the sound of the school buses pulling away from the curb. "I'm not testy," I gritted out through my teeth.

"If you say so," Dizzy said, being the peacemaker as he often was. He probably knew he had to, or there wouldn't be any peace. "Anyway, I concede your point. But you know the stuff we do in the garage isn't serious. We're just having a good time with the music. You have a serious legitimate plan, a real shot to do something bet-ter with your life."

"I hope so."

"You will, Lace. You can do it. I believe in you."

"I'm trying, Diz." I reached up and touched the side of my head, glad for the barrette that disguised the fact that I was missing a big chunk of hair. There were a lot of factors that could derail my efforts to get a scholarship. Dealing with bullies at our new school was only one of them. "Don't discount what you do with a guitar in your hands. You're the serious one, seriously badass."

"That doesn't mean shit when I don't sing."

"You sing."

"I'm not a front man." He grinned. "Or a front woman."

"True." I bumped his shoulder. I could never stay irritated with Dizzy for long. "Don't forget, I also play the piano."

"Egomaniac," he said, his grin widening.

"Pain in my ass." *Translation: I loved him like no one else.*

Dizzy's grin widened. He was fluent in Lace-speak and could read between the lines. "So, how'd your first day at Southside go? Make any friends?" He threw his arm around my shoulders.

"One."

"A girlfriend-friend?" he asked.

"No, a guy."

Bryan's mom was the last positive female influence I'd had. I didn't make friends with girls easily. I never took the time to analyze the reasons for that, but I knew that the dotted line led back to my dysfunctional relationship with my mother.

"Guys only want one thing from a girl," Dizzy said seriously, repeating the same fact he'd been drilling into my head since I started wearing a bra.

"Not this one." I shook my head. King didn't give off that vibe.

"Hope not." Dizzy tilted his head, studying me closely.

"You never want me to have any boyfriends."

"I want better for you than some Southside loser."

I had too at one time. Once, I believed in fairy tales and perfect princes who could charm you. I'd thought Bryan Jackson was different. He'd treated me nicely, spoken softly to me, and made me feel like I mattered.

But that had been wishful thinking. I was older now, and wiser. It was just me and my brother. And it was my responsibility to get where I wanted to go in the real world—without any magical intervention.

Chapter SIX

LACE

I finished my homework, even reading through the extra notes Mr. Schubert had already emailed me, so that I'd have plenty of time to get ready for the party Dizzy had thrown together. In my frenzy to find the perfect outfit, my closet had exploded. The colorful debris field on my bed contained all my clothes and all my fashion magazines.

Eventually, everything was rejected, even my favorite silver-studded black rock-chick outfits in favor of the known and familiar. Even if it wasn't really me, the sweetheart-pink schoolgirl sweater set was a good color on me, and paired well with my tightest pair of jeans.

Smoothing a hand over my curves, I glanced at myself in the full-length mirror.

My makeup was heavier than usual. A deep mauve darkened my lips, and mascara lengthened my lashes, accentuating my amber eyes. My honey-blond hair was straightened. A strategically placed bobby pin covered the missing piece on one side. The ends flipped just right to call attention to my boobs.

Bryan might not be a critical component to my happiness anymore, and his approval no longer mattered the way it once did. But

I also didn't want him to see me all grown up and dismiss me. I wanted him to be knocked on his ass.

I moved down the dark hallway from my room on the second story at the back of the house. Dizzy's room was beside it, then a small bathroom we shared between us, then the stairs.

The master bedroom, where Uncle Bruce slept, was at the front of the house, overlooking the front yard. His door was closed, I noticed as I descended the stairs. His door was usually closed, especially in the daytime when he slept. At night, he worked at a metal fabrication facility.

The length of separation between his room and ours felt symbolic . . . clear lines of delineation. His life didn't involve ours, and ours didn't involve his, even though we lived in the same house. Some might find that odd. But I was accustomed to being ignored by the grown-ups in my life. My brother was the only real parent I'd ever known.

Downstairs, I trailed my fingers over the back of the 1960s-era evergreen couch. The earth-toned plaid chairs that were paired with it were also from my favorite design era. A simpler time, in my mind, when people marched for peace, gathered at a dairy farm for free music, and love seemed to take priority over hate.

The furniture in the small living room was left by my grandparents, who had died years ago and bequeathed their house and possessions to their nonaddicted offspring. My mother had disappointed them so many times, they'd been glad to have her out of their lives. They'd never even known that Dizzy and I existed.

I pushed through a swinging door to enter the kitchen. The music in the backyard was already pumping, the thumping bass rattling a few of the glass cabinet doors. Luckily, we had nice neighbors on either side of us who wouldn't complain about the noise. Mrs. Smith was a widowed old lady who was sweet on Dizzy, and Mr. Chang on the other side worked nights, though not at the same company as our uncle.

I opened the back door and propped open the screened one with my hip. Shifting sideways, I locked the door with my key. I didn't want anyone wandering into the house. That had only happened once before, and Uncle Bruce had gone apoplectic, threatening to send Dizzy and me back to our mother. We hadn't made that same mistake again.

The backyard was roughly the same size as the downstairs of the house, boasting a bricked patio with some era-appropriate outdoor furniture. It was filled with people I didn't know. With Dizzy's admonishment about me trying to be more social running through my head, I went around to each group and introduced myself while glancing between the driveway and the garage.

Is Bryan already here or yet to arrive? Does he look the same? Will I recognize him? Will he recognize me? My heart fluttered as those thoughts went through my mind.

"I saw you in English class." A very tall guy with a slight Southern accent and thick waves of blond hair moved in front of me.

"Really?" I tilted my head. "I'm sorry. I don't remember you."

"It's hard to keep track of everything and everyone you meet on the first day." He shifted his weight from one worn high-top sneaker to the other. "It took me a couple of weeks to feel like I fit in."

"Did you move from here in Seattle?" I asked.

"No. From Portland, and Alabama before that."

"That's a big change. Two of them." I winced. "But I imagine not a good one if you ended up here in Southside."

"It's okay. My dad moves around for his work. After this last move, I went from being a junior varsity player to varsity on the team here."

"Basketball?" I lifted a brow.

"Yeah." His hazel-green eyes danced, and his full lips curved. Based on his height, he probably thought what sport he played should have been obvious.

"Cool," I said, and meant it. He was unassuming, cute, and had a nice smile. "Congrats."

"Thanks. Hey, I'm Chad. Chad Phillips." He shifted again and ran a hand through his golden hair as if I made him nervous. "I wondered if you'd like to get together and study sometime. English is hard for me. You seem good at it."

"I'd like that, Chad. Studying," I said to clarify. "School's important to me."

"Great, Lace," he said, briefly touching my arm.

My skin prickled, and not from Chad. My arm didn't tingle, but just about everywhere else did. Turning toward the source, I saw him, Bryan Jackson, and it was me that about fell on my ass.

The cute boy I'd once known and crushed on as a little girl wasn't a boy anymore. He was all man, and he was better than cute. He was absolute perfection.

The ground seemed to tremble beneath my feet as his eyes met mine, their gray-green color as dreamy as I remembered. Liquid silver pools with a shimmer of emerald, they were as mesmerizing as a magic mirror, holding all the answers to every question. Or they had at one time. I'd certainly asked Bryan loads of them that he'd patiently answered.

Currently, only one question repeated over and over inside my head.

What do you think of me now?

You can read the rest of the story on Amazon.
Free in kindleunlimited. Southside High is book 1 in the Tempest series. It is a completed series. All the individual books are available in audio.
There is an eBook box set with all 7 books inside it.

Southside High
Irresistible Refrain
Enticing Interlude
Captivating Bridge
Relentless Rhythm
Tempting Tempo
Scandalous Beat

Hot Summer
SCHOOL NIGHT

About the Book

Kyle Murphy is a drug dealer. Street level, he's a dog on a short leash, his every move controlled by his boss Martin Skellin. Handsome, resourceful, and talented, Kyle is more than he appears to be. He just can't be more.

Claire Walsh is a rich girl labeled a freak at her prestigious high school because she likes birds. Taunted and bullied, she ignores her classmates who torment her. That's the nice thing to do, and she's a nice girl, but she wishes that someday someone would see that she is more a beautiful swan than an ugly duckling.

That someday comes the night Kyle goes to Claire's school to sell drugs during her annual talent show exhibition. Claire sees more in Kyle. Kyle sees the beauty in Claire. But he's from Southside, and she's from Lakeside. He breaks the rules to survive. She follows them to please nearly everyone except herself. They are opposites from opposite worlds, a romance between them as star-crossed as *Romeo and Juliet.*

What happens when they break the rules and more than a few stereotypes on one hot summer school night?

Warning: *Hot Summer School Night* contains sexually explicit scenes, drug use, and bullying. It is emotional and suspenseful. It features a quirky heroine and an antihero. If you prefer your romance without any angst, darkness, or danger, and your romantic heroes without any flaws to overcome, do NOT read this book. Kyle and Claire's story begins on a *Hot Summer School Night* and concludes in *Breaking Her Bad.*

Never regret thy fall, O Icarus of the fearless flight.
For the greatest tragedy of them all is never
to feel the burning light.
– Oscar Wilde

Chapter ONE

KYLE

All alone, I stood in my designated corner, surveying my realm.

The walls were a depressing gray. The carpet beneath my moto boots smelled like piss and jizz, stained to a mostly uniform shit brown. No one remembered what color it had originally been before the low-income apartment became my drug den. At least, that was the story I told, and no one questioned it. The past was the past, and I kept mine where it belonged.

An orgasmic moan from the coffee table drew my attention. Four guys were on their knees around it, licking and sucking blow off the skin of a naked chick who acted like she was getting off on what they were doing. She wasn't. She just wanted heroin.

I avoided Crystal. She made the right sounds, but she gave poor head.

Most guys didn't care and took her up on her deal because she was an easy lay, but not me. Besides the fact that her baseline was barely above breathing, her eyes were all wrong. Eyes mattered to me unless the lights were off, or my eyes were closed. I did have some standards.

Pulling my gaze away from Crystal's performance, I scanned the room. A few couples were making out in the area that used to be the dining room. Two guys from the Southside High football team, my bodyguard's ex-brethren, were getting nasty with a fucked-up cheerleader by the swinging kitchen door. I looked away. It wasn't anything I hadn't seen before.

As usual this late, the den was packed. Being graduation time, there were a lot of seniors with red Solo cups in their hands. That was good. The liquor was free, courtesy of my boss. Free booze got them in the door—it was the drugs they inevitably wanted once they came inside that cost them. A few cats I recognized from school entered through the always-open front door. The breeze that accompanied them was only moderately tinted by cannabis, fresher than the stench inside.

The guys met my eyes and acknowledged me with raised fingers and chin lifts before moving farther in. I ruled unopposed in the den now. I appreciated the respect, but it wasn't anything to be proud of. The king of shit was king of shit. I did what I did because I had to. But that didn't mean I dug it.

Exhaling, I crossed my arms over my chest. I was bored. I just wanted it to be quitting time already so I could leave.

As if she sensed my restlessness, Missy Rivera signaled me from the stairs. On her ass on a step midway up, she'd been hanging around, watching me from between the rusted banister rails. With long black hair and all the curves, Missy was off-the-chain pretty, but too fond of coke. She'd blow me for it.

I usually indulged with someone at the end of my workday, and she knew it. That was why she was sticking around. It was a business transaction. It wasn't personal.

"Kyle, *psst.*"

I wanted to roll my eyes at Gary. My number-two rep was a complete dork, but you couldn't complain about his reliability.

I signaled to Randy Rhodes. Looking all menacing, which he barely was, he stepped aside to let Gary come close to me. As my bodyguard, the lumbering linebacker was improving, but he remained a work in progress.

"How's it going?" I asked Gary.

"Take's good," he said. "But less than you-know-who will want."

Gary was scared shitless when it came to our boss. Never said his name, like it might somehow magically summon him. Gary had reason to be scared. He was missing a small toe on his left foot on account of sticking it where it didn't belong, but I wasn't sure he'd learned his lesson. He was reliable but not that smart.

"Skellin's not gonna like that," I said, just to say something. Fact was, Martin would be *I wanna fuck someone up* pissed at the news. "Circulate. See what more you can move."

"But . . ." Distracted, Gary turned his interested gaze to the coffee table where things were now getting triple-X pornographic.

"Man, focus. Move the product." I narrowed my eyes. "If you don't get the job done, you'll have to answer to Skellin."

"Right." Gary bobbed his head and slunk off.

"I'm going upstairs," I told Randy, then signaled to Missy.

She stood up, looking animated rather than bored for the first time tonight.

"Need me to come with?" Randy asked, looking almost as eager as Missy. Dude liked pussy, lots of it, and he didn't mind sharing.

"No, man. I got this." I held up my fist, and he brought his up for a bump. "Keep the peace downstairs. No slacking off."

"You got it."

I nodded to acknowledge him, but I wasn't that hopeful about Randy's ability to follow even that simple directive.

Climbing the stairs, I picked my way through the group of heroin junkies sprawled on it. But getting through them wasn't any more trouble than usual.

Missy was waiting for me in front of my office. She pushed away from the hallway wall when I arrived, and I gestured for her to precede me. I could be a gentleman. Before things went really bad with my parents, my mom had insisted on it.

"You sitting or standing for this?" Missy asked, already unbuttoning her blouse.

"I'll sit. I've been standing all fucking night."

"Okay."

Blouse off, she set it on the bathroom counter, next to the rows of Ziploc bags full of drugs.

I slipped past her, undoing my belt on the way to my throne. Dropping the lid, I worked my jeans down to my thighs while she removed her bra. Her tits were more than handfuls and real. When my cock lengthened inside my briefs, her icy gaze dipped, then rose.

"Want me, baby?" she purred.

"I wanna get off, Missy." I lowered my briefs and took a seat. "It's been a long fucking night. You don't have to pretend to be into it."

"Cool."

Positioning herself in front of me, she placed her hands on my thighs and lowered herself to her knees. My cock came to life in her expert hands, and I eventually ejaculated into her mouth.

When we were done, she wiped the back of her hand across her lips. Expectantly, her eyes met mine for a moment. They weren't right, but they weren't blitzed-out wrong either.

"Coke's in the medicine cabinet," I said.

"Thanks." She popped open the mirrored door and took what she needed.

We both got what we wanted, but it was sad that the conversation and eye contact was more intimate than the blow job. I got it, but I didn't attempt to change it.

Business was business. I was the king of shit, so shit was what I had.

Chapter TWO

KYLE

A little later, I stepped off the bus and planted the soles of my Daytona moto boots on the pavement.

The concrete was dry. The waterproof black leather wasn't necessary tonight, nor the steel toes or the shin guards, but I believed in being prepared. I'd learned from experience that not being prepared could get you messed up so badly, you wished you were dead.

Popping up the worn collar on my favorite denim jacket, I glanced around. At four a.m., the sidewalks in downtown Renton were deserted. All the quaint shops and restaurants on Main Street were dark, and the carefully cultivated tree-lined street was clear of cars. The air was damp from the southernmost shore of Lake Washington, cool but not cold against my skin. Summer was officially here. But summers—even well south of downtown Seattle—came with a chill.

It took a light-rail ride and three different bus transfers to get here. It was a long, pain-in-the-ass journey, one I took every night, but it was worth it. There were no pops of gunfire here, no screams. No razor-sharp edge of violence or despair that tainted the Southside air like ozone. Renton was day-and-night different from Southside. As different as I pretended to be here.

During a normal commute time, one train ride would have taken me from Southside to Renton, but I didn't work a normal job during normal hours. Keeping my two lives separate required effort. It wasn't just the logistics involved. I also had to make sure no one followed me. Not that I—as of yet—had ever noticed anyone doing so outside Southside. But just because you didn't see the danger didn't mean it wasn't there.

The night my parents died came to mind. But as soon as that memory surfaced, I locked it down, returning it to the watertight box with all the other important things that I buried deep inside me.

Digging the hood of my hoodie out from underneath the collar of my jean jacket, I pulled it over my head. Chin down, I swept my eyes back and forth. I wasn't in Southside anymore, but I still had to be safe.

I made my way uphill along the charming-as-shit street. Colorful banners on lampposts fluttered, heralding the upcoming Puget Sound Bird Fest. Uncle Bob was excited about it, and so was I, to be honest. It was almost real, this other life I hid and protected. It certainly had the trappings of normalcy I craved.

The walk to my condo from downtown wasn't long, but it gave me enough time to switch out identities. After making two right turns and crossing a couple of quiet streets, I raked my hoodie off my head. Shaking out my untamable black hair, I removed the guardedness I wore like plates of armor. My footsteps were lighter without that burden.

I loosened my clenched fists. The fire inside me that sometimes made me do ill-advised things to defy my merciless master and rattle the bars of my unbreakable cage continued to burn. The anger and futile frustration that fueled that defiance never went out.

The entire transformative process took minutes, but I did it every night like a snake shedding its skin.

By the time I reached the wood steps that led to the deck of my condo, I was almost a different person. I breathed easier. All that remained of the guy from Southside was my rambling walk. My wide shoulders back, I timed my strides to the beat of my favorite Led Zeppelin tune.

My ramble was cooler than Warren Jinkins's glide. *I* was way cooler. Now that he had glided on to bigger and better things with his band, Tempest, and their RCA record deal, maybe people would finally acknowledge that.

A light suddenly switched on in the darkness. Caught in an unexpected spotlight, I stumbled.

Blindly, I reached inside my jacket for my blade. I wrapped my fingers around it, but when I withdrew it, it was knocked from my grip. Wheeled in a fast circle, I was shoved face forward into the wood deck. Seeing stars from the collision, I let out a grunt of pain.

"He's clear," Arturo said to his master. We served the same one. After frisking me, Skellin's bodyguard pressed his heavy weight on top of me, holding me down.

"Clear for what?" I feigned cool, but it was shit acting with splinters in my skin and me wheezing.

"Quiet, Kyle." Arturo yanked my arm back between my shoulder blades and twisted it, sending a bolt of fiery pain through me.

"What the fuck, Arturo?" My heart raced, but I slowly spaced out my words.

I needed the extra time to put my armor back on. Without it, I was vulnerable. My face was smashed and my arm burned like crazy, but I couldn't let them know I was hurting.

Never let 'em know you're hurting or who they can hurt to get to you. My father's words from long ago, the only sound advice he'd ever given me.

He had his excuses, but he'd crapped out on me as a role model long before he died. And now I was alone. I had only one person remaining in my life who genuinely cared about me. And I protected Uncle Bob, no matter the cost.

"Lay off, Arturo. How am I supposed to deal if my arm is in a sling, man?"

"Martin wants a word." Arturo cranked my arm up higher and chuckled darkly when I hissed. He was as sadistic as his master.

"Release him," Martin Skellin said from a safe zone somewhere behind Arturo that I couldn't see since my face was smashed into the deck.

"You bet, boss." Arturo gave my arm a final twist and released me.

"Thanks for nothing," I gritted out through clenched, splinter-filled teeth.

After pushing slowly to my feet, as if I had all the time in the world and wasn't afraid, I rubbed my sore shoulder as I turned around. A shadow darker than the night emerged.

"Kyle Murphy," Martin said slowly. He had a thing about full-name formality and delighted in dispensing pain unnecessarily.

I hoped tonight was more about the former and less about the latter. But with Skellin and his ilk, you never really knew and always had to be on guard. A lesson my dad never learned, and he and my mother paid the ultimate price.

"How was the take tonight?" he asked.

"Better than decent." With War out of the picture, I had no one I owed product or favors to anymore. No one except Martin Skellin, unfortunately.

"Yeah?" Skellin stared down the length of his nose, studying me.

My eyes rapidly adjusting to the moonlight, I studied him right back.

With his dark hair and eyes, chicks seemed to think he was good-looking, but I didn't get it. Chicks were fucking blind. Lace Lowell, War's ex, was now one of them. She'd gotten herself into a trap with Martin that she couldn't break free from.

"Seemed short for an end-of-the-school-year party to me," Skellin said.

"Our customers are strapped paying for graduation, along with the usual necessities." Those took priority over recreational enhancements, or they did for the graduates who weren't drug dependent like my dad had been in the end.

"Bullshit. They wanna get high off my premium shit, they pay for it. I'll just take the shortfall out of your cut."

"But—"

"You got a problem?"

In my peripheral vision, I noticed Arturo inching closer. Without a flashlight blinding me, I could see damn good at night. Like a barred owl, Uncle Bob said. Being compared to one of his favorite raptors was high praise. I didn't get praised by anyone except by him. But it was Bob. He cared about me, so his was enough.

"Got no problem." I quickly shook my head.

Those who had a problem with Martin Skellin didn't have one long because they didn't live long. And Bob was inside that condo, along with Mrs. Paczynski. She kept an eye out for him while I was working, but she was seventy-two years old. No matter how this played out, I couldn't allow any of my other life to bleed onto them.

"Glad to hear that." Martin narrowed his coal-black eyes. "Wouldn't want to bring child protective services in to have another look-see at your unconventional guardian situation before you turn eighteen, now would we?"

"No, we wouldn't." My throat tightening, I swallowed hard.

"You need to remember whose name is on the lease of that shithole in Southside, and whose cash pays for your sweet condo here. Homes and cash can disappear just as easily as people." He snapped his fingers. "You feeling me, Kyle Murphy?"

"Yes, sir." My heart pounding fast, I lifted my chin, trying to ignore the sting behind my eyes. "I feel you."

"Good boy. You're my favorite little rep. But don't forget favor must be earned." His lips curled into a reptilian grin that injected even more darkness into his eyes. "Speaking of earning, I have a job for you in a different zip code. Tomorrow night. Arturo will fill you in on the details."

Chapter THREE

CLAIRE

My hands trembling with nerves, I steered my Land Rover from the drop-off circle into the parking lot for my private school. The line of limos that had been ahead of me continued moving forward, inching their way toward the imposing multicolumnar facade of Lakeside High.

The school grounds were packed this evening. Students, teachers, parents, and former alumni were on campus for the annual end-of-the-year talent exhibition. Just thinking about my part in the show made my heart hammer inside its gilded cage.

Rolling through aisles in the nearly full lot at a crawl, I searched for an empty space. Finally, I found one near the back. Switching off the engine, I rested my hands on the steering wheel, wishing I could sprout wings and fly away.

Staring hard at the stately Western white pine in front of my vehicle, I breathed deeply. Its dark green needles blurred before my eyes. Among the many other embarrassing quirks that made me stand out rather than blend in with my peers, I tended to tear up when I was nervous.

Blinking through the wetness, I tried to envision the performance ahead and reminded myself that I only had to do this one more time before I graduated. But envisioning and reminding didn't help. My palms remained clammy, and my heart continued to race.

I sighed. If only I were a bird that could fly wherever I wanted, do whatever I wanted, be who I wanted to be . . . whoever that was. I didn't exactly have that part figured out yet.

I was only seventeen, and had a year to go before I graduated. In my mind, who I was wasn't fully formed yet. But in the privileged circles my family moved in, my identity was already established and had been before I could walk. I was trapped in a role I had to play.

Gripping the leather-wrapped wheel tighter, I held back my tears of fear and frustration. They would ruin my makeup. My mother had paid to have a professional makeup artist come to the house, an expense nearly as extravagant as my designer gown.

A Steller's Jay suddenly hopped from one limb to another, directly in front of my luxury SUV.

I went completely still like my dad had taught me to whenever I accompanied him in the field. This particular bird was a waiter and a watcher, the only North American jay with a crest. It let out a harsh, scolding call, seeming to chastise me for hiding inside my vehicle instead of getting out and doing what needed to be done.

Okay, bird. I get it.

Giving the jay a nod, I allowed myself a moment to watch it in flight. Graceful and almost lazy, it swooped through the air on its broad, rounded wings.

If only I could be as free, I would soar on the currents of my whims. Figure out for myself in my own time who I wanted to be, and what I wanted to do with my life after high school.

But that wasn't reality. Reality was me earthbound and shuffling in lockstep among a flock of geese that I'd known since our parents put us on exclusive waiting lists for the best preschools. Reality was me being a dutiful daughter, prioritizing my father's affection and craving my mother's elusive approval. One was my sure foundation. The other was higher ground that always seemed out of reach.

Go, Claire. Move. Do what needs doing.

Taking one last breath, I imagined myself as free as the jay in flight. I further imagined myself as an excellent mimic. With their calls, the Steller's Jay imitated a variety of other birds. I could do that. Mimic my classmates. Not be odd. Blend in.

With imitation in mind, I grabbed my silvery clutch and popped open my door. My high heels on the pavement, I pointed the key fob at the vehicle and clicked the locks. I smoothed a hand down my gown. The silk was a deep azure, nearly as beautiful as the jay's feathers.

Pushing my glasses higher up my nose, I turned. Walking between Porsches, BMWs, and Jaguars parked side by side was like moving through a luxury car dealer's lot. My gaze forward, I marched determinedly toward the Grecian-inspired three-story building that had been my school home for the past three years.

I was so tunnel-visioned on what I needed to do that I almost didn't see them at first, two guys standing together, blocking the aisle in front of me.

Vance Nagel, I knew. Handsome and tall, he was one of the most popular guys at school, a linebacker during football season. He also fronted a band, which was cool. Most girls went weak in the knees if he looked at them, but I just got nauseated. He was mean, and his arrogance was off-putting.

My stomach roiling, I began a pivot to avoid him and his dark-haired companion, but wobbled when his companion turned and I got a good look at him.

Wow. I sucked in a breath, ensnared by an arresting pair of eyes the color of storm clouds.

Beneath his unruly black hair, his gaze widened when he saw me. Time seemed to stop as our eyes locked.

I didn't know him, had never seen him before. With those high cheekbones, strong jaw, and firm lips, he had a devastating level of handsomeness you saw once and never forgot.

Tall and wide shouldered, he had a stance that was confident to the point of being almost confrontational. A dark prince in his tux, he'd laid claim to the ground where his regal feet were planted.

His gray eyes brewed at gale-force intensity, and his chin was tilted at an angle that dared anyone to challenge him.

"Who's she?" Mr. Devastating asked Vance in a deep voice that rumbled across the two car lengths separating us. The perfect pitch of his voice raised chill bumps on my flesh.

Vance shifted. Giving me his usual head-to-toe scan as if he were imagining me naked, even though he was dating a friend of mine, he turned back to his companion. "Nobody."

Heat burning my cheeks at that cruel assessment and dismissal, I kept walking, leaving Vance and the unknown prince behind. Vance's words were a reminder I didn't need. I was who I was. My destiny was set. Handsome, mysterious princes weren't for odd girls like me.

By the time I reached the front of the school, I was out of breath. My skin continued to prickle with awareness from my brief encounter with the unforgettable stranger.

I was dismayed to discover the path into the building was clogged by my classmates. The girls wore expensive floor-length gowns like mine. The guys wore tuxes like Vance and the prince. Everyone was clustered into cliques, none of which I belonged to.

Blocked from going forward, I glanced back over my shoulder, scanning the parking lot. When I didn't see the stranger again, disappointment washed through me, and I spun back around. My long heavy braid swished the still tingling skin between my bare shoulder blades.

"Excuse me," I said determinedly, pressing my way through the throng.

As those in front of me shifted sideways to let me pass, the inevitable quacking started. I didn't see who started it tonight, but the name calling and hurtful commentary accompanied the quacking like it always did.

Odd-duck Claire.

She's so weird. She likes birds better than people.

Just look at her. She's got a nest in her hair.

I touched my French braid and the baby's breath woven into it. I'd thought the style was pretty until now. Tears filled my eyes.

I'd earned the duck label in first grade because of my impassioned speech about local factories encroaching on the woodland fowls' habitat.

By now, I should have been accustomed to the ridicule. I should have let their words roll off me like the water-impervious feathers of my namesake. But I couldn't. Though I pretended not to care, deep down like everyone else, I simply wanted to be accepted by my peers.

Straightening my shoulders, I continued toward the entrance, wishing I hadn't let my parents talk me into doing this tonight. I wished I hadn't believed them when they said I looked beautiful.

Despite my glammed-up outward trappings, I remained the same person underneath. Always an odd duck, and never a beautiful swan.

Chapter FOUR

CLAIRE

"Hey, wait up."

Inside the school, a hand landed softly on my shoulder. Recognizing her sweet voice, even if I hadn't heard her approach, I stopped in the hallway and turned to face her. "Go back to your friends, Ella."

"You're my friend too," she said in a hushed tone. Stepping in front of me, she moved gracefully on high-heeled designer shoes she was accustomed to wearing. Her cheeks were red, and her eyes were shiny. "I'm sorry about them."

"Apology accepted," I said with a nod. Grudges weren't my thing.

"I should stand up to them." She dropped her chin. "I know that. They were being assholes. They're just jealous."

"Jealous of what?"

"Your poise. Your strength. Your unique personality that trumps their sad, boring conformist ones." Her gaze brightened. No thick lenses dulled their imploring green sheen. "Like mine. I wish I were braver like you."

"I'm not brave."

Or beautiful like Ella Skellin. In addition to her striking jade-green eyes, she had long sable-brown hair with coppery highlights and an adorable smattering of faint freckles across the bridge of her cute nose. She didn't look much like her father.

"You are so brave. You marched right through the middle of them, ignoring their ugliness with your head held high. You look stunning, by the way. That dress is gorgeous with your coloring." She reached out and tucked a stray strand of my sun-streaked gold hair behind my ear.

"I'm the same girl I was earlier in the day. Dorky Claire, only without the hideous school uniform." I captured her hand and squeezed it. "But thanks for the compliment. I like this dress. Yours is pretty too. You look beautiful."

"Thank you. My grandmother picked it out. She has my wardrobe and practically my whole life planned for me." Ella suddenly looked tired and sad. I knew she felt trapped in her life too. She jerked up her head, pointing with her delicate chin. "Are you really going onstage all by yourself tonight?"

"Yeah. My mom and dad want me to." My empty stomach lurched, disturbing the already agitated butterflies flapping their wings. "But I won't be alone. I'll have a wind ensemble accompanying me."

"You're singing alone, though. No choir, right?" She tilted her head, and the fiery highlights in her hair caught and reflected the hallway lights.

"Uh-huh." I pressed a hand to my stomach, feeling ill as I imagined the eyes of my parents, school staff, and peers on me.

"Wow," she said. "That *is* brave, putting yourself out there, revealing your hidden talent."

"Hidden, yes." I swallowed hard. "But I don't know if I'd call it talent."

"I've seen your solo parts for interscholastic choir competitions. You're good."

"Among my nerdy, grade-minded peers, maybe." I bit down on my lip. "But I'm not gifted like you are with your photography."

"That's just a hobby." Her gaze turned unfocused, which was

why I noticed Vance entering the auditorium, and she didn't. He scanned the interior, probably looking for her. "I like the world better through my lens."

"Yeah," I said. I did too.

I preferred the romantic ideals in the songs I chose to sing. The one for tonight was from my dad's favorite band. My mom and dad thought if I performed in front of everyone, they would be impressed. I didn't think that was likely. I just wanted to please them. Maybe make my dad smile. Take his mind off his worry for a little while.

"How's your dad doing?" Ella asked.

"He's all right." I shrugged as if I wasn't worried. As if he weren't.

Dad was in excellent shape. He needed to be for his job as a wildlife ecology consultant for Aranco. He often hiked into rugged and remote areas to determine where his company should run pipelines that would be least harmful to the environment. It was a job that paid well. It was important, and he was passionate about it.

"Test results not back yet?" She caught her bottom lip between her teeth.

"No." I shook my head. "But soon. The cardiologist is supposed to call with the results." We still didn't know why he'd suddenly fainted while working out a few weeks before.

"I'm sure it's nothing serious."

"I hope not."

Needing a distraction from a topic that ratcheted up my tension, I looked for the devastatingly handsome guy I'd seen in the parking lot. Head and shoulders above the others, he was easily found. He might be dressed in a tuxedo like the other men, but he stood out, even in a crowd of people. He was with Ella's father. His head was down, his expression serious.

"Who's that guy with your dad?" I asked, hoping my interest sounded casual.

"What guy?" Ella turned to follow the direction of my gaze, and her red-stained lips rounded. "Uh . . . he's one of my dad's . . . He's one of my cousins."

"I've never seen him before." I tilted my head.

Ella had had lots of cousins of varying ages who didn't look like her. They weren't usually around during on-campus school functions. This one didn't have the menacing aura most of them did, or maybe he did, and I just didn't see it because his good looks overshadowed it.

Ella dropped her gaze. "He's not from around here."

"What's he doing here?" I asked. "Does he work for your dad like the others?"

"Yeah." Her lips pursed, she said, "He definitely works for my dad."

"Does he have a name?" I asked.

"Kyle Murphy," she said, and I turned his name over and over in my head, liking it. A lot.

"What about Kyle?" Vance joined us just in time to hear her.

"Nothing." I stepped back as Vance threw his arm around Ella, almost tripping on the long hem of my gown. "I've gotta go."

Before I turned, I glimpsed Ella's mask of cool, practiced indifference sliding into place. It was the look she nearly always wore, one that kept people at a distance. I never would have talked to her, really confided to her, or her to me, if I hadn't run into her one day without her mask when she'd been taking pictures by the sound.

Setting the memory and the couple behind me, I made my way down the corridor and stopped when I reached the backstage door. Opening it, I entered the darkened area cluttered with cardboard boxes and sound equipment. There, I paused to take a calming breath.

Closing my eyes, I brought the jay back into my mind. I imagined a blue sky and flying above everything and everyone that stressed me out. Lost in my thoughts, I didn't notice the door I'd just come through opening again. But I did notice light spilling into the darkness.

Startled from my reverie, I opened my eyes and inhaled sharply. The alluring scent of a mossy wetland and the invigorating evergreen of a forest flooded my senses.

"Hey, sorry, I didn't mean to scare you," he said, and I recognized his voice. Kyle's voice. It was like earlier in the parking lot, only deeper and more intimate now as the door clicked closed and the darkness returned.

A compelling wave of heat hit my back as he touched my arm.

"Are you okay?" His touch was gentle, the connection between us sparking like a struck match.

Fire skated across my skin and rose to my cheeks as I slowly turned to face him. My eyes met his, earthy brown to cloudy gray. There was something in his gaze, a concern that calmed my fear.

I realized then that his eyes weren't merely a storm. They were a cyclone that spun and lifted me into the air, a rapid ascent from the ground to the sky that left me light-headed and breathless.

Chapter FIVE

KYLE

Fucking hell.

This chick was even prettier up close, but I'd spooked her. She trembled like a little bird caught in a predatory raptor's claws.

"I won't hurt you," I said firmly.

"I know you won't." She bravely cranked up her chin. She was tall for a girl, slender sexy, but a good six inches shorter than me.

I got why she was nervous. I was a total stranger and we were isolated, alone in this darkened corner. The murmur of others was distant, but she wasn't going to admit she was scared. Her bravado was consistent with what I'd seen earlier. She'd flinched at the bullshit name calling and quacking outside, yet she'd held her head high and marched through the group of assholes without acknowledging them.

Rich, entitled pieces of shit.

It pissed me off the way they'd treated her. I knew what it was like to be taunted. Labeled. Made to feel like a caricature rather than a person.

I was Kyle-the-drug-dealer to everyone in Southside. Most didn't even know my last name. I was more than what they thought, but I couldn't be more. Anger from that ever-present fire rolling through me, I curled my fingers into fists, though there was no enemy here to fight.

"How do you know I won't?" I asked, admiring her.

That bravery spoke to me on some basic level, telling me she was her own person. She wasn't going to let me, or those shits outside, or anyone else intimidate her.

However, I also knew what she'd done could be perceived as a challenge to those who got off on tearing strong people down. In Lakeside, on this side of Seattle, she got a pass. But in Southside, they'd eat her alive.

"I see it in your eyes." As she studied me from behind the lenses of her black-framed glasses, her eyes were wide. A soft sparrow brown in color, they were surrounded by a thick dark lashes. "I felt it when you touched me just now. You were gentle. Careful. You didn't come back here to hurt me."

Don't think about touching her again. I fought the urge, though the pads of my fingers and the rest of me continued to register the seductive charge.

"I'm not gentle." I gave her the truth, though I wanted to be gentle with her.

There was something undeniable about this girl, something beneath her strength that stirred my protective instincts. Instincts I activated for only one person now.

Sure, she was beautiful with her sun-streaked long blond hair and tiny white flowers woven into her braid. Sexy too with her body-skimming blue dress, revealing curves that made the palms of my hands burn with the desire to shape them.

Outside, I'd gone instantly hard the moment her gaze had connected with mine. My heart beat so fast and I was so distracted by her, I'd barely managed to complete the deal with Vance. Then that idiocy by her peers happened, which I'd witnessed firsthand, because of course I'd pursued her.

After that, even knowing she had some connection to my boss's daughter didn't stop me from following her backstage. I had to get a closer look. Touch her if the opportunity presented itself. Hear her voice. Determine if she was real.

God, she was most certainly real. She smelled like wildflowers, a field of them on a warm spring day.

"You can't know I'm gentle. You don't know anything about me." I took a step back, putting needed breathing space between us. Being too close to her made my mind spin with impossible ideas. I didn't do impossible. I did what I had to survive.

"I know your name," she said, lifting her chin higher.

So, she'd asked someone about me. Intrigued, I shifted closer.

"Ella says you work for her father."

I froze solid. Maintaining the mere inches between us, I nodded. The truth was Martin Skellin owned my ass. But working for him sounded better.

"What's *your* name?" I asked. She knew mine. It was only right for me to know hers.

"Claire." Her voice cracking, she swallowed. "Claire Walsh."

"Pretty name." My throat suddenly dry like hers must have been, I swallowed too. I wanted to reach up and loosen the bow tie that now felt like it was strangling me. "For a pretty girl."

Oh fuck. I sounded like a douche.

Her eyes rounded, making her perfectly arched dark blond brows rose to peek at me above the dark plastic frames of her glasses. The lenses didn't detract from her beauty. Instead, they magnified it, providing a slideshow for her easily readable emotions.

"Thank you." Her gaze warming, she blushed. Her cheeks turned the dusky rose of a new dawn. That rosy hue spread to her shoulders and the skin over them that her sleeveless dress left bare.

Her round breasts above the low-cut bodice were tempting handfuls. The rest of her skin—and there was a lot of it exposed in that dress—was dewy and glowing like honey in a mason jar held up to the sun. She wasn't a stranger to the outdoors like most of the chicks on this side of town. Her skin bore witness to that fact.

"Hey, Claire."

She jumped as an Asian boy with thick glasses approached

us. He gave me a wide berth and a furtive glance, recognizing the threat I presented like most people did, even if she didn't.

"We're waiting for you. We go on first. Remember?"

He gestured to the stage, where another boy in a tux and a girl in a green gown sat beside each other, holding instruments and wearing curious expressions. When they noticed me looking at them, they quickly glanced away.

"Right. Okay. Thanks, Henry." Claire blinked and then focused on him. "I'll be right there."

She shifted to face me as Henry went to rejoin the others. I decided to focus on her, rather than the fact that I'd let someone approach without noticing because my guard was down. Claire was a distraction. Even on this side of town, a distraction was something I couldn't afford.

"I'd better go," I said.

"Could you stay?" She licked her lips. "I'd really like you to."

My gaze dipped to her mouth.

Fuck. I'd been trying not to look at it. Her lips were deep pink like the fiery flowers on fireweed. Her top lip had a cupid's bow, and the bottom one was lush. Both were slick with gloss. More than anything, I wanted to trace her lips with my tongue. Fit my mouth to hers.

What would she taste like, a girl like her? Fresh like a flower, I imagined. Hot like fire. Bursting with flavor like a ripened cherry plucked right from the tree.

"I can't." My hands formed tighter fists to resist the temptation.

"Of course." Her head bobbed. "You're working. I remember. I've distracted you."

Hell yes, she'd distracted me, and I was working, or I was supposed to be. Skellin was going to have my ass if I didn't sell the product he wanted me to move tonight.

Blushing again, she said, "I'd like to talk to you some more. Get to know you. After I do this thing, that I don't really want to do because it makes me nervous, but I have to do it for my dad. He hasn't been feeling well lately."

She hooked her thumb over her shoulder, giving me a new source of distraction. Her movement lifted her tits. "Maybe afterward, if you're done working, we could go outside. There's an arboretum with some benches. It'll be quiet. Nice outside. We could talk."

"I don't think that would be smart." My voice dropped, revealing the strain it took to refuse her.

"Right. I guess not." The rosy pink returned to her cheeks. "But can you tell me why?"

"Claire!" the Asian dude called, pointing to the center mic. "C'mon. They're getting ready to pull the curtain."

"Shit." She stamped her foot and her breasts jiggled, making my cock jump inside my briefs.

Claire wasn't just pretty—she was an irresistible combination of cute and sexy. That combo had never attracted me before. I got what I wanted from chicks, and they got what they wanted from me. It was just business.

Until now.

You can read the rest of the story on Amazon.
It is free in kindleunlimited. Hot Summer School Night
is book 1 of 2. Breaking her Bad completes the duet.
There is also related content. Getting it Wrong and Getting it
Right is a prequel duet that tells Addy's story. She is Claire's aunt.

OCEANSIDE

About the Book

Oscar night.

Rock star legend, Ashland Keys should be on top of the world, but the blond blue-eyed SoCal surfer is disillusioned with fame, done with drugs, bored with the groupies and sick of all the fake f*ckery. A rising star, Fanny Bay is nominated for best original song in the same category as the Dirt Dogs band, but the novel redhead with the corkscrew curls and the slight Canadian accent would prefer to chart a course with a different destination.

Hollywood is not for her.

He's full of regrets, darkness and secrets.

She's full of hope and light and has mysteries of her own.

He's her reserved hero.

She's his gypsy rose.

He's water. She's fire. Together, they don't make sense.

But he's what she's always wanted, and she just might be everything he needs.

Love is the good in me
Where there is love
There is hope
Where there is hope
There is light
Where there is light
There is a way
Tomorrow Today

– Fanny Bay

PROLOGUE

FANNY - 2013

The Dolby Theatre. One of the largest stages in the nation. One hundred and twenty feet wide. Seventy-five feet deep. On one of the biggest nights of the year.

Oscar night.

Mesh bronze accents. Plush seats trimmed in plum velvet. Pure old school Hollywood glam.

Ultra cool.

What wasn't?

Me. Fanny Bay Lesowski. A twenty-year-old with red corkscrew curls and a slight Canadian accent. Even my name was the opposite of glamorous.

Under the striking silver looping ovoid structure, which supported and disguised an immense lighting grid, I felt tiny and insignificant. Clenching my fingers tighter around the mic in my hand, I willed my body not to tremble. But I was scared. I didn't belong here. Not really. Not center stage at the Oscars with dozens of cameras trained on me following my every move.

Fanny Bay, don't let your nerves get the best of you, I reminded myself, my stomach swirling anew. *Remember, you've done this song in front of cameras and audiences plenty of times since the nomination.* The trick was fooling my brain into believing that this was just one more performance, not one in front of countless celebrities and rock stars much less fifty million worldwide viewers.

Breathe in Zen. I closed my eyes and inhaled positive energy.

One.

Two.

Three.

Breathe out all the negativity. I exhaled for three counts and opened my eyes.

Better.

My surroundings seemed less intimidating with my mind cleared. My tense muscles loosened as I compiled a list:

1. The capacity inside the historic venue was only thirty-four hundred. I focused on that manageable number.
2. I had done similar shows before—minus the enormous television audience of course.
3. I wouldn't be alone. My half-sister Hollie would arrive soon to occupy her reserved aisle seat three rows back from the stage. She would be radiating positive energy and cheering for me. Our mother would be here, too. I believed that, truly I did.

Actual venue capacity. My experience. And most importantly, my support network. This was doable. When I broke overwhelming things down into less intimidating pieces, a Zen technique, it usually set me back on track.

"I love you, Mama." I brought my hand to my mouth. *"Tonight's for you."* I pressed my lips to the Claddagh ring that had once been hers but now encircled the first finger of my right hand. The metal was cold, like my life had often felt since she had left us.

Blinking back tears, I tried to envision her standing right beside me lending me her strength. But that was difficult to do. Nine months, three weeks, two days since we had scattered her ashes.

The loss still felt fresh. My emotions bubbled too near the surface and with them a pain too raw to soothe.

Focus lost, I returned the mic to its slot on the stand and backed away. I suddenly didn't feel like singing her favorite song about making your tomorrows today anymore.

"Do you need something, Miss Lesowski?" The well-meaning sound technician assigned to me suddenly reemerged from the shadows. Navy ball cap on his head, the brim low and his eyes sparkling with eagerness to please, he had been hovering nearby since I had taken the stage for my allotted ten-minute window of rehearsal time.

"Yes. Thank you." Best to give him something to do so I could try to regather my thoughts. "Would you mind taking my guitar?" My Martin D18-E, a six-string acoustic-electric featured a solid Sitka spruce top, mahogany back and sides and a Fishman F1 Aura plus pickup system. I smoothed my fingertips over the handsome finish of the beautifully crafted instrument any musician would be proud to play. I loved the warm tones it made, but mostly I loved it because it had been a gift from my mother. "Be careful with it," I cautioned making eye contact with him as I unclipped the strap and relinquished my treasure to his care.

"I will, Miss Lesowski. Promise." He gave me a reverential nod and retreated with the guitar. As he did a flash of platinum blond caught my eye.

It can't be, I thought. Only it was. It truly was.

Ashland Keys of the Dirt Dogs.

My heart leapt to my throat.

Holy shit.

I had hoped, maybe even allowed myself a little daydream about a chance meeting, but the last I had heard things had still been up in the air as to whether his band would actually perform live tonight. My eyes bugged out of my head as I stared. The drummer of the Dirt Dogs was even more handsome in the flesh, though he looked less like a rock legend right now in a crisp, white, button down shirt and dark denim jeans and more like a cover model for some upscale clothing catalog.

What to do? My heart hammering with indecision, I panicked as he moved closer eclipsing a stack of amps with his wide shoulders and over six feet frame.

I was a big fan of Ashland Keys.

Ok, maybe more than just a fan.

He was *the* reason I had gotten interested in music. I had his pictures—the band's pictures, I reflexively downplayed my obsession—pasted all over my room. I had been to so many of the Dirt Dogs' concerts that I had lost track of the count. Well, actually it was ten. The laminated ticket stubs lined the inside of the top desk drawer in my room, but don't tell. And I had indulged in a couple—okay, a lot—of farfetched fantasies in which the rocker and I met, bonded and instantly fell madly in love. If my mother had been alarmed by my fascination with the band and a man eleven years older than me, she had never let on. Though, I suspected my biweekly guitar lessons had been her way of channeling my fixation into something more constructive. Certainly nothing edifying in my stepfather's reaction. He had made his disapproval of Ashland Keys and his group of surfers turned rowdy, antiestablishment rock stars abundantly clear. But then again Samuel Lesowski didn't approve of anything that I did—that is until my nomination for best original song alongside the super successful Dirt Dogs.

Not that I desire my stepfather's approval, I reminded myself. *I didn't need or want anything from him.* He was hardly the benevolent benefactor with a heart for the downtrodden the public perceived him to be, and that he had fooled my mother into believing in the early days of their relationship. In fact, he was an egomaniac with disturbing sadistic tendencies.

"I'm marrying him for you, Fanny Bay," my mother had told me while holding her hand over a belly that had yet to swell. "For you and this little one so we can have plenty of food and a comfy bed to sleep in rather than an old car."

That had been fifteen years ago, but I actually missed the rusty 1998 Buick LeSabre land-barge that had temporarily served as our home.

More specifically, I missed her and the life we'd had together before my stepfather had entered it. Just the two of us, a typical day starting with me at her feet in the wee hours before dawn peeling potatoes while she cooked breakfast for the men working the oyster beds. Later I would take a glorious nap next to her in the backseat of the car before the evening found me standing in the shadows backstage watching her perform in the small local theater. It had been a hard way of living, yet it seemed to me that we both had been happier in those days.

"Ashland, baby, wait." A high-pitched woman's voice screeched through my thoughts like a scratch on one of my mother's vintage records. Shifting, I saw a brunette wearing ass-baring leather shorts clattering after the rock icon in her three inch stilettoes. He turned, irritation bristling his brow as he took a step backward to avoid her. But she had momentum. She barreled into him smashing her ridiculously huge boobs into his chest while grabbing hold of his upper arms—well as much of his biceps as she could curl her red tipped claws around. "Come back to the dressing room," she whined. "Do a couple more shots. Let's play some, honey." She tipped her head back and batted her glued-on lashes at him. "My sister and I were just getting started. I'll do you while she does Linc."

"No thanks." He frowned, and her overly made up face registered surprise as he decisively set her away from him.

"Whatever you want then. We're easy, honey. We'll do the whole band if you'd like. You can watch. Everyone knows how you like to."

My jaw dropped, not because her offer was shocking. My stepfather was a big Hollywood producer. I had seen plenty of women proposition him. Seasoned and aspiring actresses, some barely legal, came onto him everywhere he went hoping he would cast them in one of his films. No, my reaction was one of dismay. Being this close to my idol and having things unfold like this was a far cry from my fantasies.

"I'll pass." Ashland pried her fingers loose and lifted his chin. "Go on back and do whatever you please without me." Silky strands of platinum brushed the collar of his shirt as he turned away from her. His eyes sweeping right over me without interest or acknowledgment, he strode smoothly toward the portable riser that would be pulled onto the middle of the stage later tonight when the Dirt Dogs performed. He withdrew a pair of sticks from his back pocket and skirted around the drum kit that sported the band's name and the iconic bulldog surfboard logo before he lowered his significant frame onto the stool behind it.

Don't just stand there like a dork, Fanny. My heart rate quickened. *Introduce yourself. Get a picture with him at least.* My sister would never let me hear the end of it if I passed over a golden opportunity to meet my idol.

"Uh-um." I cleared my throat and shuffled closer. He lifted his gaze, his fingers stilling on the cymbal fastener he had been tightening. Piercing blue eyes met mine. Pinned in place, I was unable to move. I suddenly couldn't breathe. The solid floorboards seemed to go fluid beneath me. I was drowning in pools of aquamarine. They weren't the lighter shade of Lincoln Savage's, his adopted cousin and the lead singer of the Dirt Dogs. They were a deeper, more complex hue that spoke of the ocean. Not the distant view I could see out the windows of my bedroom, but the ocean in those professional surfing photos where it all seemed alive; the overspray a smoky exhalation, the currents' eddies swirling thought and the waves' cosmic forces of turbulent emotion.

I swayed, buffeted by the force of his gaze knowing that my little fantasies had been one dimensional nothings. There were layers of complexity in the 3D Ashland Keys. His eyes alone could tie me up for hours. "I'm...uh..." I found it difficult to harness my thoughts. The words stuck to my tongue as he focused intensely on me. No longer dismissive, he slipped his gaze over my body in a slow approving way that stripped me of more than just my halter top and cutoff shorts. "I'm Fanny," I managed though I sounded like I had just sprinted up three flights of stairs. "Fanny Bay." I left off the Lesowski. I wasn't proud of that association.

"'Tomorrow Today'." His intensity receding, his sculpted and-oh-so-kissable lips curved up on one side. He knew me. Well, he knew my song. Of course he did. We were nominated in the same category though my little acoustic tune wasn't near the equal of his chart-topping hit. "You're on before us." He laid his sticks on the top of his snare and stood. I lost his eyes for a moment, my gaze drifting away from them and the defined strength of his handsome face, to take in his massive shoulders, his tapered waist, his narrow hips and the untucked hem of his shirt.

"Yes, that's my song." My breath hitched as he and all his alluring male perfection approached. "And yes, I'm on before you."

"It's nice to meet you, Fanny." He stopped in front of me and my heart nearly did, too, hearing my name flow from his lips. He had such an amazing voice. Soft. Low. Seductive. "'Tomorrow Today' is a fantastic song and your guitar picking on it is perfection."

"Thank you." Heat rose to my cheeks as I lifted my gaze and found myself ensnared by the fathomless blue depths of his eyes again.

"I saw your acceptance speech at the Golden Globes." His voice rumbled compellingly lower. "I'm sorry about your mother. I know it's incredibly hard losing someone you love so unexpectedly."

I swallowed and nodded. Most people didn't know what to say and shied away from offering sympathy. Obviously he wasn't one of those. In fact, he was so confident, his commanding presence such an arrestive force, I got the impression he didn't shy away from much. "I'm sorry about Dominic." He and his band had recently lost one of their founding members. Dominic Campo, the original bassist, departed the band to join the military and had died tragically while overseas. The Dirt Dogs' song and my own were both Oscar nominated tributes to loss. Mine had been featured on a character driven film with a redemptive theme and theirs on a blockbuster WWII action film with a much more somber tone.

"So am I. So the hell am I." His eyes swam in sudden emotion that mirrored my own. "Well, I better get back to it." He hooked a thumb over his shoulder, his shirt sleeve bunching up at his elbow to reveal more of his muscular forearm and tanned skin.

"Oh. Yes." Duh. I was holding him up. "Could I get a picture with you first? Just a quick one. Otherwise my sister won't believe me if I tell her I met you."

"Sure." The heaviness leaving his eyes, the right corner of his mouth tilted his amusement again. "How about a selfie?" He didn't pause for me to answer, which was a good thing because when his lips tilted my mind whirled. "C'mon." He reached for me. "Come and stand right here beside me." My breath left my lungs in a whoosh when I felt him curl his long, slender, talented fingers around my bared shoulder. Skin to skin, an ember of heat at the point of contact ignited a deeper fire inside of me as he drew me into his rock-hard side. Being held by the living breathing man I had idolized from afar for so many years was surreal. "Don't be shy, little rose..." His amusement brightened his voice. I didn't have to glance up at him to know that his half-smile had blown up into a full grin. I realized I was too obvious in my adoration. He knew I was flustered, and he was enjoying teasing me.

"Alright." Ignoring my skyrocketing pulse and the electrical shivers racing over my skin from his touch, I slid my cell from the pocket of my shorts and took a quick shot knowing he was going to look cover model great in it while I was just going to look like a wide eyed lunatic.

"I love you." The heat already on my cheeks became searing flames. *What the hell, Fanny? Could you humiliate yourself any worse?* "I mean I love your music. It got me through a lot of rough times." I blew out a breath, ducked my chin to my chest and tried again. "What I'm trying to say, but utterly failing at, is that I'm a big fan of the band."

"Hey, no worries. I get it. You should have seen how tongue tied I got when I met Dave Grohl the first time." He repositioned so he was directly in front of me again. My eyes still downcast, I noticed that even his suede Chukka boots were sexy. "Look at me, Fanny." Not a request, a command spoken in a deepened tone I found impossible to resist. I lifted my gaze. "No reason to be nervous. I'm just a guy who plays drums. And it's cool that you like our music. It's flattering in fact." I discovered that his expression matched the sincerity of his words though his eyes continued to sparkle his amusement. "It's a total rush to be appreciated by an artist of your caliber."

"I'm not an artist." One of his platinum brows lifted in surprise. "Not like you anyway. Not that I aspire to be. I love music, don't get me wrong. When I create for myself my music gives me a space to belong. It's just not what I want to do for a living. Being in front of an audience. On stage by myself. Touring alone with a bunch of strangers. It takes the joy out of it all. You know?" Both of his brows were raised, and his ocean blue eyes didn't just sparkle now they shimmered like the water at midday. Probably because I was blathering. But I couldn't help myself, being this close to him. He was so incredibly good looking he made my thoughts mushy. And he smelled divine beneath his top note of too many shots of tequila. Like the ocean where it meets the shore. Like a summer breeze. Like freshly peeled citrus. No, like a gentle wind moving over a grove of oranges beside the sea on the most perfect summer day you could ever imagine.

"Actually, I know exactly what you mean. I've been doing a lot of reevaluating lately." He cocked his head to the side and studied me again with that unwavering intensity. And now I saw something behind those eyes, something significant, a tangle of some sort that needed unraveling. "I'm at a crossroads myself." The air seemed to crackle or at least it had for me since the moment our gazes had connected. "But I'm curious. Fanny. You're very good at what you do or you wouldn't be here. So what would you do if you didn't sing?" Eyes on mine, his expression hesitant, he slowly reached for and gently brushed aside a ruby curl that had escaped the elegant twist the stylist had fashioned to complement my designer gown.

"I'd make perfume." My words spilled out in a rush as he tucked my curl behind my ear and his roughened fingertips skimmed my smooth skin. A shiver rolled through me.

"What?" His gaze had dropped to my mouth. He seemed to have forgotten his question.

"I like combining fragrances with essential oils." His gaze lifted, his shock at my answer clearing the brief confusion that had momentarily darkened it. It was an unusual pursuit. I was accustomed to looks like his whenever I mentioned my hobby, so I explained. "There are many holistic benefits in oils and scents. So it's more than just a cosmetic thing to me. I'm only an amateur, but if I had some formal training, like an apprenticeship, and took a couple of business courses I might be able to make a vocation out of it."

"I can see it's your passion. You're lit up like a firecracker just talking about it. You should do it, little rose. We both know life's too unpredictable to continue doing something that doesn't make us happy." He was right of course, and his certainty made me want to find the courage to stand up to my stepfather.

"Fanny!" The fine hairs on my nape stood on end. Thinking of him, unfortunately, had conjured him up. I sighed. I could feel the dark cloud of his disapproval rolling toward me. I backed away from Ashland. I didn't want the inevitable shit storm that accompanied Samuel Lesowski raining reproach on the drummer, too. I turned and braced, as the director most people knew by name and loved—he had an accomplished PR department—came closer, his long jerky strides devouring the space between us, his harsh brows sharply drawn together.

Shit, I thought. What the hell had I done to piss him off this time?

"Your preshow interview with Entertainment Weekly was scheduled to start twenty minutes ago." He stopped in front of me, not a single strand of his perfectly styled jet-black hair out of place. Only his hairdresser, my sister and I knew he had started to color it to cover the grey that had crept in at the temples. "The cameras are already set up and everyone's waiting for you in your dressing room." He gave Ashland a disdainful glance that would have withered a lesser man before he returned his displeasure to me. "Don't tell me you've forgotten?"

Yes, I had, that part at least. "I'm sorry," I apologized readily. I knew from experience that he didn't tolerate excuses.

"Sorry doesn't begin to cut it, Fanny." He snorted. "It's not as if you don't have a history of being irresponsible and a penchant for finding trouble." He gave the man he no doubt considered to be my most recent example of both a condescending glare down the length of his nose.

"Father," I acknowledged the relationship though it grated, considering our dislike for one another. "I get that I'm late. I'll apologize to everyone when I get there in just a minute."

"Not in a minute, Fanny. Now."

"I just want..."

"What you want is immaterial. You're young and impetuous, though you're old enough to know to steer clear of someone with a reputation like this one."

"You're one to talk," I fired back, and his eyes widened in surprise.

"Now just a minute..."

"Exactly. Give me the moment I'm asking for—or I won't do that thing with Coppola." He had been trying to arrange a meeting for me with the one Hollywood producer that was a bigger deal than he was for months. When my stepfather wanted something from me, he would most times give me something in return. There was no love between us, but I knew he understood the value of negotiation.

"As you wish." He nodded. "But hear me well. Don't squander the success you've achieved, Fanny, my dear." He came closer. His breath blew hot on my face as he grabbed my arm. "We both know your track record of flitting from one interest to another. Your current popularity won't last if you don't nurture it." His fingers dug a deep trench into the sensitive flesh of my upper arm.

"I'll talk to him." I winced. My voice was as tight as his grip. "But I'm not signing anything tonight." Not ever if I could help it. I wanted out of the business. I didn't want to be more firmly entrenched in it. I lifted my chin. I had pretty much stopped defying him since my mother's death. Grief had stolen a lot of the fight from me. I was always so tired. I found it took less energy to give in.

"Let me remind you, daughter of the roof you have over your head. Of the food you eat. Your clothing. Your transportation. It's all because of me and my influence. Even the Oscar nomination wouldn't have happened if I hadn't included your song in the acclaimed film that I directed. If it weren't for me, you and your mother would still be combing through trashcans in that godforsaken little fishing town on Vancouver Island."

"Now you wait just a minute," Ashland said. "You're out of line." He was still standing to the side of us. I had forgotten him as impossible as that seemed to believe. "And you need to let go of her." My stepfather turned his head. The two men took each other's measure.

"Keys, isn't it?" My stepfather's expression darkened. "Samuel Lesowski. I'll thank you to stay out of my business. It's no concern of yours." He paused like he usually did after dropping his name waiting for the listener's inevitable acknowledgement.

Only he didn't get it this time.

"I couldn't disagree more." Ashland's eyes narrowed. "I've got zero tolerance for bullies. Let her go." His voice dropped to a menacingly level. "Now. You're hurting her."

"She's my daughter. You have no right to interfere in a family matter. And I don't think you quite understand with whom you're dealing. If you value your paltry career at all or that of your inconsequential bandmates, you'll turn around right now, go back to whatever you were doing and stay the hell out of my way."

The drummer's sharp jaw honed to an unyielding edge. He wasn't going to back down. Samuel seemed to have struck a nerve with him in some kind of personal way. I felt my body grow cold. It was going to be up to me to make him go away. My stepfather didn't make idle threats. He had risen to the heights he had not only because of his talent, but also because people in the business had learned not to cross him.

"I'm ok." My eyes were overly bright, my tone tinny. "I don't need protecting."

"Bullshit," Ashland spat, and he was right. I did need a protector. But it was up to me to champion my own cause after all. It was just a matter of give and take when it came to appeasing my stepfather. And I had been doing far too much giving lately.

"Samuel, let go of my arm so I can have the minute I asked for. I'm sure you don't want a scene. Tonight of all nights. And we both know there isn't a lot of time, not if you expect me to complete an interview, attend a meeting and perform my song."

"Alright. Have your one moment, Fanny." My stepfather's eyes flared. They were green like the paper he worshipped. "But don't linger." He released my arm abruptly. I shifted to face Ashland, my cheeks flaming. I was more embarrassed having him witness this interchange with my stepfather than I had been by my own ineptitude earlier. I didn't like to appear weak, though it shouldn't really have mattered what Ashland thought. What should have mattered was how I had allowed things to deteriorate to such an appallingly state with my stepfather. I needed that to change. And I needed to escape this encounter with Ashland Keys with as much dignity as I could muster. I imagined the rock star would gladly get away from me and my problems the moment I gave him leave.

• • •

ASHLAND

"Well, your old man's an asshole." I gritted out the words, my hands curling into fists. I hadn't been this upset in years. Granted I had spent most of that time in a fog—totally and completely blitzed out of my mind—instead of only mildly buzzed like I was now. But there was more to it. Some had to do with the crossroads I was at, and the rest was the way this girl somehow personified it. I didn't know why but she felt like the key to unlocking something importtant, something just out of reach, maybe something that would always be out of reach. Here I was, a member of one of the biggest, baddest bands in rock 'n' roll. I had achieved everything in my career I had set out to achieve, yet none of it really mattered. "You shouldn't put up with his shit." I hoped a word or two of advice might help her avoid some of the pitfalls I hadn't.

"I don't. You're right." Fanny nodded solemnly. Features contemplative, she reminded me of a nymph some artist had sketched in bold autumnal colors. Willowy, almost too thin, she had a recognizable inner strength. I'd seen her draw it out like a sword and wield it against her stepfather. I certainly wouldn't bet against her. "I want you to know I'm done letting him push me around. Done with a lot of things," she muttered and licked her lips. My gaze dipped to them. They were full, the bottom one more so than the top, a rich ruby color that reminded me of an expensive cabernet. Moistened, like they were right now, they glistened distractingly. Hell, everything about the fiery redhead was a distraction. One I couldn't afford right now. I should have left well enough alone and retreated to my dressing room after taking the selfie with her.

It was late. It was time to go put on my tux. Hob nob with the elites. Play my role. I had been to enough Oscars to know what was expected of me. But I didn't feel like mixing and mingling. I didn't want to get high with my bandmates. I certainly didn't want to fuck any more random groupies. I had been there, done that and look where it had gotten me. At the dead end of a road no one wanted to travel.

All the Dogs were a testament to misery each in our own way. Our lead singer Lincoln Savage had lost the approval of the one woman he had really wanted and now settled for crowd adoration and groupie hookups as inferior substitutes. Our guitarist Ramon Martinez thought he didn't know how to love, but the reality was he had given his heart away a long time ago to someone who wasn't free to return it. Our new bassist Diesel Le had been tooled around so badly by his ex-wife that he now projected his hatred onto all women. And then there was me. In love myself yet unable to man up and confess those feelings. We were really a bunch of sad fucks just lucky that enough people like this sweet girl identified with the rebellious theme in our music.

Regrets and morose thoughts spun like a carousel in my brain a lot lately. The guys in the band had noticed and were starting to speculate about the cause. That's why I had come out here alone. I wasn't ready to talk about it. I would. Probably. There was no one I was closer to than Linc and Ramon. Hell, even Diesel. He had been inside the refining fire with all of us after Patches' funeral. But not yet. After the test results came in, maybe. I might have to level with them then. But instead of finding some time to myself with my drums tonight, I had found her. And here I remained, my feet glued to the floor enjoying myself in way I never expected even with all the bullshit hanging over me. At least until her stepfather had appeared. So much like Linc's old man. If he hadn't let go of her, I would have broken his fucking arm.

"I wish I had more time to talk to you. More time to explain. There just isn't any." She threaded her fingers together as if trying to cup sand in her hands. "Time's precious, but beyond the ability of any of us to control. Right?"

I nodded, stunned by her insight.

"But I didn't want to go without telling you how much it means to me that you didn't back down from my stepfather. Most would have. Actually I can't really remember anyone ever standing up to him. And that you did it for me... Well, it means a lot is all. Thank you, Ashland." She unclasped her fingers and touched my arm. Surprised, so caught off guard by her, I glanced down at her delicate hand resting so softly on my skin and then returned my gaze to her face. She was pretty for sure, but in a more remarkable way than all the conformist clones running around backstage tonight. She had big grey eyes, a cute nose, phenomenal lips and that striking red hair. But it was those eyes of hers that were the complete show stopper. Otherworldly, they reflected her quicksilver emotions. Nervousness. Resolve. Fear. Desire. I had seen all flash within their depths.

"Ash," I corrected. "My friends call me Ash." My voice sounded gruff from the weight of the things I wanted to explore further with her. Things that I wouldn't, *couldn't* pursue. Bad timing to meet someone who so intrigued me if the test turned out the way I feared. And even if it didn't, she was too young, too innocent. Not at all right for someone like me.

"Ash," she repeated, my name sliding so easily between those recently wetted ruby red lips of hers. I imagined them wrapped around my shaft and knew I wouldn't have turned her down if she had offered to do to me the things the groupie had. My cock was certainly interested in her. It didn't care about timing or right and wrong. It was all about action.

"I'm sorry you got drawn into my mess," she continued. "I think that under different circumstances we might have been friends. It's difficult to find many of those in our profession. Genuine ones, I mean. But I think it's better if we just go ahead and say goodbye right now."

"How so?" The lust thundering through me made it difficult to focus, but I did get that she was giving me the brush off. And even though wisdom dictated that I take the hint—it was the logical thing to do after all given our differences—the alpha male in me said, 'Fuck logic.'

"Because my stepfather wasn't kidding around. He means what he says. You don't want to be on his bad side. *I* don't want you to be on his bad side. And that's where you would end up if he thought you were a friend of mine."

"Someone who steps in front of him when he's twisting your arm and hurting you, you mean?"

Her eyes wide, she nodded.

"Well, fuck that bullshit." My gaze grazed the red welt on her arm. "He's the one who should be worried about getting on my bad side."

She smiled at my vehement response and smiling she was more than just cute. She was a wrecking ball to my resolve, Prettier in person than in any of the videos I had seen of her and so enticing in that little yellow halter top with the tempting bow dangling between her shoulder blades. I imagined untying it and taking those pins out of her hair. What would those glorious red curls feel like around my.... No... I reined those thoughts back and settled for tracing her subtle curves with my gaze instead. No sex. Not with her. Not with anyone. Not for a while. Potentially not ever. I wouldn't put anyone at risk if there was even a chance they would get infected. Ironic to be sure. Divine justice for my own irresponsible behavior over the years.

The familiar icy dread returning, I had to remind myself that no diagnosis had actually been made. I had momentarily forgotten my apprehension in her presence. That song of hers was so fucking full of hope it had me expecting a miracle. And that hope sprang from within her. She was the source. No wonder her star had risen so fast. Just a handful of minutes with her was all it had taken for me to realize it.

"I...I wasn't expecting to run into you tonight." Her eyes twinkled like stars emerging in the sky as the sun relinquished its hold on the day. "I had hoped to, sure, you know, since I love...your music so much." A few more spirally crimson curls shivered free of their pins as her hands fluttered in front of her chest. "It's just now that I've actually met you for real." She gave me that utterly beguiling look. "I'll never be able to look at your picture the same way again."

"No reason to settle for a photograph, Fanny. You have your things to do tonight, and I've got mine. But afterward, there are a lot of parties. I'm sure we can manage to bump into each other again. Maybe talk some more." *Unwise, Ashland.* But yet doing the 'whoever and whatever the fuck I wanted' rock star entitlement thing was a hard habit to crush. I might not be able to take this where I wanted with her spread out on the sheets beneath me, but I wasn't ready for whatever the hell this was to end yet, either. So shouldn't I leave myself an opening? A contingency plan? I had been walking around like a zombie. But what if the diagnosis wasn't what I feared? What if I received favorable news? What then? Who then? As I continued to stare into those starlit eyes of hers, I felt something shift and lock into place that was startlingly certain. *Her*. If I had a future on the other side of this, I wanted that future to include her.

"There is a reason." She shook her head. "Samuel Lesowski. My stepfather. You two didn't exactly hit it off."

"You're an adult. He doesn't have to know everything you do, does he?"

"No." Her face brightening, she shook her head excitedly and more curls escaped.

"What do you say then? How about this? You be just you and I'll be just me. A girl from Beverly Hills and a guy from the beach. None of the other stuff. It's not important. I've got a hurdle I have to clear next week, but afterward I can come back to LA. We could meet somewhere."

"I don't know." She captured and wrapped one of her curls around her finger while blinking uncertainly at me through the thick fringe of her crimson lashes.

"There's a coffeehouse," I plowed over her reservations. "The Cosmic Cup in Manhattan Beach. It's by the water. Quiet. Close enough to where you live, but a fair enough distance from the bullshit of LA. How about Wednesday at ten o'clock?"

"But..."

"But nothing. You wrote that song, 'Tomorrow Today', right? Make every moment count. I believe that. We can't control time, but who says we can't manipulate it. We bumped into each other tonight for a reason. Don't you think we owe ourselves a chance to find out what that reason is?"

Text log

- Wednesday 10:15 AM -

Fanny: Hey, Um. I'm here at the coffeehouse. The Cosmic Cup.

- 1230 PM -

Fanny: I've been here a while. I thought you said ten but maybe I got that wrong.

- 2:03 PM -

Fanny: Did you mean ten at night?

- 8:45 PM -

Fanny: I didn't hear from you earlier. But I swung back by the coffee house again, you know just in case.

- 9:15 PM -

Fanny: The vanilla latte is pretty decent. So it wasn't entirely a wasted trip.

- 10:12 PM -

Fanny: They're closing up now.

-10:15 PM -

Fanny: Are you getting my messages?

-10:17 PM -

Fanny: If you are, but you changed your mind could you let me know?

Chapter ONE

FANNY - 2015 PRESENT DAY

I brushed aside a long wispy strand of her strawberry blonde hair and pressed a gentle kiss to her brow. Underneath my lips her skin felt hot. And as I drew back I noticed that her spattering of freckles seemed overly prominent against her pale cheeks. Worry lined my own features. Her fever was spiking again. My little sister looked worse than she had the night before.

Oh, Hollie. On my knees, I gazed down at her. Not quite eighteen, she was the soft colors of the dawn. I was the bolder hues of the sunset, or so our mother had often described us. She appeared so childlike and frail all tangled up in her thin covers on a pallet of cardboard on the concrete floor.

My flattened lips turning into a frown, I rose from her makeshift bed, took a step backward and straightened my skirt. *One more day*, I told myself. I would let her ride this fever out one more day. If she didn't get better we were going to the free clinic first thing the next morning, the risk of us being discovered be damned.

I would just have to fight him again if need be. I would do whatever it took. This time the stakes were higher than ever. My sister's wellbeing meant more to me than my own.

Fear for her, for both of us: that was why we had run. My heart hammered thinking about the night that had started with Hollie's panicked phone call. Though I had managed to get her away from him I knew that no distance could guarantee her safety.

Samuel Lesowski was more powerful now than he had been the day I had given up the rights and royalties to my award-winning song to be free from him. He had invested the sizeable proceeds of that acquisition into a multimedia company with a streaming service. His initial investment had grown into a formidable fortune. He could use that fortune as leverage to destroy Hollie's hopes and dreams, or worse if I allowed my mind to go there. But I couldn't. I couldn't focus on the things *he* could do. I had to focus on what *I* could do. I had been in rough spots before. And I had come through.

Dig deep, Fanny Bay. My mother's sweet voice echoed her advice inside my head. It was fainter nowadays, but I still remembered everything. *Find your Zen. Sweet are the uses of adversity which, like the toad, ugly and venomous, wears yet a precious jewel in his head.* Yoga and Shakespeare, her two favorite philosophies. She had melded then into one uniquely her own. The sound of her voice might have faded over the years, but her memory never would. I wouldn't allow it.

I closed my eyes and imagined her beside me. Imagined further that my feet were roots tunneling beneath the cold concrete to the nurturing soil beneath it like the ancient cedars of Cathedral Grove on Vancouver Island. The oldest in British Columbia, they stood strong through the tests of time. They had weathered many hardships. I could manage this one.

Centered, my determination restored, I opened my eyes and my other senses to the rest of my surroundings like my mother had taught me. Scent first. It had always been scent first with me. I took in the brine of the ocean and the unmistakable fragrance of Coppertone. Then the sound of the roaring waves, the cry of the gulls and the muffled shouts of the surfers outside our hut. Last, the damp humidity seeping through the cracks around the door and the slats of the louvered window and settling deep into my bones.

My heartrate slowed. The beats became steadier. My next breaths came easier though the pressure of tears still threatened.

"I miss you, Mom," I whispered, longing to see her one more time, to be held by her one more time. But it was just me and my sister inside the small, ten-by-ten-foot pumping station we had been hiding in for the past several weeks. Weeks we hadn't intended. Time we had planned to spend on the other side of the border farther from Samuel Lesowski's reach. But Mexico wasn't an option anymore. Not since my purse, along with our passports and every bit of our money had been stolen. We had to regroup. Once Hollie was better we would find another way.

"I'm going out," I said out loud, firming my shoulders. "I'll be back soon."

"M-kay," Hollie mumbled a groggy reply. My leaving each morning was part of the routine now. She was more recognizable. We had agreed at the beginning that I was the one who had to go out. Her fever complicated things. I'd had it, too, but I had gotten over it quickly. As it lingered on in her so did my worries. My brow creased as I watched her turn over, pulling the measly blanket I had salvaged from a dumpster up over her head. "But turn up the heat before you go, Fanny. It's cold."

There wasn't any heat. No electricity. No running water. No food. None of the necessities beyond a case of bottled water someone had left behind on the beach, which I had dragged up here. Going without basics wasn't a completely novel experience for me, the way it was for Hollie. Our house in Beverly Hills, the nannies, chauffeurs, a chef. That posh life was all she had ever known.

But thinking about what we once had wasn't going to get us what we now lacked. I grabbed a bottle from the case, loosened the cap and left the water nearby so she could find it easily when she awoke.

Time to get going. No use stalling, though a large part of that stalling was hesitance about leaving Hollie alone when she was so weak.

1. Food.
2. A drink with electrolytes.
3. Pain relievers.
4. Getting Hollie better.

My current list. Priorities. Broken down. Manageable. To that end I needed chicken soup, Gatorade, Tylenol and cash to purchase them. Beyond those items and a more difficult task to achieve, I had to find someone to go into the Rite Aid to get them for me. I couldn't do it myself. Even with a knit Lakers cap covering my distinctive hair, and a thick layer of grime blurring my features, there was a chance someone would recognize me.

Another obstacle.

But I had the will. The motivation. Hollie needed me to be strong. I would find a way.

Opening the heavy metal door a smidgen, I stuck my head out and glanced around checking to make sure the coast was clear before widening the gap and slipping through it. Outside the building, I pressed my back to the closed door and scanned my surroundings. The sub-pump structure was at the far end of the public parking lot, and the lot was full of vehicles. The property of the early morning crew of surfers, at least twenty out on the water today. Nearly that many already peeling off their wetsuits underneath beach towels that functioned as dressing rooms. A few locals and some strangers I didn't recognize were sitting on the low concrete wall that bordered the sand. Some were drinking coffee out of paper cups, the steam rising in the crisp early spring air. Others had their hands shoved in their jacket pockets as they stared out at the water. But whether they were locals, strangers or just interlopers like me, we all had a bottom line commonality. We all paused at the sand where the land met the sea to acknowledge the majesty of the ocean.

I took my own moment. The ocean churned today like my thoughts. Lighter blue in the shallows, but darker where it became deeper. Reminding me of...well, I had to let go of that otherwise I wouldn't be able to find the peace I sought. The surfers bobbed on the rolling waves in their dark wetsuits like sea lions. The concrete pier jutted out like an arrow pointing to the vastness of the waters. The rhythmic sound of the surf lapped the shore.

Tempting, it was so tempting to rest and commune. I was so weary, so hungry. But moments could turn into hours and entire days could be lost here.

Get a move on, Fanny. This isn't some vacation. Everything you need isn't going to conveniently fall into your hands. I had learned that lesson at a very young age. If you wanted something, you had to work for it. Often sacrifice to defend it. And as hard as you tried, sometimes you didn't get what you wanted but only what you needed to get by.

• • •

ASHLAND

Sun bright against the back of my eyelids, I gave up trying to sleep any longer and rolled out of bed.

I liked—no, loved—the view of the water. The OB pier and the horizon of blue beyond it out my penthouse windows could have cost me tens of millions to procure. But the building that housed it had been vacant so long and required so much work to bring it up to code that I had gotten the entire apartment, including the offices downstairs for Outside, at a fraction of its worth.

My only regret—ok, I had a shit ton of them to be honest—but my most pressing one regarding the apartment was the absence of retractable blinds. They were currently on back order. I couldn't wait for them to arrive so I could sleep a little later than the butt crack of dawn.

Abandoning my bed and the sheets I had tangled shifting restlessly back and forth during the night, I shuffled into the attached master bath and took care of my morning business: pissed, washed my hands and shaved. I dried my face with a hand towel and clasped the counter as I stared at my reflection in the mirror.

You've got a good life, Ashland Keys. Set the what-ifs and the other bullshit aside that fucks up your brain at night. Live in the moment. Count your blessings. Your glass is half-full not half-empty. Your physical needs are met. Emotional ones, too. Linc. Simone. Your parents, Ramon and Karen. Everyone you love and who loves you are nearby. That other something more that couples have, it's not for you. You have your part to play. You're the loyal son. You're the one who stands strong for your friends. You're the one who keeps a level head when all hell breaks loose for everyone else.

A flash of purple and a delicate but intriguing dirty face beneath it came immediately to mind. Ok, so maybe my head wasn't entirely level when it came to the Lakers Girl. But only because she was a mystery I had yet to solve.

Why did she always run? What was she so scared of? She was afraid of me in particular that much was obvious. She often paused and listened when the others spoke to her. But not me. Those unusual purple high-tops of hers that Ramon had mistaken for Converse practically kicked up fire when I got near her. But why?

I shook my head. There were no answers in the mirror to solve the mystery of the homeless girl. No answer to what ailed me, either.

Today, I reminded myself. *Not tomorrows. Just today.*

Refocused, I reentered the bedroom. I dropped my boxers and pulled on my running gear. After I laced my shoes, I stood and grabbed my favorite OB ball cap from the dresser, turned it backward so the brim was out of the way and headed straight to the kitchen. Simone would be here soon and besides it was time to take my medication.

A few quick strides down the short hall and to the left brought me into an open galley style kitchen, with all the amenities. Six-burner gas stovetop. Cool hammered copper hood. Seafoam and terra cotta hand painted Mexican tile backsplashes. Wrought iron fixtures. Black granite countertops. The previous owners had started a remodel that gave the entire apartment cream colored walls and dark hardwood floors for a knock your socks off understated Southern California Spanish Mediterranean vibe but then abandoned it when their funds had run out. Outfacing floor to ceiling windows framed the sunrise that had woken me while the back wall of the kitchen was lined with distressed wood cabinets of varying size. I opened one and reached for the bottle. Same pill. Same time every day. Miss a dose and the infection could come roaring back. This was my life, the reality I woke to every morning since my diagnosis. A routine I had come to uneasy terms with.

A knock sounded on the outside door. My running partner had arrived. Monday, Wednesday and Friday each week. Just she and I whenever we were both in town, less a given now with her revived singing career and with me out scouting the SoCal coast for new talent for Outside.

In a couple of steps I was out of the kitchen and through the adjoining living room. My previous melancholy dissipated as soon as I opened the door and saw her.

"Hey, Mona." I leaned in and gave the curvy brunette a quick kiss on the cheek. The only type I gave, and they were only for her.

"Hey, Ash." Her amber eyes glittering, she lit up the dingy outer hallway with her beautiful smile. "Ready?"

"I'm always ready," I returned, holding up my apartment key. "But I gave you one of these. You don't have to knock like a stranger. You can just let yourself in."

"I know. But what if someone's with you?" she asked, her brow creasing. "I wouldn't want to interrupt anything."

Ah, so that was it. I captured her chin before she could drop it. "No one spends the night, Simone."

"No one ever?" Her expression was incredulous, her eyes now wide.

"Never. Not my scene. There's only one girl I ever would consider inviting for a sleepover and she's taken. Yeah?"

"Yes." She nodded. She knew that girl was her. "But..."

"But nothing. I've got my life just the way I want it." I didn't much care for the troubled look on her face. "You're not feeling sorry for me, are you?"

"No of course not." She shook her head. "It's just that with Linc and me together now, and Ramon and Karen..."

"You've been thinking I'm the odd man out." I filled in for her stumble.

"Yes, I guess. If not for yourself, think of your nephew Chulo," she gently chided, trying to lighten the mood. Chulo was Mona's adorable, fourteen-pound, fluffy canine companion. "He could use an aunt at some time in the future. You know how he is. The only thing better for Chulo than one person petting him is two. And you've got so much to give Ash. If it weren't for Linc..."

"Don't feel sorry for me. I get it regularly, Simone." She paled beneath her golden tan. I had been too blatant, too abrupt. I softened my tone. "What I mean is that I'm content with my life the way it is."

"Just content?" The crease between her eyes deepened.

"Content, yes." I wasn't going to lie to her. She was a friend. She could have been more. There remained that undercurrent between us, but I would never act upon it. I loved her too much to give her less than the best of my affection. "A state of peaceful happiness is a good place to be." A much better place than I had been after the diagnosis. Under water. Drowning. The crash that hadn't really been an accident. My prized self-control lost for a time. The long arduous rebuild of my life without the worst of my coping mechanisms. "But enough of this." I took her arm and turned her, steering her out into the exterior hallway. "I think you're stalling. Today's the stairs at Narragansett at the end of our run. You lose and you're buying breakfast. And just to let you know upfront it'll cost you. I'm starving."

Chapter TWO

FANNY

Ducking my chin to my chest, I quickly scurried past the police trailer in the middle of the lot.

Pretend you belong and slow down, I reminded myself. In a second-hand broom skirt and a zippered hoodie from the thrift store, I blended in for the most part with the others who made the streets of Ocean Beach their home.

Leaving the lot, I turned right and took the sidewalk uphill through the palm tree lined center of downtown. Beneath the shelter of colorful shop awnings, I matched my strides to the wet sandy footprints someone had left behind. I wondered if I should risk making a quick run by the surf shop to see if the two best friends who managed it, Simone Bianchi, Lincoln Savage's fiancée, and Karen Grayson, the surfer girl who belonged to Ramon Martinez, had left anything for me.

You shouldn't, my inner voice cautioned. *It's too risky. What if he's there today?*

He was Ashland Keys. A today that had never come. Retired from the Dirt Dogs. Now a musical mogul, the co-owner of Outside, an independent record label he had formed with his cousin Lincoln Savage. The offices for Outside and the penthouse apartment Ashland lived in were housed in a four-story building that was uncomfortably close to the sub-pump structure where my sister and I were hiding.

Familiar regret lanced through the center of my chest whenever I thought of Ashland Keys.

C'mon, Fanny, I chastised myself. *Forget about him already.* That was a long time ago. He had forgotten all about me I was sure. Why he had asked me to meet him at the coffee house in the first place and then never shown up, I would probably never know, and it shouldn't really matter. I had a life now far removed from the music business. I had a boyfriend, too, a serious one, or at least I hoped I still did. Who knew what was going on inside Tristan Murphy's head or how the story was playing out for him and everyone else in the media? Everything traceable Hollie and I had we had left behind. Our cell phones. Credit cards. Vehicles. Our ID's. My mom's Claddagh ring. Everything had been abandoned in a rush to my sister's rescue after her fateful late-night phone call.

Passing by the front of the Ocean Beach Hotel with its trio of Mediterranean style arched windows, I nodded once to Charlie. He nodded back, scratched his long grey beard and continued shuffling along the walkway in his bedroom slippers on his way to his favorite spot near the sand. Head ducked low, I avoided making eye contact with the rest of the people I encountered especially the guys at the lifeguard station. They didn't tolerate the homeless congregating around the nearby public restroom. In singles we were ok. Invisible even. But in groups we gave the city a headache it didn't relish with a potential to spook the paying tourists.

When I reached the Deck Bar, I stopped and scanned my surroundings again. No one was around the popular second story restaurant that overlooked the water. It wasn't open yet, but the trashcan beside it was full to overflowing from the previous night. After one more furtive glance around, I unzipped my hoodie, threw it on the ground as a catchall and started combing through the contents of the receptacle. Glass bottles were a low score worth only ten cents each. They clinked together as I dropped them on my jacket. Plastic bottles netted a dollar each. Aluminum cans were the best. I could get a dollar fifty-seven for them. Discarded food inside sacks or takeaway containers I had avoided in the beginning. I didn't anymore. Desperation made me less picky about what I put inside my stomach.

It was near midday and the rays from the rising sun were hot on the exposed skin of my neck and shoulders by the time I had sorted through everything.

I stuffed fries and a quarter of a burger wrapped in crinkly paper inside my pocket to eat on the way back. I didn't trust such fare for Hollie. In her present condition, it might make her sicker. I put everything I didn't want back inside the can. Someone else might come along and find the ten cent glass bottles or the leftover moldy bread worthy of their attention.

Feeling exposed in just my tank and skirt, I gathered the sides of my hoodie and hefted it like a knapsack over my shoulder. I glanced at the sun and sighed. I was running later than usual. A wealth of broken bottles in the trash had slowed me down. Wanting to make up time, I broke into a jog, slowing only to take a bite of my food. My purple Chloés served me well, but my unwieldy bounty bounced awkwardly against my shoulder blades as I increased my pace.

When I finally arrived at the church, the line had wound around the entire complex. I bypassed it. Those on the sidewalk were waiting for a free lunch and entering their names into a lottery for a cot tonight. I already had a place to sleep, and I had eaten. The char-boiled hamburger and greasy fries now sat heavy in my stomach, but it was sustenance. As long as it stayed down, not a given unfortunately, it would do.

Behind the sanctuary, the side door to the warehouse was propped open with a cinderblock brick. I ducked inside and scanned long rows of bins for recycling. There were only two people inside the small office by the entrance and both had their backs to me, a blonde and the usual security guard. I could clearly see them through the glass half-wall. They gave cash on the spot for recyclables here. The guard was a necessary precaution. Most of the street people were harmless like myself. We had our own ethical code and looked out for each other as best we could. But there were other factions around—dangerous ones—at the ready to take advantage or do us harm.

I knocked on the glass and dropped my gaze to the ground. Outside or inside, I tried to avoid eye contact or conversation. A pair of flip flops with sandy feet and pink toes appeared in my field of vision.

"It's you," a recognizable voice stated.

I jerked my head up.

Karen Grayson. The owner of Offshore. Ramon's surfer girl. I had once pushed her out of the way of a moving car that had almost hit her. She had only been knocked unconscious. It could have been much worse. Everything was ok now, but at the time Ramon had completely lost it.

I started to back away toward the door, but found my retreat blocked by the security guard. My eyes went wide. Panicking, I jumped away from him and dropped my knapsack/hoodie. Plastic bottles clattered and aluminum cans pinged on the concrete. I barely noticed over the sound of my racing heartbeats.

"It's ok, Lakers Girl," Karen said gently. That was what she and her OB friends called me. "I'm not going to hurt you. We're not gonna hurt you. Are we Jackson?"

The security guard shook his head.

"Then have him move away from the door," I demanded softly, my voice warbling in my near panic. Swallowing, I shook my head and spoke more firmly. "I don't like being cornered."

"Sure. It's ok." Karen lifted her hands spreading her fingers wide in a placating gesture. "Jackson, I know this woman. She's the one I was telling you about. The one I've been looking for. Can you give us two girls a moment alone?" She was talking to him, but she didn't take her gaze off of me.

"Sure Miss Grayson."

"Thanks."

Wary, I watched him retreat. When he was outside she spoke again.

“I’m Karen Grayson, but I think you already know my name.” She took a step closer, both hands clasped in front of her now. “I’m not going to hurt you. I just wanted to thank you. Your quick thinking saved my life.”

“You’re welcome,” I whispered. She was pretty. Blonde hair, light brown eyes, golden skin, toned body. A SoCal surfer girl through and through, she didn’t have a bit of trouble blending in Ocean Beach. Ramon’s nickname suited her. But more importantly to me, she had a gentle manner. I had seen her at the beach teaching kids how to surf. I’d seen her walking hand in hand with Ramon downtown. I had accidently seen them doing more much more than hand holding down by the pier. They were hot together. But thinking about that didn’t conjure up longing thoughts of one of Tristan’s kisses like it probably should have.

“What’s your name?” Karen asked.

I shook my head.

“You don’t wanna tell me, huh?”

I nodded.

“You in trouble of some sort?”

I nodded.

“With the law?”

“No.” I shook my head. I didn’t think so, but who knew what my stepfather was telling people to try to get Hollie back.

“No surprise there. You seem way too industrious and smart to be a criminal.” She scanned me head to toe, thoroughly as if taking notes.

“Your face is dirty. But the rest of you is clean.” She was observant, and I kicked myself for stopping to wash up in the public restroom last night at Dog Beach. But I couldn’t sleep when I was grimy. “If you could keep your appearance presentable and come into the shop reliably each day I could really use some help organizing.”

My eyes got large. She was offering me a job.

“I’d like a chance to pay you back at least in some way for what you did. When I think of what might have happened...what I could have lost....” She trailed off, bringing one of her hands up and placing it on her lower abdomen. Protectively. Like my mom had all those years ago.

Was Karen pregnant?

"Well, anyway," she confirmed when I didn't speak. "It seems to me you could use a little help, and I could, too, honestly. Simone is gone so often with her singing. I couldn't pay you a lot. I'm still trying to make Offshore profitable again. But I think I could pay you more than you make turning in cans, and I would provide meals, too."

"Why would you do that? You don't even know me. I could be dangerous."

Her lips slowly lifted into a sweet smile. "I don't think a dangerous person would warn me that she's dangerous or bother pushing me out of the way of a moving car. Do you?"

I shook my head and grinned back at her. She was kind and funny, her humor contagious.

"So what do you say?"

"I can't." Without the dirt on my face, someone might recognize me. I wasn't the celebrity Hollie had become with her acting. Most people had forgotten me. My success had been short-lived, my fame a flash that had come and gone. The way I had wanted it to of course. I glanced at my feet where the cans and plastic bottles had scattered. "Can I turn these in? I need the money, and then I need to get going."

"Alright, Lakers Girl." Karen looked and sounded disappointed. I was, too. I liked her. A lot. She and Simone had been leaving gifts for me, clothing and food inside a box behind their shop. Neither looked through me pretending I didn't exist like a lot of people did. They didn't seem to think less of me because I was dirty and combed through the trash for cans and food. "But I want you to know that the offer stands. If you change your mind all you have to do is come by the shop."

"I'm sorry." I shook my head. "I appreciate the offer. But I can't accept it. I can't explain why. If you need someone to help don't wait on me. You should hire someone else."

"Alright." She sighed. "Let me get Jackson back in here. He's got the code for the cash drawer. We'll get you your money so you can be on your way."

Moments later, I left the recycling center with a wad of bills and coins jingling in my pocket. Yet, my heart ached. It hadn't been easy to refuse Karen, and to leave her friendly face behind. I felt so lonely. Overwhelmed. Frightened. Karen would be the first person I would turn to if Hollie didn't get better.

Toughen up, Fanny girl, I admonished myself. *And get going*. I was even more behind schedule now. It would be busy at the gym where I used one of the rental lockers to store my guitar. The beat-up pawn shop find had cost me only thirty-five bucks. But that had been everything Hollie and I had scraped together after my purse with most of our cash had been stolen. You had to have money to make money. The acoustic wasn't pretty like the Martin I had left behind. It had a cracked headstock which was why I'd gotten it so cheap, but it played well enough.

And isn't that a lot like me and my life right now? I mused philosophically. Yet, Karen had noticed there was more to me than met the eye. And didn't her ability to see beyond the grime and the tattered clothes say a lot about her and who she was as a person?

Lost in my reverie, I almost didn't see the two men coming out of the gym. Two handsome blue-eyed blonds, one with platinum hair the other golden. Ashland and Lincoln. *Holy shit*. I quickly dashed into the thick underbrush beside the building.

"Leg seems better. You don't favor it at all anymore."

"Yeah, brilliant suggestion about the rowing machine. It's been a good exercise for it. You wanna hit the beach and do some surfing with Mona and me later?" Linc asked his cousin, cracking open a water bottle and tipping it back for a long swig. I scooted further into the dense foliage not wanting to leave but not wanting to be spotted, either.

"Nah, I appreciate the invite, but I've got stuff to do," Ashland replied, opening a water bottle of his own with his long slender fingers. My eyes burned as I stared at him. Mesmerized, I was unable to look away. He was just as striking as ever. He wore a navy

OB ball cap on backwards, his platinum hair skimming his broad shoulders. A black workout tank and grey cutoff sweats revealed his sculpted arms and muscled thighs. With his sleek skin, golden tanned strong body and ruggedly handsome face, he could have easily been a model for the gym.

"Oh yeah, like what? We do own the record label. We can set our own hours."

"Yeah I know, if I were content to rest on our laurels and not grow, that plan would be fine. But I promised Ramon I'd listen to the new mix on his album." And that voice. Deep. Smooth. Devastatingly sexy. My stomach fluttered.

Stop it, Fanny. He might not have changed, but you have. You are not the same infatuated fangirl you were back then.

"I can't believe you talked him into recording again. He was so adamant about being done with music."

"Our guitarist protests too much. I read between the lines. It's the traveling he's done with."

"Being away from OB and Karen you mean."

"Yeah, no doubt."

"What about you?"

"What about me?"

"You know what I mean. Always holed up in that palatial penthouse with way too much space. You found anyone to share it with you?"

"I don't know about palatial. It's only got two bedrooms, Linc."

"It takes up the whole top floor of the building, Ash. Two if you count that cool rooftop. And no computer and not a single TV in that huge place. That's just plain weird. Seems to me you enjoy disengaging from the outside world just a little too much. But you're avoiding the real issue. What about you and Renee?"

"Nothing to tell, cousin. We have an arrangement that works for both of us. It's never been anything more."

"It could be if you wanted it to."

"Give it a rest, Linc. You've got the best girl in OB locked down, and Ramon's got one who's a near tie for that title. And anyway,

I'm not looking. My heart belongs to you and Simone. My life's full. I don't need anyone else in it."

Lincoln said something more, but I couldn't hear it. They had moved too far away. My curiosity overriding my caution, I took a step forward. A crack. A loud one. I had stepped on a fallen tree branch and broken it in two. My eyes went wide as both men snapped their heads in my direction. Ashland stared right where I was cowering as if I had an inner homing beacon that he was attuned to.

Chapter THREE

ASHLAND

"Hey!" I exclaimed. It was her. The Lakers Girl. "Wait!" I shouted, but predictably she was already on the move, running in the opposite direction. I dove into the underbrush right where she had been standing only a moment before. The foliage was thick. Branches that she ducked gracefully beneath slammed into my chest as I pursued her. I reached out to grab her as she slowed to skirt along the edge of the building, but I got nothing but a handful of air. She dropped to her rear to skid down an embankment. Staying on my feet, I barreled after her scraping my palms on the loose gravel. Reaching the bottom before I did, she picked up her skirts and ran full out. And the girl could sprint. However, I had an advantage. My legs were longer. Plus at midday the streets were crowded with people. Trying to avoid a collision with a mother and a baby carriage, she tripped and went sprawling, face first, palms out in front of herself to break her fall.

"Ash, stop." Linc grabbed my arm. Gripping it firmly, he yanked me back. I didn't even realize he had been right behind me. "What the hell? She's just a girl. You're scaring her. Look."

"I am looking." My adrenaline was humming. I was in chase mode. I needed to catch her. I felt like she held the answer to some important inner question, and then I wanted to...well, I wasn't sure exactly. Speak with her, I guess, hear her voice, remove that cap and wipe the grime off her face to see what the hell she really looked like underneath it all so maybe I could let go of this nagging curiosity about her.

"I need to get to her." She was less than a dozen feet away. I'd never gotten this close to her, never had her hold my gaze like she was doing right now. Her silver eyes glowed like a magical mirror primed to reveal her secrets. I had to know what they were. I had to get closer. I tugged my arm free.

"Why, Ash?" Linc asked, knowing he only held me from her because I allowed it. "I mean, what the hell?"

I ripped my gaze from her to give him an incredulous look. "To thank her for saving Karen's life." He knew that. I'd been trying to catch her for weeks. I shouldn't have to explain myself.

"Really?" He frowned. "You have to chase some homeless girl through the woods and scare the shit out of her to thank her?"

Well, hell. Now that he had put it like that I felt like a complete ass and paused to contemplate my motives. She didn't wait for me to finish my introspection. Nimbly she flipped over. Leaves dislodging from her knit cap fell to the ground as she regained her feet. My own stumbled toward her as if our movements were connected.

"Wait..." The plea clogged in my throat when I saw the bloody handprint on the concrete. *Her* bloody handprint. Guilt slowed my steps to a halt. I forced myself to stand still. Hands clenched at my sides, my eyes burned as I watched her escape. Her skirts kicked up high above her purple triple buckled high-tops. Darting in, out and around the people clogging up the sidewalk, I could practically feel her panic, and the further away she got away from me the more my uneasiness rose.

"What's really going on with you?"

I turned to fully focus on the man I loved like a brother and desired like a lover, though I knew now that his heart would always belong to Simone.

"What do you mean?"

“Well, if you’re not busy chasing some poor little homeless girl around you’re pouring every waking hour into Outside.”

“What’s your point?” I felt a crease form between my brows.

“My point is.” He blew out a breath. “You need to get a life, man. A real one, stop drifting around on the periphery of everyone else’s.”

“I’m not,” I huffed the denial though his criticism struck home.

“You are. And you’ve been doing it for too fucking long. Especially since your diagnosis.”

“I’m sick, Linc.”

“So what, asshole? I mean alright it sucks. But it’s under control. Your t-count is stable and as long as you take your meds like you should, it’s not a death sentence. I went with you to those sessions with the doctor and all of the follow-ups with the psychologist. We went through the steps of rehab and rebuilding our lives side by side. You. Me. We’ve been through hell and back. Kicked addiction. Levelled with each other about our feelings. There aren’t any secrets between us anymore. There shouldn’t be any bullshit, either.” He studied me a long moment. “You haven’t moved on, Ash. You’re stuck in place. The same place, for almost two years now. It’s time. Take a chance and try for something real.”

“HIV is my reality, cousin. Day to day I do what I need to. But relationships? The kind of happiness you and Simone have found, that kind of romantic shit? It isn’t in my future.”

“Ash...” he protested. “It could be if you want it to be. People aren’t facts and figures. Relationships aren’t equations. It’s not always about A plus B.”

“I’m fine. No need to psychoanalyze me.” I ignored my attraction to him and the appeal in his light blue eyes. “Stop trying to get up in my headspace.”

“You’ve got a big heart. It’s the motivation behind nearly everything you do. There’s a lot of love inside of you. Sacrificial love. I’ve been the fortunate recipient of it over the years. We all have. I wouldn’t be with Simone now if it hadn’t been for your encouragement.” His expression softened. “Don’t be defensive. I just want the best for you. I believe there’s someone out there for you, someone that likely needs you as much as you need them. But you have to be willing to look to find them. Willing to let that person in when they come along. And willing to really get on with your life in order to live it."

• • •

I tossed my keys on the desk and turned to stare out my window at the view of the water. I'd been trying to clear my head of Linc's well intended advice, but I wasn't having much luck. Wasn't having much success getting the girl with the purple hat out of there, either.

My cell buzzed in my pocket. I withdrew it, saw who it was and took the call.

"Hey, Ramon."

"Dude. Seriously. No. Just no. You practically mixed the guitar out completely. I can barely hear anything but my voice."

"Yeah. Exactly. I mean to emphasize it." I spun my chair around and sat down, leaning back and putting my feet up on my desk. My studio. My office. My rules. If I wanted to drag in at noon in my exercise clothes that's what I did. If I wanted to shake up my artists a little, well so be it. And I might as well get comfortable. Ramon was stubborn. This would likely take a while.

"I'm not Linc, *hermano*."

"No. He has his gifts as a frontman. You have your own."

"I'm a guitarist. I'm just messing around on vocals."

"Whatever. We've had this conversation before. Your woman told you, and she's right. You've got that raspy singing voice chicks love."

"But the chord progression is dope, and it'll get lost with the lyrics cranked up that high."

"The chords are still there. It's about balance." In music and life it took the right composition for harmony. So why couldn't I follow my own advice? "Put the headphones on. The good ones I got you. Not those shitty ear buds you favor. Listen to it, the entire arrangement a few times with an open mind, then sleep on it. In the morning if you still don't like it, we'll bring you back into the studio and redo everything. Alright?"

"Alright." He let out a breath. "Hey, speaking of my woman, she ran into the Lakers Girl at the church recycling center today."

"Oh, really." I feigned a casual interest, but I put my feet on the floor and sat up straight.

"Yeah, so you don't need to chase her anymore. Karen thanked her, even talked to her a bit. She offered her a job."

"Did she take it?"

"No. She mentioned being in trouble and was really skittish about being cornered. Karen thinks maybe she's a runaway."

"She's no kid." I might be living my life on the periphery, but I had definitely been close enough to the Laker Girl's to see that she had some serious curves.

"Not like that. On the run from an abusive situation. A boyfriend or a spouse."

My fingers clenched into fists. The thought of that twisted my guts. No wonder my pursuit had frightened her.

"So about the second item on the agenda from my woman. You gonna finally take her up on the invite to come over to the house and share a meal with us?"

Fuck. That was the last thing I needed, though I loved them both. But I didn't relish the thought of sitting down at a table with all their romantic bliss front and center given the complete lack of anything like it in my own life. "I appreciate the offer, but I've got a lot going on right now." I still wanted to finish up early so I could swing by Stump's Family Marketplace. I'd heard there had been a girl with a guitar over there doing a compelling cover of 'Lonely Island', an old Dirt Dogs' number. Talented female performers were hard to come by. If she was decent I might bring her into the studio. "Can I take a raincheck?"

"Ok, *hermano,*" he agreed as my other line bleeped. "But you're going to have to answer to Karen if you keep making excuses."

"Hey, I've got another call."

"I get it. You're busy, but Ash. Listen. Being busy doesn't mean your life is full. No matter how many new artists you sign or how high they go on the charts, at the end of every day and the beginning of the next what really makes our lives meaningful is who we got beside us to share it. Right?"

"I hear ya."

"Good. So don't wait too long to come over here and share some time with your friends."

"I said I gotcha."

"Yeah, I know you do. You've always had my back. I'm here alive and kicking today with beauty in my life in large part because of you. What you too often forget is that I'm here for you, as well. Right beside you for the long haul, bro."

He hung up and I switched to the other line.

"Ash. You there, my boy?"

"Yeah. Hey, Dad."

"Hey, son. Haven't talked to you in a while. Saw more of you when you were still touring."

Yeah, because I had stayed at the house when I was in town back then. He and my mom had been surprisingly disappointed about me finding new digs. Nearing the midpoint of my thirties, yet they still thought of me as their little boy.

"What have you been up to?"

"Not getting any work done," I grumbled, putting my cell on speaker mode so I could shuffle through the daunting pile of mail on my desk.

"You sound like your mom."

A compliment. "She doing ok?

"Yeah, it's just the busy time of the year for her. Lots of new zoning applications for the city council to comb over. And her birthday's next week."

Fuck. I had forgotten.

"I thought we might take her to *El Prado* for lunch. You know how she loves their pisco sour."

I did. "Count me in Dad."

"Can you get Linc and Simone to come?"

"I'll see what I can do."

"You're a good son."

"You're a great father." My parents were the good guys, loving and supportive. My dad would never turn down anyone who needed help, and my mom had an empathetic streak to match his. That was why she used her law degree to serve in the public sector instead of taking a higher paying job with a private firm. And that empathy wasn't just reflected in her career. After growing up in foster care she had vowed that our house would always be a safe haven for anyone who needed one. We'd had Simone over for family meals when her old man had kicked her out. For years Linc slept in the twin bed beside me, more adopted brother than cousin after his mom had died and his father had physically abused him.

"I'm proud of you and all you've accomplished. Just..." He hesitated. He wasn't one to talk just to fill in the silence. His words might be few, but they were considered and meaningful when he spoke them. "Just don't get consumed by all those multimillion dollar music deals. Remember why you started Outside in the first place."

"To give other SoCal artists a chance to create music that made a difference."

"You told me you can change the world with a simple song."

I'd been waxing philosophical after rehab. Both Linc and I had. Outside was a new phase for both of us. We'd done enough raging against the wrongs in the world as a band. That was exhausting and didn't leave you with much of anything to hold onto in the end. We wanted to be about building something positive and lasting.

"Motivations matter. The reasons why we do the things we do can be as important if not more so than the accomplishments themselves. You know what I always say. Motivations reveal our hearts."

"I know, dad. I remember."

"Good."

Our conversation turned briefly to the prospects of his favorite baseball team, the Red Sox, before we ended the call the way we usually did with back and forth I love yous.

I got back to work. Mail first. Most of it junk. More than a few inquiries for follow up interviews about my appearance on the Rock Fuck Club. I hadn't wanted to do it, but Linc had been right, being on the show had been great for the label. Giving us visibility with the entertainment industry and the music crowd. We had signed a couple of promising bands on the heels of it. A plus professionally. A minus personally. Ever since my booty call, Renee had paired up on screen with the RFC star, she had been acting weird with me.

Once I cleared the mail, I moved onto the budget. No worries there. We were kicking ass across the board, and despite just starting out, Linc and I had several artists on the hook. Other labels like Black Cat Records and Zenith Productions had to be watching us. I wouldn't be at all surprised if one or both tried to buy us out.

Next, I tucked into the current concert schedule and the studio calendar. Logistics focused tasks. Things that came easy to me. Things I enjoyed. A plus B stuff. Back in the early days of the band on our mini-tour up the SoCal coast, I had been the one setting up the gigs, negotiating with the club owners. Dominic had been in charge of keeping my dad's VW bus running. Ramon had been our PR guy tacking up fliers. Mona with the camera I had given her had served as our historian. Linc, well, he had been just holding on, a mere shadow of his former self trying to recover physically and mentally from the injury that had cost him his dream of being the world's best professional surfer.

Nostalgic thoughts weighing me down put me in the mood for some musical therapy. I logged out of my computer, stood, stretched and headed out of my office and down the hall. Studio three was free. It had a decent kit. I was going to work on some of the drum fills for Ramon's album.

I was on the second to the last track when our receptionist and accountant shuffled out the front door, done for the day, heading home to their families. I'd completely lost track of time. I clicked off the recording equipment with the remote, set my sticks on my knees and grabbed the bottle of water beside me. The liquid was room temperature now but still refreshing. I drank it all and tossed the empty into the recycling bin. Grabbing a towel from the table beside me, I wiped the sweat from my brow. That's when I noticed my cell all lit up and dancing, still on vibrate mode.

"Hey Mona," I said, sliding open the call without hesitation after seeing her pretty face on the screen.

"Hey, Ash." Her sultry speaking voice was nearly as sexy as her singing one.

"You ok?" I asked. "Where are you? There's a lot of noise in the background."

"It's the ocean. You do remember the ocean, don't you? Look out the window, you old plow horse."

"Who you calling old? I wasn't the one wheezing like a geezer on the stairs this morning, darlin'." I stood and took in the view from the huge picture window that overlooked the beach. Simone and her cute little black and white Havanese waited on the sand just a couple of feet below the studio. She was wearing a shortie wetsuit with the Offshore logo, her long brown hair tied back. She must have walked over from giving surf lessons to the little ones. Smiling, she waved at me, and I waved back returning her smile with a grin.

"You coming out to join us or what?" she asked into her cell. Of course I was coming. How could I say no to her? I'd only managed it that one time in the shower and only then because I had known if I had slept with her I would have lost both of them, her and Linc.

Chapter FOUR

FANNY

"I'm better." Eyes nearly the same pewter shade as my own were no longer glazed with fever, and her pretty features firmly reflected her resolve. "You don't need to go back out at night."

"It's dusk not night, Hollie."

She raised one strawberry blond brow.

"Ok. It'll be night by the time I get all the way there." And later, dangerously later, for me all alone on the way back. "But don't try your signature eyebrow thingy on me. It doesn't turn my brain to mush like it does all those hormonal teenage boys who stalk you on social media. And anyway, my mind's made up. We need the money, Hols or we're never going to get out of here."

"We'll find another way."

"There is no other way. I earned enough cash the first time to pay for another set of clothes for each of us."

"Yeah, I know, but you've also had those gang bangers tailing you ever since looking for their cut."

"It's a risk." I nodded, conceding her point.

"A big one, Fanny."

"But worth it." If I did it a couple of times and made as much as before, we could get new fake passports. We could get across the border. Money would stretch further in Mexico. He'd have a harder time finding us there. We could lay low until Hollie's eighteenth birthday, then tap into her sizeable accounts. Get a high-powered lawyer willing to take on our stepfather. Turn the tables on Samuel Lesowski once and for all.

Hopefully.

Leaving Hollie behind, I hurried through the parking lot but then froze beneath the shadows of the cliffs when I heard his deep booming voice and Simone's laughter. The cute fluffy white and black dog I'd seen around the surf shop was bounding around her ankles on the sand. Ashland was standing across from her. They were both wearing wetsuits. The way his fit him left little to the imagination. Wide shoulders, strong arms, powerful legs, tight ass. When I brought my gaze back up to a safer zone, I realized Linc had joined them, his darker blond hair dripping wet and slicked back like Ash's. He draped his arms around Simone, pulling her into himself and looking like a man who had everything he most needed in the world. Ashland, well. He looked the opposite. Alone. Isolated. A one-man island though he was standing on the shore among his friends.

I shouldn't have been lurking in the shadows staring at them—him—like a stalker. I needed to get moving, retrieve my guitar and earn some cash. But yet here I lingered, watching and wondering about Ashland Keys as I had done far too many times in the past and way too often lately.

Who is Renee? I wondered. The woman Linc mentioned Ashland had an arrangement with. What kind of arrangement did they have? Whatever it was it sounded like it had been going on for a while. Why didn't he want anything more with her? Was it the same reason he had never shown up to meet me?

Her.

Simone Bianchi.

The woman he was staring at so intently, so longingly.

The beautiful brunette with the golden eyes who belonged to his cousin.

My heart belongs to you and Simone, Ashland had told Linc while I had been listening.

She was the one. The one he could never have. The one who apparently ruined everything for the rest of us. The reason no other could ever measure up.

He had come to terms with it. I could see it in his eyes. He would never cross the line and betray his cousin's trust. But he watched her the way I watched him, even now unable to look away from the truth though the sharp pain of finally knowing it gripped my heart.

"There is a tide in the affairs of men
Which taken at the flood, leads on to fortune;
Omitted, all the voyage of their life
Is bound in shallows and in miseries".

Shakespeare had it right. I needed to get on with my voyage, on with my life. I had more important pressing issues to deal with than wallowing in my misery. I had my stepfather to worry about and gang members on the lookout for me. I didn't have the luxury of wasting any more time on Ashland Keys.

Slipping back into the shadows, I skimmed the cliff walls along the water until I reached the concrete stairs at Narragansett. I took them two at a time, a steep ascent. I was huffing when I reached the street level several stories above the sea. Sprinting past the green roofed rental cottages, I hooked a sharp left at the alley that backed the downtown shops. I stopped when I reached Bacon Street and looked both ways before crossing.

As the alley narrowed, I slowed my steps and started scanning more cautiously. I'd almost gotten caught by thugs from the street gang once while running away from Ramon back on this side of town.

Tonight, there was no one here, nothing but the dumpsters and walls of colorful graffiti for company.

I quickly ducked under the carport behind the gym, opened the back door, checked to make sure the storage room was empty and then marched straight to the oversized locker where I stored my guitar.

"Hey, what are you doing in here?" a grumbly voice barked.

"Nothing," I replied automatically, swallowing hard and turning to more fully face the man who had grabbed my arm. "I just need to get into my locker."

"Who gave you permission to be in here?" Bald, tall and imposingly built, I recognized him as the owner of the gym.

"Your wife." My hands shook as I held up my key. His eyes narrowed. "She..." I swallowed again. "She said it would be ok for me to keep my guitar here. I...I don't have any place else safe to store it. I'm sorry."

His expression remaining hard, he studied me for a long uncomfortable beat. My eyes wide I didn't drop my gaze though my heart beat rapidly.

"I saw you earlier. At the Deck Bar putting the trash back inside the can after you took all recyclables out. Took you a good long while."

I nodded once in acknowledgement.

"Hardworking, conscious kid."

A compliment. Not a reprimand. I let out the breath I had been holding in.

"I could use some help keeping the back room swept and clean. You think you might be able to do that for me?"

I nodded vigorously.

"Alright then. Tuesdays and Thursdays. I'll need you to be here early before we open. I'll pay you ten bucks. It's not much but if you show up on time and do a good job I'll let you come in and wipe all the equipment down in the evenings, too, after we close. Sound good?"

"It sounds great." Tears pricked my eyes. It was perfect. Before everyone got here and after everyone was already gone meant no one would be there to potentially recognize me.

"Ok." He gave me a nod, turned away and used his key card to enter the main part of the building Stunned by the unexpected kindness, I lost a few moments staring at the spot he had just vacated.

Ten dollars would help a lot, but it wouldn't get Hollie and I where we needed to go by itself. Out of OB. Across the border. Beyond our stepfather's reach.

I got my feet moving, inserted my key, took out my guitar and returned to the alley. Long sinister shadows had crept in beneath the street lamps. There wasn't much performing time left. There was only the one place with enough traffic at this time of the night that would be worth my while. Stump's Family Marketplace on Voltaire. But it was on the outer edge of the street gang's territory. Dangerous, sure. Hollie had gotten that right. But I had no choice. It was a risk, but one I had to take.

• • •

"*Hola,* Lakers Girl."

I froze. The crowd had dispersed. I had been just about to close up my guitar case. On the sidewalk in front of me, it brimmed with cash. Cash it had taken me well into the night to earn. Cash Hollie and I desperately needed but that apparently the three Hispanic guys in grey and black gang colors thought they needed more. The confrontation I had been hoping to avoid. Times three. Their wallet chains jingled as they strut-glided straight toward me.

My heart rapped hard against my chest with each step that brought them closer. The one I knew only as *El Jefe* led the way. He wore a rolled black bandana to hold back his long black hair. He wasn't tall, but he had a sturdy frame that was packed with ropy muscle. He lifted a finger in some kind of silent command and the two guys flanking him separated. The taller leaner one moved to my right, the heavier one with the tear tattoos on his cheeks moving to my left. *El Jefe* stopped directly in front of me, his dark brown gaze slowly slithering over my form. The tips of his black shoes nearly touched my purple high-tops. I wanted to retreat, but there was a chain link fence directly behind me. I was hemmed in. Trapped.

"Hey." I gulped. "*Qué onda*?" What's up? I had lived in LA long enough to know basic rudimentary Spanish. And though I might not know a lot about bullies, I had grown up with my stepfather. So I had learned an important lesson. Never let someone stronger than you know that you're afraid.

"Looks like you had another good day in my territory, *güera.*" *El Jefe's* menacing gaze dipped to my guitar case full of money then rose, his expression even angrier than it had been a moment before. He and I had been playing cat and mouse like Ashland and I had been. Only with the gang banger it was no trip down memory lane, and it wasn't a game. He was deadly serious.

"Grab her, Nieto," *El Jefe* commanded lifting his chin. He grinned slowly. "It's time for her to pay."

"*Claro.*" Rough fingers immediately latched around my upper arm. Nieto squeezed, and I hissed. Even with my hoodie providing a layer of protection his grip was tight enough to sting.

"You need to learn a lesson about working my corner without asking for my permission and paying me my fifty percent." The *El Jefe's* harsh features sharpened and his dark brown eyes practically glowed with steely anticipation. He enjoyed hurting people. I had seen that same type of creepy fascination in my stepfather's eyes when he had threatened me.

"I'm sorry." I licked my dry lips "Take what I earned tonight. You can have all of it."

"I will have all of it. And you need to understand. It's not what you earned. It's what we earned. You sit on my corner. You play your guitar and sing your sad white girl songs in my hood. You pay." He even sounded like my stepfather. "You disrespected me, *güera*. And this isn't your first offense. You getting me?"

"I'm sorry." I nodded. "Truly sorry."

"Oh you will be." He leaned close. I smelled alcohol on his breath and the pungent stench of cheap marijuana on his clothes.

"What's underneath this thing? I wonder." He reached out without warning and ripped off my Lakers cap. Spirally curls tumbled free to my shoulders.

"*Roja.*" Both his enforcers took a step back, making the signs of the cross on their chests.

"*Madre de Dios*!" Nieto exclaimed. Remember the fortune teller. She said..."

"Callete Mex," El Jefe snapped, but his thick lips were pinched flat now, and his bronze skin had turned ashen.

"Maybe we should let Carlos handle her alone," Nieto hooked his thumb sideways.

"Sí." Carlos grinned darkly and the tatted tears beneath his eyes glistened in the street lamp lights as if they were real ones.

"No," *El Jefe* decided after studying me a long moment. "Carlos doesn't know when to stop. He just wants to earn more tears. But I don't want to kill her. I just want to hurt her. Rough her up *muy malo*, but not so bad she can't walk. That way she can still make me *mucho dinero, comprende*?" Fear trickled down my spine as he circled a finger and Carlos and Nieto came closer.

"*Pobrecita*. Poor baby. All alone sleeping on the street digging through the trash like a dog for her food." He dropped my cap on the ground and stomped on it. "Shame." His gaze lifted. "Such a shame. All that pretty flame. Sad that it has to die." His arm flashed out again. This time a switchblade appeared in his grip. The metal caught the light, the brightness piercing my eyes. "Hold her still, *mis hermanos*." She's not going to like what I do." Rough hands curled around both my arms. "But when I'm done, you two can have your fun." He grabbed a fistful of my hair, yanked it and sawed it off slicing the top of my ear in the process. My stomach clenched. I couldn't see how deep the cut was. It felt like a wasp sting but then a significant amount of warmth trickled down the side of my neck. Stomach turning, I leaned forward, grabbing the only thing I could, *El Jefe*. I retched, heave after dry heave my fingers curling around his forearms and my eyes bulging out from the force of it. If there had been anything inside of me it would have come up.

"Oh, she likes me, Nieto." He put his hand on the center of my chest and shoved me backward. I swayed, but remained in place, since I was strung up tight, my arms outstretched as far wide as they would go between Carlos and Nieto. "Stand up straight," he barked. "I don't like little white girls." He grabbed another lock of my hair, sliced it off and grinned. "But you're in luck, 'cause Carlos does."

Chapter FIVE

ASHLAND

I pumped my cock harder, my gaze on Renee and hers on me.

"Yes!" the naked blonde panted from her bent over position between my spread knees. Her face was so close to mine I could feel her hot breath on my skin. "Harder," she begged, her passion glazed eyes dipping to my lap where pre-cum slickened my shaft. "Fuck me harder."

"Babe." My lip curled. I slowed my strokes. "You forget who's in charge of this scene?"

"Ash, please don't tease. I'm so close."

"Grip her hips harder," I lifted my chin making eye contact with the guy who was fucking her from behind. "She likes it a little rough."

The guy groaned. His eyes were nearly black. He was beyond talking, but he complied with my directions. He slammed his cock inside her.

"Oh!" Renee approved whimpering then crying out as his thrusting deepened. Her breasts bounced in front of my face, but she didn't lose her hold on the leather ottoman that separated her from me. I stroked my cock faster. The sounds of their heaving breathing and flesh slapping together was the only other sound besides my measured respirations inside the room.

"Faster. She's nearly there." The guy grunted and picked up the pace. He started drilling her. Renee squeezed her eyes shut. She was there and so was the dude. His body stiffened. He planted himself deep. His fingers dug into the skin at her hips. She moaned low and long. Her thighs quivered. Shuddering, I watched her come. Then I closed my eyes a couple of seconds, used my imagination and felt the wet heat of myself as I erupted all over my hands.

A moment later, I opened my eyes and snapped a couple of tissues from the box on the table beside me. After doing what I needed to do, I drew my jeans up, buttoned a couple of buttons and stood. "I'm getting cleaned up in the master bath. You two are welcome to use the guest room for whatever." No one went inside my room but me. Not even Renee. Without another word, I stalked from the room. I made it to the mouth of the hallway behind the kitchen before it hit me, the flicker of disappointment in Renee's expression and the shit-ton of it inside of myself.

Suck it up, Ash. This is your life. And this was our arrangement. A consensual arrangement. She knew the score. The guy she had called up on Tinder and brought in had certainly been apprised. Voyeuristic scenes where I called all the shots and watched someone else get fucked used to be a preference. Now they were all I had. All I allowed myself anyway.

Inside my room, I tried to strip off the feeling of dissatisfaction as I peeled off my jeans. I folded the pants neatly and dropped them in the hamper. The hardwood floors felt cold beneath my feet as I continued toward the bath. No reason to linger in the bedroom. It was an uninspired space. King mattress on a frame, boxes for nightstands, a dresser with a mirror. I hadn't gotten much beyond the living room with furnishings that had a cohesive vision. No time. Not much interest really. The only personalization within the bedroom space that really mattered to me was the floor to ceiling windows that faced the ocean that I loved and had missed so much during all those years on the road.

I stopped in front of them, naked though it didn't matter since the windows were unidirectional. I could see out, but no one could see in. Much how I had structured my life. I stared out into the cloudy night for a moment. I couldn't see the stars just the waves crashing into the concrete pier. The water churned, almost as if it were angry. It would be cold. The spray that lifted into the arcs of light from the pier would sting exposed skin. My thoughts drifted. *Her* again. Even my thoughts pursued her. Was she cold? Had she tended to the abrasions on her hand? It had clawed at my insides all day that she had been injured trying to get away from me. And the way she had looked at me, her eyes stormy like the ocean was tonight. Stormy like my thoughts. Did she have somewhere safe to go on a cold, unsettling night?

As much as I loved the ocean, I found no answers to my questions in the waves. Shaking my head, I sighed and almost wished I had taken Ramon up on his offer. It would have given me a distraction from my own tumultuous thoughts.

I turned away from the windows and entered the bathroom. Going straight to the shower, I popped open the door and flicked the dial all the way over to hot. I avoided my reflection in the long mirror over the double sinks. No way in hell did I want to acknowledge, let alone confront the me who stared back. "You got off," I mumbled at him. "Get the fuck over yourself."

I got in the shower. I scrubbed. I lathered. I washed my hair, rinsed and got out again. Snagging a big white towel from the heated rack, I dried off, tucked it around my waist and reentered the bedroom.

"Shit, Renee." I stopped short. "What the hell?"

"He's gone. The guy I picked up for us on Tinder."

"That's well and good, but..."

"Don't you even want to touch me anymore, Ash?" Her expression crestfallen, her voice hitched on my name. My fingers twitched. Renee and I had been through a lot. Over the years, I'd allowed her in more than most, but the boundaries were set, established. She could come to the line, but not go across it. No one could. That was a place reserved for only one. Me. I kept my arms by my sides.

"You know that's not the way we are," I reminded her.

"One time..."

"One time that didn't work out and that was before my diagnosis." I could feel my expression hardening as I recited the facts the doctors had given me. "I'm HIV positive. I can continue to be sexually active with minimal risk to my partners as long as I use protection. I can live out a life as normal as anyone else provided I take my antiviral meds religiously."

"This isn't normal, Ash. And you're barely living. You've taken it to the extreme, these parameters you've set for yourself. The no touching thing during sex we do now, I don't understand it. And I don't understand why you gave up the band when you love music so much."

"I only gave up touring," I corrected. "It's too exhausting and makes my body too susceptible to secondary infections. I still have my music. I just produce and compose it now." My eyes narrowed. "What is this really about, Renee?"

"This isn't working for me anymore."

"It was working for you just fine fifteen minutes ago."

She flinched, and I felt like an ass.

"I'm sorry."

"I am, too, Ash. I need more from you. That connection we used to have grows fainter each time I come over. It's almost like scening with a total stranger now." I didn't argue with her. She was right. I felt exactly the same way. "I can go clubbing if I want something like that. Just do a hookup with someone random like that guy tonight."

"That's not smart, Renee." My fingers curled into fists. I wanted to grab her by the upper arms and shake some sense into her. But I wouldn't touch her or anyone else when I was pissed. I was in control of myself. A man wasn't a man if he wasn't the master of himself. Another valuable truism from my father. The clincher on that lesson had been seeing the marks Linc's father left on his body and deeper ones on his soul. My cousin and I both had damage we carried on the inside from our childhood. His from his drunken old man. Me from my mother's struggles with mental illness. "Promise me you won't put yourself at risk like that."

Her shoulders went back." You don't control my decisions outside the things we do in our scenes, Ash."

"I know that."

"And you're fine with that?" She cocked her head to the side. "You've got your life arranged just like you want it." She sighed. "I guess that the fact that I'm in love with you doesn't fit your neurotic narrative."

I stiffened.

"Case in point." She rolled her eyes. "My emotions are my own. Deal with it. But unlike you I want to nurture my feelings not neglect them. I won't keep going on like this. We either move beyond the lines you've drawn or we fall back to just being friends without benefits."

I watched her stomp out of my room, then glanced at the rustic hardwood beams and scalloped ceiling as if there were answers up there about how to deal with women. Renee. The homeless girl. It seemed all I had lately were women running away from me.

Fuck it.

I grabbed a set of sticks from the dresser and headed for the rooftop where I had my kit. I didn't want to rot in my own thoughts anymore. I didn't want to worry about what I was going to do about Renee's ultimatum. And I sure as hell didn't want to consider what it meant that I couldn't stop obsessing about the Lakers Girl, and that it had been her not Renee or anyone else I had been imagining tonight when I had closed my eyes and jacked off into my hand.

Chapter SIX

FANNY

I stopped at the pier. The truth was I collapsed. At least the pavement wasn't as cruel as they had been.

I continued on my hands and knees. I wasn't too proud. Not anymore. Not after what they had done to me.

Eyes forward. Keep going. You've picked yourself up before. You can do it again, Fanny.

Mother? The voice inside my head that kept prodding me sounded a lot like her. I squinted through the slit of what remained of my vision. With both my eyes nearly swollen shut, I was lucky I could see at all.

Don't freak out. Don't panic.... It is held that valor is the chiefest virtue. And most dignifies the haver.

Alright. Valor it was, and dignity, even in the current state that I found myself. Thank you, Mom for insisting I memorize Shakespeare.

1. Crawl.
2. Breathe—even though each breath felt like I had to suck in the air through a straw—a straw that was on fire in the

center of my chest where Nieto and his counterpart had kicked me.

3. Don't think about it.
4. Don't cry. I tasted salt between my lips but pretended it wasn't there.

Only 1, 2 and 3, Fanny, feeling sorry for yourself only makes the rest more difficult.

My goal. I had to focus on my goal. Get to Hollie. Hide. Rest. Get better. Then get out of OB and never come back. I tried to gauge the distance to the sub-pump again. Why wasn't it getting any closer?

A sudden gust of wind cut right through me, but I turned my face into it. The wet cold air felt good against my skin. The swelling was making my face feel like it was stretched too tightly over my skull. Pulling in another shallow breath, I tried to crawl forward some more. An inch. Two. Then a rest. Just for a moment. My eyes were drawn to the lights on the pier. They flickered like distant stars. The sound of the waves soothed me. And just on the edge of the wind, I imagined a steady beat like someone drumming. Or maybe that was only the pounding of my heart.

"Fanny! Oh my God! No!"

"Hollie," I mumbled, lifting my head. Had I dosed off? Had I made it to my destination? But if I was inside the sub-pump structure, why was it still so cold?

"No! No! No!" she wailed.

"I'm ok. Shhh," I tried to reassure her, but I sounded like a punctured tire with the air rushing out. She gathered me close. I hurt everywhere, but I didn't complain.

"Help me!" she cried. "Someone please. My sister's hurt. Help!" Her pleas were caught up and carried away on the breeze.

"What the hell!" I knew that deep voice. I tried to focus. It seemed important. But everything was dark now. I couldn't pry my eyes open. My teeth chattered together. My entire body shivered uncontrollably.

Hollie said something, but I couldn't process the words.

"She's going into shock. She needs a doctor. Let me get her inside until the ambulance comes."

"No hospital," I protested. "Hollie, no." I quieted as warmth suddenly enveloped me. I felt so light, so detached it felt like I was floating on the surface of a warm ocean current.

"I'm here," my sister said, and I sagged with relief. "I won't leave you. I'm right beside you." Why did she sound so far away and strange, her voice scratchy like she had been screaming in a smoky concert hall all night? "Relax. Stop worrying. I've got you this time. Let me take care of us for a change. Let me be the strong one."

• • •

"Ow. No. That hurts," I whimpered. Woken from a dream where I had floated somewhere safe and warm, I tried to pull my tank back down. Someone had been running practiced fingers directly on the tender skin over my ribs.

"Just bruised. Not broken."

"There, there little one." I heard the deep soothing voice and felt my hands captured, enveloped by much larger ones that gently returned mine to my sides. "Don't interfere. Gloria just needs to make sure you're alright." I felt my shirt being smoothed back into place.

"Poor girl," a kind feminine voice said. "Rest now."

A good plan. I didn't argue. My back felt like it was cushioned on a soft surface but the rest of me felt crushed, crumbled and weighted down by a mountain of trouble.

"I cleaned her up. Washed her wounds. Put antibiotic on them. Only one that's deep. The cut on her ear. The amount of swelling she has around her eyes concerns me. Her nose might be broken. But her pupils are responsive to light. It tells me those blows she took to her head likely didn't result in internal bleeding. But you really should take her to the hospital to be sure, Ashland. I'm only a paramedic. I mostly just do physicals for life insurance now for your dad. There might be something I'm missing."

Ashland Keys. "No!" I struggled to sit up again. "Where am I?" I still couldn't see and that added to my panic. "Where's my sister?"

"Shhh. You're ok." That deep reassuring voice again. "You're safe. *She* is safe." Strong hands curled around my shoulders. "Take it easy." Not a suggestion, a command. His warm breath spilled into my ear. His gentle thumbs swirled a comforting circle into my skin. Tingles rolled through me as firm but undeniable pressure pushed me back down into the bed. Was I in *his* bed? "She's here." A barely spoken whisper, but I heard him. "In the other bedroom. Scared for you, but out of sight. She said it's what you would want. She insisted on it."

"Ok," I exhaled a shaky breath as the comforting patterns on my skin continued. His voice and Gloria's seemed to drift far away on a tide. My limbs felt languid. My thoughts scattered. I slid back into the void. It seemed the only thing I could do.

You can read the rest of the story on Amazon.
Free in kindleunlimited. Oceanside is book 3 in the Rockstars, Surf and Second Chances series. Each book features a different couple. Books 1-3 are available in audio.
It is a completed series.

Outside
Riptide
Oceanside
High Tide
Island Side

Find ME

About the Book

• • •*Complete Series Now Available*• • •

Almost forty-one-year-old Annabelle Morris, wife to multi-billionaire record label executive Charles Morris of Zenith Productions, and mother of two is at a crossroads in her life.

Separated from her husband after walking in on him having sex in the public restroom of a charity event she was hosting, she has arrived on the island of St. John alone and rejected, determined to re-evaluate her life and her marriage. She's tired of being her husband's showpiece while he pretends she doesn't exist. She's tired of trying to make their marriage work for the sake of their two teenage boys.

When she meets Johnny Lightning, a sexy but mysterious piano-playing, bearded sailor, she is tempted to break vows she has never before broken. But Johnny is much younger than she is and seems to be hiding more than a few secrets of his own.

From the laid-back sandy beaches of the Caribbean to the elite circles of Dallas high society, Annabelle is forced to make critical choices.

Is a chance for happiness worth the risk of giving up the life she has always known?

Worth jeopardizing her own and possibly even her children's future?

In the end, will she stay on her present course or brave a new and uncharted one?

Find Me, Remember Me, and Keep Me is a reverse age gap romance, a full and complete story in three separate parts.

FIND
/find/

: to discover (something or someone) without planning or trying to : to discover (something or someone) by chance

: to get or discover (something or someone that you are looking for)

: to discover or learn (something) by studying about it

Chapter ONE

The expression on my face reflected the emptiness I felt inside. I peered out the first class window watching the baggage handlers load the trolleys, while trying to summon the energy to get up out of my plush leather seat and deplane.

"Mrs. Morris?" I shifted to look at the uniformed flight attendant when she called my name. She wore a nervous frown. "Everyone's already exited. Can I get you something else?"

"Oh, I'm sorry. I didn't realize." I had gotten lost in my thoughts, lost inside the confusing maze my life had become because of my marriage. I retrieved my light blue Gucci duffle from under the seat in front of me. When I straightened, my mask was back in place. The one that made me appear indifferent. My preferred pretense ever since I walked in on my husband having sex with his twenty-something new artist's coordinator in the women's bathroom of a charity gala I had been hosting.

Outside on the mobile stairway the bright sun blinded me, and I teetered on impractical spiked heels that got caught in the metal slats. Pulling my Bvlgari sunglasses from the tangle of curls piled atop my head, I took another step, and nearly toppled as my other heel got hung up, too.

I cursed under my breath, took off my Louboutins and went down the stairs barefoot. The sharp metal stung, but I wasn't dumb. I could adapt, like Charles always wanted me to do in our marriage, though adapting felt more like continuing the denial.

At the bottom of the stairs, I slipped my damaged designer shoes back on. No luggage to retrieve I made my way around the still empty carousel, past the other passengers chatting excitedly about vacation plans.

White shuttles and yellow taxis were lined up at the curb, and not a one of them had a sign displaying my name. This wasn't a planned trip. It was an escape. An excursion to re-evaluate my life. One that my best friend insisted I needed. One that I knew she hoped would help me reach the decision to make the yearlong separation between Charles and me permanent. Claire was the only genuine friend I had outside the status-seekers that had comprised my social circle for the past fifteen years of my marriage. Claire had made all the arrangements for me and offered to take care of the boys while I was away. I didn't want to think who might be "taking care" of my *husband* now or how they might be doing it. It was hard enough to get the one visual out of my mind. But I wasn't naïve. I knew the coordinator hadn't been the first. I was just reluctant to tear apart my family and scared to start all over again at almost forty-one.

I approached the curb, slid my sunglasses down my nose, and leaned over to speak to the first driver in the taxi queue through his open window. "Excuse me."

He set his sandwich down on a paper bag on the front seat and gave me a warm smile. "Yes, Miss? How can I help you?" A bit of the icy-tight knot in my stomach thawed.

Thank you, Claire, I thought, *for choosing an English-speaking island.*

"I need to get to the ferry terminal downtown...to St. John."

"Sure, I'll take you." He exited his side and rounded the front end to open the back door for me. He tried to take my bag, but I preferred to hold onto it. It had been so long since I had traveled alone without Charles, without the boys, without piles of luggage, and this duffel was serving as my only shield. I would feel more naked and exposed without it than I already did. The bag gave me something to hide behind not unlike all the designer flotsam Charles insisted I wear.

"How far is it?" I asked situating myself in the backseat as the driver barreled away from the curb.

He steered his weathered land-barge around potholes in the asphalt and stray chickens crossing the road as he answered. "Not far. Fifteen minutes. You should make the last ferry."

I hoped so. I stared out the window and tried to relax. I wanted to appreciate the too turquoise to be real ocean I glimpsed briefly between breaks in the buildings. But I couldn't. I leaned my head back against the plastic-covered seat. I had been up since four a.m. in order to make the connecting flight in Miami from Dallas. My Armani linen dress was wrinkled, my eyes felt gritty, and I was soul-weary tired. I just wanted to lie down and sleep, preferably for about a week straight.

The cab driver's estimate had been accurate and within minutes of being dropped off, I was on board a sun-bleached, paint-peeling passenger ferry named Speedy. It sat about fifty in tight rows with barely any leg room. I closed my eyes, tuned out the sounds of the few other passengers, and lifted my face to the salt spray out the slider window. Hugging my bag as if it were a life vest and not a cumbersome loadstone representing the life I was trying to come to terms with, I let the up and down motion of the boat and the diesel fumes lull me to sleep.

"Miss." I opened my eyes to the same woman with coffee-colored skin and warm brown eyes who had taken my fare when I boarded. "Are you okay? The boat's about to go back to St. Thomas. Did you want to stay on?"

"No. I'm getting off here." I stood, face sticky from the salt spray and dress more wrinkled than it had been before. "Thank you for waking me." Stumbling because of the subtle rocking (high heels were no more practical on board the boat than they had been on the airplane stairs), I scooted down the empty row, attempting and failing to smooth my skirt as I exited.

Out on the dock, I took a quick look around. The harbor at Cruz Bay was much smaller and less commercial than the one in Charlotte Amalie on St. Thomas. The downtown started at the waterfront and crawled up the steep hill. The buildings seemed taller than the zone restricted three stories of height I had read about. A parking lot lay straight ahead, occupied by a few vehicles. Tropical trees and a few villas crowned green rolling hills in the distance. An open, pink building with a red roof sat on the dock at my left. Half a dozen sailboats and a few motor-craft bobbed on the smooth crystal water on my right.

Teetering on the uneven wooden slats of the dock, I carefully made my way toward the shore. I frowned when I reached the loading and unloading zone and didn't see a waiting car. Claire had promised that I didn't need to arrange a pickup. The caretaker of her brother's villa was supposed to meet me with a jeep I could use during my stay. Apparently, he lived on the property somewhere out of view of the main house.

I glanced at the mother-of-pearl dial on my Philippe Patek watch, realizing it was later than I thought. Maybe the man had come and gone already. Afternoon sun beating down on me, I moved under the awning of a nearby jewelry shop when a rusty topless jeep pulled up alongside the curb.

"Are you Mrs. Morris?" The driver, a heavily bearded man wearing a *Quiet Mon Pub* ball cap, peered at me through his wraparound sunglasses. In his late twenties or early thirties, he looked much younger than I had imagined a caretaker to be.

I nodded and moved toward the jeep.

"You ready to go?" He dipped his shaded gaze slowly, sliding it over me. "Or do you need some more time at the jewelry store so you can find a more expensive watch with bigger diamonds?"

"No, I'm ready." I frowned at the snide comment that implied I was as status conscious and shallow as all those social-climbers I had such contempt for. It was an unkind and unwarranted remark. He didn't really know me. How could he presume to after only one glance? Then again, I looked at myself every day in the mirror and hardly knew who I was anymore.

"You're late," he complained. "You're lucky I decided to swing back by the dock one more time, especially since the ferry's been in for over a half hour. Still I wouldn't have wanted to miss that fancy dress and the sun reflecting off that flashy watch of yours. Get in." He gestured with his chin toward the passenger side. Moving my bag to one arm, I grabbed the handle and yanked, but the door wouldn't open.

"Probably used to your chauffeur opening the door for you, huh?" He raised his bearded chin and lifted his shaded eyes to the heavens as if petitioning the island gods for patience. "It usually works better if you unlock it first, fancy face. The power feature is broken. You'll have to do it manually." His voice was a low baritone, but the insinuation was as unpleasant as his lack of manners.

I blew the humidity dampened curls out of my eyes and did as he suggested. "Why even bother to lock it?" I grumbled once I was in the seat, twisting around to grab the seatbelt.

"Because hardly anyone ever sits there," he answered absently, glancing in the side mirror. He scanned a quick look for traffic and then pulled away from the curb.

I can certainly understand why, I thought sarcastically as I settled into my seat. He meticulously steered the vehicle around the busy shopping area alongside the dock, and I took advantage of his distraction to look him over. He wasn't bad. Well, at least from what I could see of his face underneath his untrimmed beard, thick mustache, and long layers of unkempt midnight black hair barely contained by the ball cap. He reminded me of Pierce Brosnan. Pierce Brosnan as James Bond, to be more specific. Well, if I wanted to get really technical about it, Pierce Brosnan as James Bond in to *Die Another Day* after he had been captured and tortured for fourteen months by the North Koreans without the benefit of a hairstylist or a razor.

In other words...quite possibly hot.

Maybe.

But who could tell what was lurking under all that scrunge?

Maybe instead of Pierce Brosnan, the guy was actually Steve

Buschemi. I chanced a second look to be sure...and felt a delicious, rippling heat along my spine.

Definitely *not* Steve Buschemi under there.

His lips were particularly interesting, a rich crimson hue that drew my attention. I wondered if they were as satiny smooth as they looked. I felt a warm, unexpected stomach flutter as I stared at them. His mouth flattened into a displeased line seeming to sense...and to disapprove of...my interest. “Is there a problem, Mrs. Morris?”

“What? No.” I shook my head. “I’m sorry. I didn’t mean to be rude. I’m just tired. I zoned out. It’s been a long day.”

He didn’t reply or make any attempt to make me feel any less awkward. I hugged my overstuffed bag tighter and tried to swallow back the bitter tears that seemed so near the surface most of the time lately.

The jeep had a stick shift, and he worked the gears confidently as we steadily climbed one hill and then another. The view of the sparkling ocean through the trees was breathtaking. I just wished I could get out of this jeep and away from him so I could try to relax and really enjoy it.

“Here we are,” he announced unnecessarily as he finally pulled the jeep into a driveway and turned off the engine. The one story villa was a simple structure with white-washed walls and a red tile roof. It was even more charming in person than it had been in the pictures Claire had shown me.

“It’s beautiful,” I whispered as I took it all in, the house and the verdant landscaping. I let myself out of the jeep, and for a brief moment completely forgot the irritable man by my side. He murmured something in a surprised tone, but I didn’t catch the words. I was determined not to care, refusing to let him ruin the moment for me.

The steady, salty breeze lifted my hair and refreshed my flagging spirit, bringing with it the sweet fragrance of the flamboyant tree blossoms. Two of them framed the villa forming a natural awning, their fiery orange flowers and delicate fern-like leaves kissing the turquoise shuttered windows that apparently had been left open for cross ventilation. Just beyond, on the other side, I could hear the siren's call of the surf. Pink Bougainvillea and lush tropical foliage embraced the house, making it seem as though it were a part of and not just an addition to the island's vibrant natural landscaping.

"You're taking excellent care of Mr. Lawton's property. I'm sure when he comes back he'll be grateful to you." Claire didn't talk much about her brother. She only told me that he had built the house intending to live in it with his bride after they got married, but that the girl had broken it off with him right before the wedding, thereby ruining the place for him forever. He rarely used it anymore but didn't want to sell it, either. Claire was unusually tight-lipped about her sibling. I think she only shared select personal information so that I wouldn't worry about imposing on or running into him while I was staying at his villa.

The door slamming behind me was the only response I got to my compliment from Mr. Irritable. Pebbles crunched beneath his flip-flops as he crossed the drive. Without glancing at me, he inserted the key into the lock to open the gated entry into the property. I didn't understand why he was being so rude. If he treated everyone who rented the villa the way he had treated me so far, I could certainly understand why the house remained vacant when most were rented out during high season. I should probably mention his behavior to Claire at some point. But for now I told myself I wasn't really offended by his dismissive manner. My husband had ignored me for the better part of our marriage. I had lost the confidence that I was in any way interesting to the opposite sex beyond my role as my husband's representative.

The iron gate swung open soundlessly, and I followed the caretaker inside without being told. An arched breezeway covered in concrete provided a lovely postcard frame for the view of the ocean on the other side.

"Spectacular. I love you, Claire," I whispered. My feet compelled me forward over the rough Saltillo tiles, my eyes widening as I scanned the seemingly limitless slate of brilliant blue. Without realizing it, I reverentially kicked off my shoes as if the spot I stood on was hallowed ground.

"Are you and Claire really good friends, fancy face?"

"Yes," I replied without hesitation. "The best." I moved toward the water, laying my hands on the railing. It spanned the length of the villa and kept people from walking off the elevated deck. Pulling in deep breaths, eyes feasting on the glistening ocean, ears lulled by the crashing of the waves, I also admitted, "She and my boys are my life. My whole life. All that gives it purpose. Besides my older brother and younger sister, I mean."

I was too tired to notice how sad my words probably made me seem. The sun was setting, and my mind was lost in the mesmerizing orange and pink kaleidoscope of color. I wished I had unpacked my camera. If I could get the caretaker to give me whatever instructions I needed before he left, I might have time to take a couple of shots before the light disappeared.

"Sir, do you..." I trailed off, surprised to find the spot where he had stood just a moment before empty. The jeep in the driveway was the only witness to my sudden consternation. I retraced my footsteps back through the entryway and found a set of keys on top of a flat rock, a piece of paper with a masculine scrawl of written instructions beneath them.

"That was weird," I muttered. He was strange. Though he physically resembled my favorite secret agent the first time he had ever appeared on screen sporting a beard, he certainly didn't have the suave smooth demeanor to go along with it. He hadn't even bothered to say goodnight. I closed the gate and latched it, not wanting to have to deal with him anymore anyway.

He lived on the property. But how far away? I suddenly wanted to know the answer, hoping it was far enough that I wouldn't run into him again. He didn't seem to like me much and after the way he had behaved, the feeling was entirely mutual. I was sure we could manage to avoid each other if we both put some effort into the task.

I padded back to the railing at the edge of the deck and dropped wearily onto my rear on the tile. I would get my Canon out tomorrow. It needed time to acclimate to the temperature and humidity so the lens wouldn't fog up.

I tucked my legs beneath me. I didn't care that I was probably getting red tile stains all over the expensive ivory linen of my dress. I just wanted...needed to decompress.

Hugging my bag to my chest, I stared out at the rolling waves and laid my forehead against one of the iron rails. It felt cool against my skin. As my thoughts drifted off on a lonely tide, I offered a prayer that while I was here I could find both the answers and the solace I sought. The sky turned light pink and then black before the rhythmic crash and gurgle of the surf eventually soothed the raging maelstrom within my heart.

Chapter TWO

I woke up with my head resting not on the railing as expected but on a cushiony pillow. Confused, I sat up and gaped at the sheet that covered me. I didn't remember getting it or the pillow. Tossing the sheet aside, I lifted my arms and stretched them up to the pale pink sky, taking a breath of fresh ocean air.

The sea was much calmer this morning, mirroring my thoughts. The last thing I remembered before falling asleep was talking to my boys and hearing about their day. Connecting with them somehow calmed me.

My older son, Trent, had been more talkative as usual. He was excited about his physics class and about pursuing his passion next year at college. His grades were good enough that he might even gain admission to SMU. His younger brother Charles Junior, CJ, was a dreamer, more prone to be fanciful-minded like me. Well, more like how I had been before my disappointing marriage. CJ wrote stories and hoped to be a film director one day. He had answered the questions I had posed but hadn't stayed on the phone very long, just long enough to tell me how much he already missed me and to ask when I was coming back home.

"Soon," I had told him after admitting how much I already missed him, too.

I got up, feeling stiff and a bit silly about sleeping under the stars now in the bright light of the new day. I folded the sheet, picked up my shoes and bag, and padded into the one-room villa. No wall separated it from the deck, though there were floor tracks and a sliding louvered door that went over them in case of inclement weather.

Inside, there was a large, mahogany, canopied bed with mosquito netting and a galley kitchen with modern stainless steel appliances and an island bar with two barstools. Turning and looking back the way I had come, I noted the large umbrella out on the deck along with a circular cushioned lounger big enough for two with pillows. I wished I had taken advantage of that setup last night, but it had seemed too far away from the ocean at the time.

I opened a couple of teak cabinets and got some coffee brewing. My gaze drifted to the bed. It was strange that I didn't remember pulling the sheet and pillow from it. I must have been more tired than I had realized.

In the small but functional bathroom with teak cabinetry that matched the kitchen, I washed off last night's makeup. My complexion sans raccoon eyes was an improvement, but I made a face at my reflection in the shell-framed mirror. Why bother reapplying my makeup? Who was here to notice? Back home in Dallas I wouldn't have gone out to get the newspaper from the driveway without being fully dressed, including makeup, and my hair styled. But this was the islands. I wasn't here to make a fashion statement. I was here to get my life together. To find myself again. To find a better me for my family and for myself.

I ran a brush through the nighttime snarls and piled my reddish brown curls back up on top of my head using a decorative elastic band I always carried around in my purse for emergencies. I filled an earthen-ware mug with coffee and went back to the rail with my camera. I wanted to snap a few shots of the sailboat that had just appeared at the mouth of the crescent-shaped bay.

Watching the boat through my viewfinder, rapidly clicking shot after shot, I tuned into the surf and the chirping of the birds, quickly losing track of time. The heat of the sun on my skin warned me that I needed to apply sunscreen. But then I realized something else. The boat I had been taking pictures of wasn't turning back out to sea. It was headed straight for the small dock directly in front of me. Feeling embarrassed with the pilot of the boat close enough now that he could probably distinguish the color of my eyes, I put the lens cap back on the camera and let it dangle from the strap around my neck. I leaned down and snagged my forgotten mug of coffee grabbing it by the handle, taking a sip and grimacing when the cooled beverage hit my tongue.

I hated cold coffee.

When I straightened and peered back at the boat, the sailor leaned into view, tossing a thick rope to the dock as he expertly aligned the hull of the boat alongside it. My eyes widened. My morning diversion was none other than Mr. Irritable himself. Only he didn't look irritated this morning. He looked relaxed and cover-of-*Men's-Fitness*-scrumptious. Impressive chest, traceable abs, and athletic legs that looked like they had been carved out of stone, but were more likely the result of hours upon hours of wrestling with the wind and the waves on his boat. His thick black hair was wet and slicked back from his heavily-bearded face. Unlike the day before when his wide shoulders and lean torso had been mostly concealed by a faded, v-neck cotton t-shirt, this morning there was nothing to cling to or cover any of it, just acres of smooth sun-kissed skin above a pair of low slung swim trunks.

I started to duck out of sight hoping he hadn't caught me staring...again...but he had. He snagged me like a fish on a hook with his aviator-shaded eyes. He returned my perusal, his gaze slowly scanning my rumpled, slept-in clothes from last night. I felt as naked as if he had undressed me. I didn't move. I couldn't move. I felt like I was in a daydream. Awareness of myself as a woman and him as a man crashed over me like a warm wave. I surrendered to the sensation, letting myself be swept away by the intoxicating current.

After his behavior toward me, I was surprised when his lips lifted into a roguish grin as if he could guess the direction of my forbidden thoughts. Or maybe, if I was totally giving into the dream scenario slash fantasy, he was having some of those same kinds of thoughts himself...about me.

Heat flooded my cheeks that suddenly transformed into the unwelcome burn of embarrassment, when I glanced down at myself and realized why he had been staring. Not because of some sweet blissful musings. Not because I was some beautiful siren summoning his inner Ulysses, but because the position of the sun made my gauzy linen dress completely transparent.

I spun around and scurried into the house like a crab to its hole in the sand, and my mortification kept me there for the better part of the day. Suffering in silence in the sweltering heat, I didn't even risk a trip down to the ocean to cool off.

By sunset, I was mostly over it. My stomach grumbling helped me make the choice to move on. I needed some supplies. I couldn't survive on just coffee, sugar and cream. Scooping the car keys off the kitchen counter, I locked up the villa and marched determinedly to the jeep.

Once behind the wheel, I frowned. Morning Sailor slash Mr. Irritable was wrong about me being dependent on a chauffeur. I drove myself around except for that one time when I had accompanied Charles to the Grammys, but it had been a long time since I had driven a vehicle with a stick shift. Not only that, I had to remember to drive on the left side of the road as the local laws required. I stalled the engine at the first stop sign. After a couple of attempts, I started it up again, and once I got it into second gear with some momentum down the hill, I was golden.

An hour later, having been distracted by the interesting selection of tropical produce, I had a basket filled to the brim with stuff to make salads and sandwiches, nothing too fancy or hard to prepare.

After loading up the jeep, I returned the way I had come. Only this time, I stalled out going up a hill instead of down, and I had a terrifying moment of panic as the jeep rolled backward before

I eventually got it going in the right direction again. I prayed the clutch would hold out for an entire week.

By the time I emptied the trunk and put the groceries away in the kitchen, my Alexander McQueen paneled dress was stuck to my skin, and my Prada sport sandals that were supposed to be comfortable were killing me. I kicked them to the side vowing that I was going to town for a pair of flip-flops at the first opportunity.

I took a cold shower and slid on a fresh pair of Chantelle panties but abandoned the matching bra on the bed after wrapping one of the sarongs around my breasts. I felt a lot better and cooler after the shower, but I was almost too tired to fix anything. I was standing in the kitchen staring at the fridge trying to summon the energy to make a turkey sandwich when I heard *his* deep voice.

"Yo, fancy face. You alive up there?"

I went to the railing and peered over to find Mr. Irritable Sailor on the sand beside a portable grill holding a spatula. His shaded gaze lifted. My cheeks flushed with warmth. I made a quick, investigative glance to make certain nothing was amiss with the olive sarong that matched my eyes. I exhaled my relief noticing as I returned my gaze to him that he still wore the same swim trunks from earlier, but his muscular torso filled out a Skinny Legs Bar & Grill t-shirt now.

Dressed up for the evening.

Island style.

Thank goodness.

"I didn't hear any movement upstairs. I was afraid you might have expired from the heat. Too many people come down here to the tropics and try to do too much their first day. Heard you take the jeep out." He grinned, a flash of white teeth within the dark frame of his beard. "Glad you made it back. You know there *is* actually a gear between first and third."

"Yeah, I found it." *Eventually.* "Thanks for the concern." I was proud of the sarcasm I managed considering how badly I was reeling from the realization that his apartment was just below my own. From the front of the house, the second unit beneath mine hadn't been visible.

"I caught some snapper this morning. I'm almost done grilling it. Would you care to join me?"

My jaw dropped. Was this the same guy who had been so judgmental and annoying the day before?

"I'm sorry I was so irritable with you yesterday." And could he read my mind? I certainly hoped not. He would know how pathetically fixated I was on him...a sexy and way too young for me guy, even if I wasn't married. "Let me feed you," he added when I didn't reply. Oh gosh, the inappropriate images those words engendered showed just how quickly my fascination had grown out of control. I covered my heated cheeks with my hands before my blush could give me away. "I need to make it up to you, or Claire will never forgive me."

"No. I'm not hungry. The heat has taken away my appetite." The heat I was having a problem with had everything to do with him and nothing to do with the ambient temperature. "Wait a second." My sexy sailor haze cleared. Why would Claire care if the guy managing her brother's villa was rude to me? "What did you say your name was?"

"I didn't." This time he was the one who looked embarrassed. "Come down and I'll introduce myself. You need to eat. My sister mentioned that you've been skipping too many meals lately."

Sister? So he *wasn't* the caretaker. He was Claire's brother! He must have decided to move back into the villa. I wondered when and why. And if Claire had known he had returned why hadn't she warned me?

Questions flitted through my mind as I found and took the path down to the bottom apartment. It wasn't hard to reach. A couple of stepping stones along the side of the house and I was there. Claire's brother was placing perfectly grilled filets onto a platter. He looked up at me, and his engaging grin made my stomach flutter.

I stumbled on the sand.

"Let's eat inside." His gaze swept over me. I tried not to fidget, though I knew I had to look horrible. My hair was extra curly from the humidity, and the sarong and my bare feet were a far cry from sophisticated, but it didn't really matter. He wasn't interested in me that way and wouldn't be even if I had been decked out in the sexy silk Gucci gown that hung in my closet back home.

"Sure. That sounds great." I tried not to stare overly long at him though the porch lights revealed that he was holding up much better in the heat and humidity than I was. I guessed if I stayed a while I would get acclimated to the tropics and wouldn't pour buckets of perspiration every time I moved.

"Mosquitos are a problem at dusk," he explained. "I'm surprised you didn't get eaten alive sleeping out on the deck last night."

I tripped on the step up into the lower apartment but righted myself quickly enough to remember to close the door after I entered. One seamless wall of glass faced the ocean and the interior was completely climate controlled. The cooler inside air was invigorating. "Did *you* cover me with the sheet?"

"Yeah." He stroked a hand over his beard and avoided my gaze while setting the platter of fish on the round glass top table that was already set for two, a sprig of pink Bougainvillea in the center for decoration.

"Thank you," I said softly. "That was very thoughtful."

He shrugged as if it hadn't been a big deal. "Would you like a Carib?"

"What's that?" I asked.

"A local beer."

"As long as it's not a dark beer." I made a face. It had been my favorite style until I had contracted a stomach flu right after drinking it the last time.

"No. It isn't."

"Okay, but let me get it. After all, you did all the cooking. Is it in the fridge?"

He nodded and I went straight to the kitchen. His apartment had the same layout as above, so it wasn't hard to figure out. The floors were cool marble instead of red Saltillo, and his bed looked like it had actually been slept in. The neutral toned sheets and botanical comforter were rumpled as if he had tossed and turned. A lot. There was also a shiny, black baby grand piano. I tried not to gawk though it was as impossible to ignore as the tangled sheets, given the direction of my thoughts.

I grabbed two brews by the neck and the bottle opener lying out on the speckled granite counter. “Do you play the piano?”

“You could say that.” He gave me a long and searching look almost as if he expected me to know the answer before he had provided it. “I took extensive lessons as a kid and used to play it all the time, but I don’t much. Not anymore. Not for the last couple of years anyway.”

“Why not?” I blurted before realizing the question might be too intrusive. I couldn’t begin to imagine the expense and hassle of getting something that big and fragile down to an island that had no direct flights or large cargo ship deliveries. It must have been a logistical nightmare. Why bother if he wasn’t going to play it?

“I guess I just don’t enjoy it as much anymore,” he stated enigmatically, taking off his sunglasses and laying them on the glass top table. I almost tripped on my own feet without the sand or a step up as an excuse. His eyes were striking, a storm grey fringed with thick black lashes.

“I’m sorry to hear that,” I said quietly, something in his gaze cautioning me not to press him further. This wasn’t an insignificant matter to him. “It’s a beautiful instrument.”

He nodded once and reached for the beers, opening one and passing it to me before he popped the top off the other. I took a sip of mine enjoying the cold crisp flavor. He drained his nearly dry in that same amount of time. He held out a seat for me then sat on the other, setting his bottle down and leaning forward. “So what do you think of the island so far?”

I laughed. “I haven’t seen anything but the inside of Starfish Market and the view off my balcony, but so far it’s more beautiful than any place I have ever been.”

He smiled slowly. “Well as beautiful as that view is, there’s a lot more to see.” He speared a large filet for me and took another one for himself, shoving a huge bite in his mouth before asking, “You seem to be settling into island life rather quickly. I like your new dress.”

"It's just something I picked up at the market." I glanced down at myself and then back at him. "It's more practical than the things I packed."

"Nothing practical about the way you look in it. I thought it was only the designer clothes, but now I can see that you make everything you wear look fancy." He leaned back in his chair so he could slide his gaze slowly over me. "Although I will admit I liked the one you had on this morning a little better," his tone lowered, "only because of the way it let the sun shine through it."

Compliments. Provocative ones. I was unaccustomed to them. I shifted in my seat feeling those same seductive tingles of awareness I had felt earlier. Only they were stronger now with him so close.

"What are your plans while you're here?" His sudden question was accompanied by another lingering appraising look. "Do you enjoy hiking or snorkeling?"

"I do." I smiled, relieved to be on a neutral subject and more familiar ground than how he thought I looked. "I've discovered that I like nearly every new kind of outdoor activity I've tried since I met your sister. Just not mountain biking." I took a smaller bite of my fish than he did. It was flaky and moist. I closed my eyes. "Mmm. This is delicious. What did you do to it?"

"Just shook on some St. John's seasoning." He took the last swig of his beer, went to the kitchen and snagged another bottle. He seemed awfully thirsty. Did his mouth get as dry around me as mine did around him? Or had I embarrassed him with my appreciative moan about the fish? "Are you ready for a fresh beer?" he asked.

"No, I'm good." I took another bite and chewed while trying not to stare at him, a temptation for me apparently. He had a rolling swagger that testified to the fact that he spent a great deal of time on the ocean. He was nearly a foot taller than me and his legs were long and covered in fine hair as dark as the long strands on his head. He had kicked off his flip-flops when we had come in, and his feet were as tan as the rest of him, golden brown against the sleek ivory tiles. But he seemed a lot older without the sunglasses. His eyes seemed to hold depths of knowledge that I knew came only with experience, and those years of wear and tear did not show on his body. I tried to recall, but I couldn't remember Claire ever saying how old her brother was. I did know that when he was of age he had adopted her to get her out of the foster care system after their parents had died in the private plane their father had been piloting. They had both hated the foster system.

He reclaimed his seat and drained half his beer before leaning forward to scoop salad from a bowl onto my plate first and then his own. His portion was huge. He speared another filet, too.

I smiled wider. I had two teenage boys who had appetites just as big as his. Charles wasn't home for dinner often enough anymore for me to make a comparison.

"Ranch dressing?" he asked.

I nodded. "Yes, thank you."

"I'm Johnny by the way. But my friends call me Lightning." Again a searching glance and a pause as if maybe that revelation should mean something to me. "What's your real name, fancy face?"

"Annabelle." I smiled as I chewed enjoying his company. "But your sister calls me Belle."

Chapter THREE

"Well, I can't very well call you that, can I?" he asked, his tone teasing. "Isn't that the name of the Disney character from *Beauty and the Beast*?"

I nodded.

"The one who goes around with her head stuck in a book," he confirmed. He placed his napkin on the table next to his empty plate while studying me with unnerving intensity. "Are you a reader, fancy face?" He seemed very curious about me, determined to delve deeper.

"Sometimes," I admitted. "If it's a good mystery with lots of clues to put together and some action to make it interesting."

"There aren't many mysteries on the sleepy island of St. John. But I'll see what I can do about adding in a little action to make your stay here interesting." After cleverly turning my words around, he tapped a finger to his chin. "You don't seem like a Belle to me." His voice rumbled low, and the inflections he used added to the intimacy of the moment. "You're too sophisticated and sexy. Definitely not G rated."

Me? Sophisticated and sexy? Was he flirting with me? I had been out of practice for too long to be certain.

"Don't get me wrong. I've got no problem with a girl who likes to read. That usually implies that she's intelligent, has an imagination, and a predilection for creativity."

I wanted to fan myself with my hand despite the air conditioning. Everything he said, everything he did made my mind careen around one thought. *Don't look at the bed,* I warned myself. Again. The strain from the day before when he had seemed to develop such an instant dislike toward me had turned into dangerous tension of another sort, if I was reading the situation correctly. Had it changed because of something Claire had told him? I felt at a distinct disadvantage not knowing exactly what he knew about me.

"You said you'd spoken with Claire recently?" I probed after taking a swig of my beer.

He nodded. "I called her today to let her know I was on island. We had a short conversation. Well, mostly she did the talking."

"That's Claire."

"Yeah, bossy since birth."

"Opinionated," I softened.

"Yeah if by opinionated you mean her way is the only way."

I laughed. Claire was headstrong, but she was a good friend. A steadying influence. Our friendship had begun around the time he had moved away. "She misses you, badly I think."

"How do you figure that?"

"She's never really said so, but whenever you come up in conversation, she gets a really melancholy look on her face." I tilted my head inquisitively watching him, awaiting his response. "Not that you come up very often. She's only spoken in broad generalities about you." I didn't want him to feel awkward or get the impression that we sat around and gossiped about him. "She just shared how rough it was for you both after the crash..." I trailed off as his expression turned guarded, much like hers whenever we talked about that time. "What I mean to say is...that..." I stumbled for the right words. "She speaks very highly of you and how well you took care of her. I think in her mind she was a burden to you back then so she doesn't want to say anything now, but I can tell that she wishes that she heard from you more."

"She never lets on whenever we do talk." His brow furrowed. "But then again she's always been so self-sufficient."

"Siblings are important," I stated gently. I knew he believed that too, or he never would have taken care of Claire like he had right up until she'd left for college. "Sometimes they're all you have. I know that pretty well," I explained giving him a little background that I usually didn't share. "I grew up in a house with two alcoholic parents. My older brother Cooper was my shield, and my younger sister Faith was my refuge. I don't know what I would have done if they hadn't been around."

"I'm sorry, Anna." We shared a moment of empathy and something more. It was wrapped up like a pretty package deep inside his eyes as he had spoken my name so softly. He seemed to see me in a way no one else ever had. But I couldn't acknowledge that. My mind scampered away from the idea faster than it had from the realization that my dress had been see through. A shadow of regret seemed to pass over his gaze, but whether it was because of our conversation or something else I couldn't tell.

Johnny said there weren't many mysteries on the island. He was definitely one of them, one that intrigued me more than I should have allowed. But I couldn't help myself. I was as curious about him as he seemed to be about me. It was strange. On one hand, I felt comfortable with him because he was Claire's brother. On the other hand, I was more than a bit unnerved by how attracted I was to him. My mind kept wandering off on tangents it usually didn't go to. I was overly conscious of my movements. My legs turned into uncoordinated blocks of wood. My heart beat too fast, my lips got too dry and my breathing became too shallow.

"It's ok." I needed to focus on something else. "I'm sure Claire would love to see you. She could come here," I suggested. "Now that you're back."

"She could," he allowed. "That's actually a good idea. Thank you, fancy face. I'm really glad I decided to return to the island when I did." He abruptly pushed back from the table and picked up his plate. I got the impression that maybe he had shared more than he had meant to. His gaze dipped to my plate. "You done?"

"Yes, but I'll get it." My reply was notably breathy as if I had just finished a quick sprint. The amount of pleasure I experienced from his praise revealed much. My lips parted in order to usher in the extra oxygen my lungs suddenly demanded to keep up with my racing heart. I stood to gather dishes, following him into the kitchen when I had an armload, trying to find a safe zone for my gaze. There wasn't one. Wide shoulders. Narrow hips. Long legs. Perfect ass. All of him sexy. All of him impairing my ability to reason. All of him an indulgence I couldn't afford.

"You can set those down on the counter. I'll wash them later." He gave me a long searching glance.

"Why don't we just do them now?" I looked away trying to regather my thoughts. "It won't take long."

He agreed, but I could tell he was surprised by my offer. I think we were both a little surprised by the other. I got the hot water running insisting on washing while he dried. My arms up to the elbows in a sink full of suds, we worked efficiently side by side as if we had done so dozens of times.

"It's probably still too hot for you to fall asleep upstairs," Johnny said as he put the last pan in the cabinet.

"Maybe," I agreed, taking the stopper out of the sink while he threw the dish towel he had been using onto the counter.

"If you're not too tired, we could watch a movie together. I won't keep you up too late. I want to take you to my favorite beach for some snorkeling early in the morning."

After a little debate about selection, he popped a movie into the Blu-ray that we had both already seen, but one that I had chosen because it was an action flick with a decent romance. Perching on one side of his small beige leather coach, suppressing my excitement about spending more time with him the next day, I hugged my arms around myself. He took a seat on the other end, sprawling his long legs out in front of him. I was acutely aware of his presence. He radiated heat and the air conditioning was freezing. Or at least that was the lie I told myself.

"You're cold," he remarked during the first chase scene, the one I barely noticed because I was too busy sneaking side glances at him.

"No, I'm not." I shook my head.

"You've got goosebumps on your arms." How had he noticed that? Was he watching me as closely as I was watching him? "So either you scoot over here and let me warm you up, or I get a blanket for you. Your choice."

I chose the blanket. I might have spontaneously combusted had I taken him up on the other. He retrieved it from the bed I had been trying to ignore. The material was soft and smelled like a blend of fresh ocean breeze and citrus cocktail. Exactly the way he did.

"How old are your boys?" he asked, shifting suddenly to more fully face me, the television bathing his handsome features in a blue glow.

"Trent is eighteen. CJ is fifteen." The question was a little unexpected. "Why do you ask?"

"It's obvious they're important to you and I heard you talking to them last night." He shrugged at my arched brow. "Sound carries pretty well from the upstairs unit." His gaze seemed serious though his tone was light. "You wear a wedding ring, but you didn't mention a husband, and I didn't hear you talking to one, either. Did something...happen to him?"

The easy groove we had fallen into since cleanup dissipated instantly. It suddenly seemed as though Charles was an actual presence on the sofa between us.

"Yeah something," I replied bitterly, twisting the three carat round Tacori engagement ring and matching band that was just for show these days. It meant nothing now...at least to Charles, and it had been that way almost from the beginning of our marriage. But I didn't go into all of that. It was too painful to admit, too humiliating.

"What about you?" I asked him, deflecting. "Is there anyone else?" I remembered what Claire had said about the fiancée who had broken his heart and his comment about no one ever sitting in the passenger side of his jeep. Those details plus the fact that the upstairs and downstairs apartments seemed to be devoid of any feminine touches strongly implied that he remained unattached. After having gotten to know him a little bit better, I couldn't really understand why.

"No children. You've got to have someone you can trust. Someone who you know will also be a good mother before you can consider starting a family, in my opinion. I've never met a woman like that."

His answer was nearly as vague as mine, though telling. Obviously his fiancée hadn't measured up to those standards. I settled deeper into the couch and went back to pretending to watch the movie, but mostly I peeked at him through my lashes and wondered.

Chapter FOUR

"How much food did you put in there?" I asked Johnny the next morning as he hefted the cooler into the back of the jeep, his biceps flexing beneath the weight. "I can tell it weighs a ton. I thought we were going to the beach for the day, not an entire week."

"Who knows what will happen today." His eyes gleamed with rakish intent. "Maybe we'll stay longer. Maybe we'll find other things to do and burn more calories than we anticipate. It's best to be prepared, Anna." I tried to pretend I didn't like his playful teasing or the way his voice sounded when he abbreviated my name. But I think my flushed cheeks gave me away. He seemed amused that I was flustered. His gaze lingered on my face, and he was still grinning after he closed my door and climbed into the driver's seat.

I shifted to watch Johnny like I had too many times the night before. The morning sunlight only improved the view. Sunglasses shielding his eyes he drove the jeep confidently, his strong fingers working the stick shift more capably along the up and down two lane road than I had. He didn't turn on the radio and I was glad. I enjoyed the muted early morning sounds of the island and the easy comfort of his presence.

When we reached downtown Cruz Bay I tried to focus on learning the maze of confusing streets as Johnny zipped the jeep through them, instead of memorizing every detail about him and wishing I could photograph him. His profile serene, the wind sifted through the long layers of his thick black hair like invisible fingers. He wore a plain grey v neck t-shirt that looked like it had been poured onto his chiseled chest along with a pair of long swim trunks. This time they were light blue. He rested one arm on the sill while he steered with the other. Masculine wrists. Strong veins on the backs of his hands. Long fingers. Blunt nails. Musician's hands, despite his admission that he didn't play much anymore.

He took the steep hill up from town and turned into an empty parking lot when we reached the bottom on the other side. Angling the jeep into a spot next to a sea grape tree with a twisted trunk and large, fan-shaped leaves, he popped off his seat belt and exited well before I did grabbing the cooler and the tote full of beach paraphernalia. I followed behind him a little less enthusiastically. It was still early, and I hadn't yet finished my travel mug full of caffeine.

I perked up when I saw the view framed by more sea grapes. I had never seen sand so purely white or felt any so fine between my toes. The water started as a foamy ribbon of lace at the shore, and then became clear for a bit before turning light blue and then brilliant turquoise further out by the reef. I hadn't realized I had stopped with my toes buried deep in the sand, mouth open in awed wonder, until his low chuckle broke the spell.

"That was my reaction the first time I came here. Hawksnest is one of my favorite beaches. It gets overlooked because it's so close to town. It's not always the hard to reach places that are the best ones, you know?"

Under one of the trees he laid our towels on the talcum textured sand and hung the tote from one of the branches. "Ready to snorkel?" he asked, looking as eager as my boys when the three of us climbed onto the oversized sectional in our recreation room and got ready to watch *JoJo's Bizarre Adventure,* our favorite Japanese anime series.

"Sure." I smiled. His enthusiasm was contagious. "But let me take a couple of photos of the beach while I choke down the rest of this coffee. I need the caffeine to counterbalance your youthful energy."

He frowned. It didn't seem as though he liked being reminded of the age difference between us. "How old do you think I am, Anna?"

"I don't know," I stated truthfully feeling caught off balance by his directness. "A lot younger than me."

"I'm thirty-three. Last I checked that wasn't all that young. Legal, certainly. How old are you?"

"A gentleman never asks..."

"I'm certainly no gentleman. Of that I can assure you. If you knew what I've been thinking since I first saw you this morning in that black bikini..." His eyes looked sinfully dark in the shade beneath the tree.

"But I've got on a cover up..." I reminded him, my voice a little breathy.

"I don't know why women wear those things." He snorted. "It's mesh. It's like a peep show every time you move." He stroked his beard as he regarded me. "What's beautiful to a man never changes. Curves, soft hair, smooth skin, heat that blooms because of our touch. But nothing is more seductive than looking into the eyes of someone you're attracted to and having the desire you're feeling mirrored back at you."

I swallowed to moisten my throat. The present topic and the undercurrent between us, whether real or imagined made my mouth go dry. Though older, I felt less experienced somehow, I guess since he had been on his own from such a young age. I definitely felt completely out of my league with this handsome, much younger man. "I'm nearly forty-one," I confessed. "My birthday's coming up soon."

"Mine was nearly a full year ago. So I'm almost thirty-four. Seven years isn't much." He took my mug and set it aside, then reached for the zipper on my cover up. "Need some help getting this off?" He lifted an inquiring brow.

"No. I'm alright. I can get it myself." My voice sounded high and panicked, exactly the way I felt.

"Okay, but hurry." He grinned. I loved being on the receiving end of one of his smiles, even if I didn't really know what I had done to amuse him. He grabbed a pair of fins and a blue snorkel from the hanging tote. When he reached between his shoulder blades and took off his t-shirt, my jaw came unhinged.

Again.

What kind of exercise routine did he do besides the boating to get muscle definition like that? I saw lots of the same guys in the gym back home nearly every week. They worked out constantly like I had since the boys got older and I met Claire, but none of them had a body near as amazing as his. Luckily he was already halfway to the ocean and didn't see my response. I had a feeling if he did that grin of his would have grown wider.

"Meet you in the water, Anna," he yelled kicking up splash as he jogged out into the flat crystalline surf.

I practiced breathing techniques and polished off the last of my coffee before talking myself into unzipping my cover up. Trying not to look at him, I stumbled and slid ungracefully down the sandy slope into the water with my snorkel equipment in hand.

I hoped Johnny already had his mask in the water. No such luck. His mask was up on his head. He was treading water, and he was staring...at me. He looked so long that my cheeks grew warm, and my mouth got dry all over again.

You're imagining his interest, I told myself. Sure the two piece swimsuit was sexy. Claire had talked me into the demibra-like top and the Brazilian cut bottoms. But my hips were too wide, and my breasts were too full after two pregnancies, no matter how much I worked out. Nothing I had could possibly hold his attention.

I glanced behind me expecting to see some slim supermodel walking into the ocean, but there was no one. Just me. And damn if that hot look from him after all I had been through in my marriage wasn't a balm for my ravaged ego.

As soon as I was deep enough in the water, I slipped my head back to wet my curly hair. Donning my fins and then my mask, I put my face in the water and swam out to him, about twenty yards from shore.

I removed the snorkel from my mouth. "What's to see here?" My voice had a husky quality to it that I blamed on the snorkel and the exertion to reach him though it hadn't really been all that far.

"Lots of variety at Hawksnest," he replied, his tone a lower rumble than I had yet heard it. He touched my arm, fingers skimming softly over my wet skin before he adjusted the straps on my mask.

I stared into his gorgeous grey eyes through the glass, and he stared right back at me for several protracted moments. The world seemed to hold its breath...or maybe it was just me. I noticed everything in those moments. The water droplets on his dark lashes. The mix of grey and blue in his eyes. How the ocean lapped against parts of me that had awakened because of him and how much I ached for a man's experienced touch.

His touch.

"Reef squid. Turtles. Parrotfish. Angelfish." He cleared his throat almost as if he had been as lost in me as I had been lost in him. Then he smiled softly, and I noted how his eyes had crinkled white lines around the edges. "Let's stay together." His lips formed a compelling frame that I suddenly had an ill-advised desire to taste. "I'll squeeze your hand and point if I see something interesting, if you promise to do the same for me."

I nodded, though I hadn't really focused on what he had said. Not when his gaze had dipped to my lips as I wet them. Warmed by the dark charcoal his eyes had become, I held my breath. We were so close, and he hadn't let go of me since he had adjusted my mask. His hands were on my shoulders as we both treaded water. His grip felt significantly warmer than the tropical water.

He leaned closer.

Was he going to kiss me?

Would I let him?

"You'll need this," he advised, sliding the snorkel with its plastic mouthpiece toward my lips. I felt foolish and guilty for the forbidden direction my thoughts had taken me.

However, I didn't remember ever letting out that breath that I had taken in thinking about the possibility of him pressing his lips to mine. It burned bright inside my chest throughout the hours of snorkeling that we did together. He was always nearby making sure I didn't drift too far out to sea. He glided his fingers along my arm or grasped my hand to point out something interesting, his methods of communicating underwater where words were impossible.

I liked his method. I liked it a lot.

After a while, I started to do the same thing. I tugged on his wrist when I spotted an octopus peeking out from under the fire coral, and I grabbed his hand when I saw a French angelfish he might have missed. I forgot there was another world outside our watery one until I turned the corner and nearly slammed into a four foot long barracuda. Eyes wide, I swam as close as I could get to Johnny and pointed frantically toward it.

Tucking me into his side, he led me several yards from the perceived threat and lifted his head out of the water. I did the same but glanced back in the direction where the fish with the razor sharp teeth had been, afraid it might have followed us.

He touched my face, and I turned back to regard him, knowing my eyes were still wide behind the glass of my mask. He removed his snorkel and lifted his mask on top of his head. Water sluiced in enticing rivulets from his thick black hair to his broad shoulders. "It's okay, fancy face." He removed my snorkel for me, his thumb brushing across my parted lips. My heart rate sped up, but no longer from fright. "That barracuda is always there because that's where the reef squid hang out. It's not interested in having you for dinner. If you ignore it," he gently lifted my mask onto my head, "it will ignore you."

Yeah, I thought wryly, *that strategy might work for the barracuda, but it probably won't work for all of the jumbled feelings and desires you have stirred up in me.*

Later on the shore, unaware of my secret thoughts, Johnny rinsed and stowed away the snorkel equipment. He took the beer I popped open for him, and I began to get our lunch out of the cooler.

"Get yours first, Anna," he told me when I handed him a plate. "We snorkeled a long time. You've got to be starved."

"I am, but I like taking care of whoever I'm with." My breath came in on a sudden rush when he curled his finger under my chin and lifted my head so I had to look at him instead of at the sandwich I was making.

"I can see that." His piercing grey eyes held me captive.

"Part of the mom in me," I explained. "It's not a big deal."

"Maybe not to you, but to me it certainly is. The women I used to hang around with cared more that they were...that I was...well, they cared more about a broken nail than they cared about me as a person or being kind enough to think to serve me before themselves. Yet you do it like it's second nature." He tucked a wet curl behind my ear. "And you look beautiful doing it."

"I've got snorkel mask indentations on my face. I'm all sandy and my hair's a mess. You've been by yourself too long, I think."

"Just because I've been out of circulation for a while doesn't mean I can't recognize true beauty when I see it."

"Thank you. That's very nice of you to say."

"I can see you don't believe me," he concluded after his eyes searched mine. "It's as much about your words and actions as it is your pretty features. Calling to check on your boys even though you were so exhausted you fell asleep sitting up. The way you speak so lovingly about your family and my sister. Forgiving me for being an ass *and* helping me mend things with Claire. That's not just superficial. It's deeper. Real beauty always rises up from what lies inside, fancy face. Don't you know that?"

If he was right then he had a lot of beauty inside of him, too. I had a hard time not gawking at this man with a swimsuit model's physique and a poet's heart. While my lunch remained mostly uneaten in front of me, he finished his in a couple of quick bites. Then he laid on his side on the beach blanket, and the photographer in me had the urge to snap a photo, except that the shadows from the sea grape tree would have interfered with the shot.

While he relaxed, I busied myself throwing away our trash, stowing away the uneaten parts of our lunch and fumbling when I found his eyes on me.

His dark brows dipped, and he turned his head away, reaching for his sunglasses and rolling onto his back.

I swallowed, deciding I must have imagined the serious look in his gaze. He certainly couldn't be as caught off guard. Fumbling in my mind like I had fumbled with our supplies, I felt like I suddenly needed words to fill the awkward silence. I glanced out at the sparkling water and listened to the waves lapping at the shore. The question automatically drifted into my mind.

"Why St. John?"

"Hmm," he murmured lazily as if drunk on the one beer and the sun.

"It's an island paradise, but why did you choose it as opposed to somewhere else?"

"Because it felt right. Like home, from the first time I saw it." His biceps bunched tightly as he lifted up onto his elbows to regard me for a long moment from behind the dark barrier of his sunglasses. He seemed to be trying to work something out in his mind, or maybe he wanted me to pick up on something, but before I could figure it out, he continued. "Life had gotten out of control for me at one point. The slow pace here, the simple lifestyle, it was just what I needed to help me put the scattered pieces of my life back together."

I nodded. I could understand that. I could feel it beginning for me.

"Then when things didn't work out the way I thought they would, I came back, and here I have stayed." His explanation was vague, but I got the idea he was probably talking about the woman he had almost married. "What about you? What do you like about Dallas, and what do you do back there besides take care of your boys and keep my sister in line?"

I told him how I loved the wide open spaces of the Metroplex. I talked about my charity work and how much I enjoyed the specialty water aerobics class I had begun to teach at his sister's insistence.

While we packed up the jeep, he told me details about some of the islands he had visited and how he liked to sleep on the front netting of his boat so he could look at the stars.

I listened attentively as he continued to describe his favorite beaches on the way back to the villa, thinking how the open jeep somehow felt like a bubble in a private universe just big enough for the two of us. I realized that the way I felt, the breathless effervescence, had begun all the way back when he had first stared at me through my snorkel mask and that it had not lessened all day. Being with him and getting to know him was like discovering something wonderful. Something that you never knew you needed but now that you had found it realized you didn't just need it, you needed it desperately.

"I've got some things I need to take care of, Anna," Johnny told me back at the house without meeting my eyes as he rinsed off the cooler and the snorkel equipment with the garden hose. "Will you be alright by yourself tonight?"

"Yes, absolutely." I hid my disappointment. Maybe I had misread things. The lingering touches. The soft whispers in my ear. The hot glances. The connection. "I need to check on my boys and I should get to bed early." For what reason I didn't really know, but it seemed like the appropriate thing to say.

He shut off the hose and straightened a lock of his hair that had escaped the sunglasses and fallen into his eyes. He stared at me for a long moment. His gaze seemed conflicted almost as if he were wrestling with himself about something. "Have a good evening, Anna," he said low like a permanent goodbye, stepping close and grazing his warm knuckles softly over my cheek before he turned away and took the path around the villa to the lower level.

"You, too," I said softly to the emptiness that remained after his departure, standing in the driveway feeling unsure and strangely bereft.

Get a clue, Annabelle. He's hot and thirty-three-years-old. He took pity on you. He's going to run back into town and grab his twenty-five-year-old girlfriend and fuck the hell out of her. Newsflash, you're not even an afterthought in his scene.

Only later I wondered if maybe I had been wrong because after I had my shower and called my boys it wasn't male groans or feminine giggling that drifted upstairs from his apartment down below. It was the sound of the piano. Soft, tinkling high notes and a few somber, wistful low ones. A tune began to coalesce that I had never heard before. Did he write music? He started humming, and his voice was rich and soulful, somehow reminding me of the way he had looked at me before he had said goodnight.

You can read the rest of the story on Amazon.
Free in kindleunlimited. Find Me is book 1 in the
Finding Me series. All the books are available in audio.

Find Me
Remember Me
Keep Me

Strange
MAGIC

About the Book

Billy Blade is a hardworking, hard living, razor sharp musical force. Mysterious behind his dark shades, the rough around the edges Texan mesmerizes with his haunting harmonica and tantalizes with his dangerous looks and smooth country charm. His latest album is topping the charts. He's the newly crowned King of the Bacchus Krewe. He's definitely living the rock star dream.

Exotic Creole beauty Thyme Bellerose couldn't be more content. She has it all. An adoring grandmother. A handsome Tulane medical student beau. A satisfying job in the heart of New Orleans' French Quarter. Her life is as rich as the ice cream she creates. She's got everything under control. But control is an illusion. Dreams can turn into nightmares. And now during Mardi Gras, otherworldly powers stand ready to shape their destinies in ways they could never imagine. Shadow and light.

Magic and mystery.

Reality and myth.

All come together in a place where rules bend and lines blur.

Even those between life and death.

We love life, not because we are used to living but because we are used to loving.

- Friedrich Nietzsche

Part ONE

PROLOGUE

BILLY

Heard melodies are sweet, but those unheard are sweeter.
- John Keats

"Dammit, *de'pouille.*"

I quickly grabbed a pillow and covered my lap while Arla Gautreaux rolled his eyes to the ceiling as if searching for the patience he required within the recessed lighting of the tour bus.

Access to my dick denied to her, the brunette kneeling on the floor between my spread legs rocked back on her spiked heels. She wasn't wearing anything else. Neither was the other brunette on the bed next to me, but she wasn't as bold as her companion and pulled the rumpled silk sheet in front of her too big to be real breasts. The entire scene too familiar to be shocking to him anymore, my manager continued to voice his displeasure peppering the air with Cajun curses strong enough to make my eyes water.

"Next time maybe try knocking," I mouthed lamely. It wasn't much of a defense. He had it right when he called me a hot mess. I was a pedal to the floor, picking up major momentum, barreling headlong down a predictable path to its natural dead end disaster.

"I'll start asking your permission to enter," Arla tapped his watch and jerked his chin over his shoulder to emphasize his point, "when you start taking your commitments seriously, no? You forget you have a show tonight, Billy?"

I shook my head. Of course, I hadn't. "Excuse me, darlin'." I tossed the pillow aside and moved Brunette One out of the way so I could yank up the Rock 47 jeans from around my ankles. She and her eager friend might have told me their names at sound check before they offered me their services as a two for one deal, but I'd be damned if I could remember either one. In fact, I was already regretting taking them up on it.

"I gotta go. Playtime's over," I announced gruffly despising the weakness that made me screw up everything in my life. Untamable strands of dark blond slid forward effectively shielding my eyes from my manager's condemnation as I carefully tucked my dick back inside, buttoned my fly and re-buckled my Nocona belt.

"If you wanna keep your fans and tour sponsors you need to stop pulling stunts like this, *podna*." Arla continued to dish out the well-deserved verbal lashing ignoring the brunettes as they sifted through drifts of empty liquor bottles and six months of accumulated tour clutter for their discarded clothing.

"You're right, Arla. I screwed up. I know." I swiveled at the waist snagging my favorite wadded up black Fender t-shirt from where it lay on the bed behind me. Bunching the soft cotton between my fingers, I punched my head through the frayed collar. Before I could get my arms into the sleeves, one of the white gold bands from the silver chain I wore around my neck got caught on a loose thread. Guilt burned inside my gut as I paused to untangle it.

"I hope so, Blade." Arla slammed me with a censuring gaze the moment I looked up, his dark scowl eradicating the trio of laugh lines that usually framed his muddy brown eyes. "I surely do hope so, but lately it doan seem like anything I say gets through to you." Arla's lazy way of drawing out his words and stressing the last syllable came from time spent deep down in the Louisiana swamp and was even more noticeable than my south Texas twang.

Arla's disappointment stung. I didn't really care what most people thought about me, but he was a loyal friend, one of the few who had stuck by me when everyone else had written me off as a lost cause. For nearly a year I had taken a sabbatical from everything, holing up in the old tool shed behind my parents' house, drowning my sorrow in alcohol. The only breaks in the monotony were the regular visits from the one man who had refused to give up on me. If not for his stubborn persistence, I'd probably still be languishing within the ramshackle confines of my self-imposed exile.

Walkie talkie sputter crackling in his hand, Arla made a rolling gesture with the other. I knew the drill. Best get moving. Arla wasn't some label lackey that I could brush off or push around. We'd been together too many years for that, since the very beginning of my career when I had been seventeen and winning the Professional Bull Riding world championship had been my goal. Singing had just been more of an afterthought, something I did to impress the chicks. Pathetic now that I thought about it, how my pickup technique hadn't changed in all this time.

Anyway, Arla had convinced me to hang up the spurs, placed a guitar in my hands and insisted I learn to play. He had showed me the basics of songwriting, and not long after I got the knack of it he had negotiated my first record deal. The latest one with Black Cat Records was his doing as well.

"Blade, take us backstage with you," Brunette One whined blocking my exit, a pile of clothes in her arms, but still as naked as the day she'd been born. Brunette Two in her bra and jeans hovered beside her friend chewing disinterestedly on a raggedy red thumbnail.

"No can do, darlin'." I stepped around her snagging sunglasses from the shelf and lifting my black Stetson off its stand. I raked back the thick layers of my hair to get them out of my eyes before shoving the hat down on my head. "We leave for Houston directly after the show tonight." I slid on the dark aviator shades I always wore on stage, dismissing her, but more importantly shielding my glacier blue eyes from Arla's scrutiny.

He barked an order to event security on his handheld before addressing my companions. "Ladies, you've got two minutes to get dressed and get off the bus. I'm sending someone back here in case you need some encouragement." He turned and made his way down the center aisle past the sleeping bunks to the front lounge without pausing to look over his shoulder to see if I followed. He didn't need to. I might be on the slow road to ruin but I didn't have a death wish.

My three man security detail and my personal assistant, Lorraine, fell into place around us as soon as we stepped onto the pavement. As a unit we set off across the gated lot where all the buses were parked. The steady roar of the outdoor crowd grew louder as we approached the scaffolding of the stage but I knew it would be even crazier once I stepped out in front of them.

A warm wind with just a hint of brine from the bay rolled a discarded Outside Lands festival cup across my path. I stepped over it just beginning to run through the set list in my mind when Arla spoke again.

"Just got the call from the Bacchus Krewe Captain." Hearing the edge of excitement in his voice I knew it had to be good news. "They chose you, *podna*."

"Seriously?" That was cool but it wasn't something that came totally out of left field. Arla had buddies who were on the committee. Each year the thousand or so members of the Bacchus Krewe chose a top tier celebrity to be their king and fashioned their theme around him. Because of Arla's connections I knew that my name was on their short list, but then so were a lot of other notables.

"Yeah, Blade. When's it goan sink in that thick skull of yours how big of a deal you done become? Country entertainer of the year. Grammy for song of the year and best rock album. Cover of Rolling Stone. Top of the list for rock and country sales for over half the year. Why wouldn't Bacchus want you?"

I shrugged. I didn't put a lot of stock in awards and shit. It was nice to receive those honors, don't get me wrong. It was just that I tried not to focus on stuff that was outside my control. It was hard enough to manage the things that I could. But I knew this one was a big deal to my native New Orleans boss.

"Don't make any plans in February. It's not just the parade you'll be officiating. You'll also be performing at their masked Rendezvous Supper Dance in the Morial Convention Center. Your ceremonial duties aren't quite as complicated as those in the older more traditional Mardi Gras Krewes, but we'll still have a ton of stuff to go over as the event gets closer." He shot me a serious look and held out his hand. "Here." I took the coin he offered me. "That's just a prototype. When you're in the parade you'll wave your scepter and the other riders on your float will toss those wherever you point."

I studied the silver dollar sized doubloon. I knew the ones from Bacchus were some of the most collected and valuable of all the carnival throws. They sold for thousands of dollars after Mardi Gras on auction sites. Mine was black and had a silver imprint of me in my cowboy hat and sunglasses on the front. That same side also had the year twenty fifteen and the parade number. The flip side was engraved with an image of my harmonica, the date again and the theme 'Celebrating Mouth Harp Charmers'.

A blast of icy wind that came out of nowhere suddenly lifted the hair underneath my hat and raised chill bumps on my arms.

I glanced around to see how everyone else was reacting but oddly no one else in my entourage seemed to have been affected. "Arla," I began. "Did you feel that..."I trailed off as the ground started to roll like a boat on a choppy lake beneath my feet. I swayed and my vision tunneled. I heard three long protracted harmonica notes. A beautiful woman's face materialized within a smoky haze that I knew had nothing to do with the famous San Francisco fog.

Though I'd never seen her before she seemed strangely familiar. Haunted violet eyes locked with mine as if it were a two way exchange, as if she could really see me. Not just the man I was now, but also the man I had been, the one who used to give a damn, the one who had been buried under the rubble of his demolished heart.

"Help me," the violet eyed beauty intoned faintly with an accent I couldn't place. "Please."

"Hey, Billy." Arla put his hand on my arm. I jumped. "You ok?"

The spell was broken.

"Where the hell is he?" The voice on the other end of Arla's walkie talkie exploded with high volume disembodied displeasure.

The sounds and sensations of the here and now effectively swept away the lingering traces of whatever the hell had just happened. Just one more freaky occurrence I'd have to chalk up to alcohol and my overactive imagination.

No more mixing tequila and whiskey, I vowed.

"Relax. We've got him. We're coming down the corridor now. He'll be there in five," Arla responded calmly, his wrinkle free western shirt and pressed Wrangler jeans outward reflections of his inner chillaxed attitude. Though he had an intricate tattoo spanning the entire length of his spine that told me there was a little unexpected rebel beneath the polish. I could always count on him to keep his head despite the chaos that I or anyone else threw at him. Irate record execs, clingy groupies, condescending rehab administrators who didn't appreciate me checking in wearing only boxers and boots; no one kicked my boss from the bayou out of his steady groove.

"You're thirty minutes late this time." Arla shook his head, the ends of his dark brown hair brushing his collar. "You're lucky Blackberry Smoke extended their set to cover for you." He gave me another censuring glance that might've had me quaking in my boots a couple of years ago, but not anymore. Not these days. Not the soon to be crowned Bacchus monarch, the prince of the rock and country airways Billy Blade. The no longer down and out, scraping out a meager living playing nothing but cash songs at BYOB honkytonks out in the boondocks. These days I was the comeback sensation everyone was talking about, a headliner selling out maximum capacity stadium sized venues. A mega huge superstar.

Fucking fickle fame.

It was all due to the success of my latest album *Never Too Dead to Dance*. The title sucked wind, in more ways than one I could assure you, but I was proud of the songs I'd written for it after crawling away from the wreckage of my life post rehab. I'd channeled all the bad stuff, all the broken dreams, the heartache and the anger into my music. The only time I really felt like my old self anymore was when I was up on stage playing those tunes. If I wanted to continue having the privilege of doing so I would do well to pay attention to the boss. People were counting on me. Loads of them. The crew. And my fans. It was time I stopped being such a self-hating, self-absorbed bastard.

Arla took off to negotiate the next big deal on my behalf while I jogged up the steps to the stage. Rodney, my guitar tech, handed me my custom black and silver Gibson hollow body. I threw the strap over my shoulder and clipped it into place, not missing a step as I strode out onto the brightly lit stage, an earsplitting boom from the Golden Gate Park capacity crowd nearly blowing the hat off my head. I still hadn't gotten used to it, even though it had been like this at nearly every stop for over a year now. As low as I'd been, I'd never take it for granted.

I tipped my hat to the audience out on the grassy lawn to show them my respect and the sea of fifty thousand Outside Lands festival fans cheered even louder. Cell phone cameras flashed from the bikini clad chicks on their boyfriend's shoulders upfront and the tented VIP booths on the far sidelines where the rich cats paid thirty-six hundred dollars a ticket.

It was wall to wall people in every direction, a massive swarm of living breathing humanity.

Well, not all of them were living and breathing. There were others out there, too. Ones only I seemed to be able to see. Ones I refused to dwell on. They were nowhere in sight at the moment, but I knew from experience that they wouldn't remain hidden for long, not if I blew into my harmonica. So I just wouldn't play it.

"Howdy, San Francisco!" I threw my right arm up into the darkening sky, thumb and pinky out, three middle fingers curled into my palm. "We got any southern rockers out there ready to shake it?" I queried.

While they screamed their affirmative replies, I put my pick between my right index finger and thumb and strummed the first chord of "Hell". The stage lights pulsed in time to the rhythm. The crowd roared their approval and the Billy Blade Band crashed in following my lead, tight as usual.

We took it through three straight songs from the set list without pausing before someone shouted the inevitable request I dreaded. 'Midnight Serenade'.

Shit. Every muscle in my body went tense.

Someone always asked. No matter what city we toured or what venue we played, it was nearly impossible to get off stage without pulling out my harmonica and performing that godforsaken tune. I wished I'd never penned the damn thing. Wished I'd never laughed at Arla when he warned me not to be mocking death. Especially now that I was confronted with it every time I played the song. But there was just no stopping me from being a damn fool.

I had been headstrong all my life, taking up the bull riding, or eight seconds of sanctioned suicide as my ma liked to call it. Leaving school prior to graduation. Digging my boots into the fertile soil of the Rio Grande Valley whenever she or my pa used the words 'can't or 'don't' with me.

Sweat dripping into my eyes from the intense heat of the lights, I lifted my hat from my head and mopped up the wet with the absorbent material of my sleeve. Hoping, hoping, hoping that the request wouldn't catch on.

But as I reached down behind the center speaker, grabbing the bottled water a roadie always placed there for me, I heard the crowd chanting in unison for 'Midnight'. Ignoring them I unscrewed the lid and chugged half the cool liquid before pouring the rest over my steaming hot head.

"Midnight. Midnight. Midnight."

Damn. Looking out over the audience I pulled in a deep breath. It didn't do anything to calm my nerves, and it sure as hell didn't stop the chanting. Giving in was easier than expending the effort to try to steer fifty thousand people in a different direction.

I half turned and gave my drummer Daryl the nod. He twirled his sticks in the air to acknowledge my cue, and I swiveled back to face the audience, sliding my harmonica from my jeans pocket.

I didn't really want to do it but I it was almost as if I were playing a game of chicken with myself and the universe, knowing what was going to happen, but daring it not to.

The delusion of choice was all I had left in my descent into madness.

They began to materialize with the first notes that I played, emerging from whatever depths that held them. Shadowy outlines rising like smoky wisps of steam, they filled in all of the available spaces in the audience, in some cases overlaying their living counterparts, their number equally vast.

Their ethereal forms flickered like holographic projections. Each individually distinguishable. Every age, gender and race represented. Some appearing the same as they had in life but more often than not they wore the evidence of their mortal wounds. The more gruesome those wounds, the harder it was to keep my expression neutral while looking at them.

Seeing just one ghost would have been bad enough, but no, for me there were thousands. Their phantom heads all turned towards me as I played, cocking to the side as if they were listening to the music and finding the tune too intriguing to resist, their mouths opening and closing. They were trying to communicate, that much was clear, but the eerie howling that accompanied their arrival sounded like screeching feedback inside my brain. It was extremely difficult for me to play through.

They started to line up tonight and that was when I really started to get weirded out. My heart raced as I watching them form vaporous rows, like a ghost army ready to do my bidding or maybe to spirit me away with them.

I searched among the sea of expectant transparent faces for the ones I would give anything to see once more, the ones I had tried to summon repeatedly after discovering my disturbing talent. But they weren't there. They never were. Had they come it would have meant that my talent was a gift instead of the curse I suspected it to be.

A week earlier I'd gotten shit faced enough to risk asking if anyone else in the crew saw dead people when I played that damn mouth harp. Bandmates, roadies, everyone within earshot that night had looked at me as if I'd gotten thrown off a bull and cracked my head open.

Arla had a bit stronger of a reaction. After not so subtly suggesting that I avoid playing the harmonica for a while, he had stormed to the bus and poured all my Jack Daniels down the drain. When I explained later in detail what had been happening, an unidentifiable emotion had flashed across his face. Not surprise. The opposite maybe. It almost seemed as if that had been what he had been expecting me to say. But like a lot of things lately I didn't trust my own take on the situation.

Unmindful of my introspection the apparitions continued to march forward. Adrenaline streamlined into my bloodstream as they drifted closer to the stage, passing through every obstacle in their path. People. Trashcans. Light poles. Nothing slowed or deterred them.

Morbid fascination kept me frozen in place. I broke into a cold sweat despite the hot as a Texas summer sun spotlight on me. What did they want from me? What would happen if they actually touched me? And why did I find their dark energy so strangely appealing?

Maybe because I was nuts. Certifiable. Hello, Mr. Blade, right this way to the padded cell we have prepared for you.

Fear dogged my heels as the mob of specters surged forward. I began to rush through the notes, praying that I could get to the end of the song and pocket the harmonica before they got any closer.

But what if they didn't go away when I stopped this time?

And what if I started seeing them when I wasn't playing?

Chapter ONE

THYME - AUGUST 2005

You were made perfectly to be loved — and surely
I have loved you, in the idea of you, my whole life long.
- Elizabeth Barrett Browning

Fogerty's "Graveyard Train" bluesy rhythm rolling through my body, work clogs tapping on the linoleum floor to the beat, I swayed back and forth in front of the steaming work kettle that reminded me of a witch's cauldron, pretending the oar sized wooden paddle was my dance partner.

When the thick custard began to bubble around the edges, I stuck my nose into the light steam, inhaling deeply, savoring the rich aroma of the ice cream base. Lately I swore I could distinguish each individual ingredient: the heavy cream, half-and-half, egg yolks, sugar and a dash of salt, by the way it smelled.

I laid my stirring stick on the butcher block prep station careful not to drip on my worn copy of Browning's *Sonnets from the Portuguese.* I'd cracked it open earlier while waiting for the machine to churn out a batch of mint chocolate chip.

I crossed the kitchen quickly going up on my toes to snag a heat resistant plastic tub from the steel drying rack above the sink.

The tub was nearly as big as I was, but I wasn't afraid of transferring it by myself anymore, even though it weighed over eighty pounds when full.

I pulled the lever to tilt the kettle pouring the steaming base into the tub I'd set on the floor. Once full, I toted it by the built in handles over to the commercial fridge where it would need to cool overnight.

I loved the order and discipline it took to precisely follow the steps in the ice cream recipes that I used each day. But I also enjoyed being creative and dreaming up new flavors. I could barely wait to try out a new one that I hoped would mimic the flavor of a blueberry Old Fashioned cocktail.

I lifted the base above my shoulders to place it on an empty shelf and closed the freezer door.

"Oh!" I jumped back, heart rate spiking, hand to my throat, startled by my *mamere's* unexpected appearance in the kitchen. She wasn't usually up this early and I hadn't heard her enter over the sound of Creedence.

She shook her head, intelligent caramel eyes twinkling with amusement, but her expression was stern. I was going to get an earful from her about something. Grasping one of the iPod strings she plucked a bud from my ear. "You need to wait until Tony comes in to move the tubs," she fussed, tapping a disapproving finger to a rounded cheek a shade lighter than my own. "They're way too heavy and it's dangerous for you to carry all that hot liquid by yourself. You could trip and burn yourself, badly, *non*?"

"I'm ok, *Mamere*." And I was, truly. In the past, I wouldn't have dreamed of doing that chore alone but lately the batches just seemed lighter and lighter.

I put stubborn hands on my aproned hips. Mine were more in proportion to my petite frame. *Mamere's* were much wider, a testament to her love of food in general. She'd been sampling the ice cream we made at *Chantelle Glace* in the historic *Vieux Carre'* section of New Orleans for a number of years before I came along. I myself had never been as tempted by sweets as she was. Fried seafood, shrimp and okra were my weakness. Though my morning runs and robust metabolism seemed to burn off most of those guilty calories.

"I know you can do it, Ty Boo, but it's not wise. Don't be *tete dure*."

"Sorry, *Mamere*. You're right. I'm being hard headed. I just don't like waiting around till Tony comes in, especially when I don't really need his help with them anymore. And today, I need to get everything already done early so I can..."

"Have time to get ready for your big date with your beau," she interjected. "*Oui*?"

I nodded, blushing. She knew me very well. There wasn't much I didn't share with her. She was loving and encouraging, the type of grandmother I'm sure every girl wished she could have.

"Did you do any more thinking about Mr. Johnson's offer?" She must've seen my spine stiffen after she posed that question because she rushed on before I could get a word in edgewise. "It's a lot of money. Enough to reopen the shop somewhere else."

"No. The location is too good here. That's why he wants it so badly. Prime spots in the French Quarter are hard to come by. We discussed this last night. I thought we were both in agreement."

"We are. I'm sorry I brought it up again. I just worry what you will do someday after I'm gone. Here, let me help you." She grabbed the other scrubber, and we worked quietly and efficiently together as we'd been doing for years bringing loads of soapy water from the professional sink over to the kettle to wash it out.

Though my gran was sixty-two now, except for the grey accents in her tight chignon, a style I mimicked with my own long brown locks while working, you wouldn't be able to guess her age by her appearance. Her complexion was smooth and youthful reflecting her Creole heritage. The faint laugh lines around her mouth and eyes only added depth and interest to her lovely face. Most days it seemed as if she had nearly as much energy as I did.

The ten by ten foot kitchen space sparkled when we were through cleaning. I could even see my reflection in the silver finish of the kettle. I didn't linger on the flash of my violet eyes or the complexion that had darkened considerably this summer as I set aside my towel and untied my apron strings. “Are you sure you and Tony can handle the Sunday rush alone?”

“You know we can. I want you to take the day off. Help Mr. Hill like you’ve been wanting to for an age. And buy yourself a new dress. You deserve it. Don’t rush getting ready for tonight.” She ran a gentle hand over the hair I’d let down, tucking a wayward strand behind my ear. “*Tu es jolie*. Your Shane is a lucky man.”

“*Merci, beaucoup, Mamere.*” I caught her hand and placed a soft kiss in her work roughened palm, my cheeks warming from the compliment. “I’m pleased you think so.”

She made a tsking sound. “You don’t realize your beauty, Ty Boo. I don’t understand it. What do you see when you look in the mirror?”

I ducked my head avoiding answering, staring down at my practical but unattractive work shoes. I’d been saving up and planning to buy a new pair of heels in addition to the dress I’d had my eye on for tonight. Shane liked me in heels. Said they made my legs look incredibly sexy. That was fine by me, since I was nearly as obsessed with pretty shoes as I was with my handsome beau.

As to what others saw when they looked at me, I couldn’t say for sure. I just saw a young woman on the verge of her twenty-first birthday. Average looking. Mixed heritage like my *mamere’s* forced me to walk a tightrope between two worlds and two identities, not black or white enough to easily blend into either. Certainly not pretty enough to turn heads in my opinion. Brownish hair, glossy and long. My violet eyes were probably my best feature, but I didn’t believe Shane would’ve given me more than a passing glance if we hadn’t known each other for so long.

He had taken pity on me when he’d been a fifth grader. I’d just entered kindergarten, a silent, shrinking little oyster after my mother abandoned me on the doorstep of *Chantelle Glace*. I remembered that my *maman* had always seemed a bit flighty, moving us around from place to place as if she were afraid to stay in one place too long. She was uncomfortable indoors, always wanting to be outside with her bare toes touching the grass, especially along the banks of the river after it rained when the current was strong. But despite those idiosyncrasies, I'd loved my mother dearly.

It'd taken me years to come to terms with her abandonment. I so wished that she'd have come back at least once, if only to explain why she did it. At that tender of an age, I had blamed myself, wondering if she had not wanted me because of the obvious differences in our skin tones.

Back then, a couple of the older neighborhood boys had found it amusing to torture me. They'd pulled on my braids, tripped me, called me names and made fun. Typical stuff. But Shane had stood up for me. He had let everyone know I was his friend and not to mess with me or they'd answer to him. I think I'd been a little in love with my knight in shining armor ever since.

"*Je t'aime, Mamere.*" I kissed her cheek. "Shane says he has something special planned after dinner with his parents. I might be late. Don't wait up for me."

Chapter TWO

THYME

My soul has grown deep like the rivers. - Langston Hughes

After pulling my long hair into a ponytail on the upstairs landing, I turned the key to lock the door to the two bedroom apartment *Mamere* and I shared above the shop. I didn't need to use the iron hand rail as I tromped down the wide dramatic spiral staircase and didn't slow my pace to linger over the view to our tropical courtyard where the fountain was bubbling softly. Hand on the smooth wooden newel at the bottom, I was just about to breeze through the tile foyer on my way to the outside door when I passed Tony coming in to work.

He flashed me a warm smile and we exchanged brief pleasantries before he turned to go into the shop. I continued outside breaking into a jog as soon as my running shoes hit the uneven slates of the banquette.

Today, we had all the turquoise shutters thrown open downstairs and up but I didn't think either level was going to cool off. The air was too still. There was absolutely no breeze which was unusual even by late August standards. The atmosphere seemed oppressively humid, heavy and expectant, even more than the previous day when everyone had begun complaining about it.

Given the temperature and the early hour, I had the gallery lined street of the *Vieux Carre'* practically to myself though I knew from experience hordes of tourists and locals would clog the streets soon enough. Mr. Hill was out in front of his three story home, one of the most colorful B&B's on the Rue St Philip, even more eye catching than our white washed building with its red paint and whimsical bright blue gingerbread trim. He was using his garden hose to spray his sidewalk clean.

I waved and he waved back.

"How's Chantelle doing this hot and humid morning?" he asked.

"She's doing well. Feisty as usual," I replied as I jogged in place. "How's your back?"

"I can't complain, Ty Boo. Every day's a gift, right?" He shooed away a pesky fly that'd tried to land on his wiry grey hair.

"I gotta run." I smiled. "I'll catch up with you later." I started jogging backward. "After I get cleaned up." I'd finally convinced him to let me help him clear out his basement. He had a large space under the first floor of the B&B he hoped to rent out long term for extra income.

The *Vieux Carre'* was a small community. Some celebrities owned seasonal homes and kept to themselves when visiting, but among the locals everyone knew each other. We helped each other out like a great big family, sharing when we could and bartering for what we needed. It was a system that drew us closer together and served everyone well, with the notable exception of Mr. Johnson. But then there was always at least one rotten egg in any basket.

Sprinting hard, passing Spanish colonial buildings like our own on either side, I headed down St. Philip, stepping down into the middle of the narrow deserted street since the banquette was so uneven. I crossed Decatur where the road split into two, the green and white awning covering the outdoor seating of the French Market Restaurant on the neutral ground on my left. On my right, a gold likeness of Joan of Arc sat astride a horse, a gift from our sister city in Paris. Locally we'd affectionately dubbed her 'Joanie on a pony'.

I dashed quickly between the break in the shops, across an asphalt parking lot, over the tracks of the riverfront street car line, and then up the steps to the Moonwalk, the elevated flood embankment that'd been repurposed as a scenic trail for Woldenberg Riverfront Park.

Feet pounding the red pavers, I pulled in deep breaths of heavy moisture laden air. I loved it here. It was just a short distance away but it felt as if it were miles and worlds removed from the hustle and bustle of the Quarter. There was an aquarium and an IMAX theatre at the end of my route along with a couple of statues on the way. The eighteen foot Carrera marble 'Old Man River' representing the power and majesty of the Mississippi was my favorite. But it was the water itself that really spoke to me.

The wide expanse of the river on my left, I ran past the Toulouse Street wharf where a coast guard vessel lay docked alongside the slumbering Natchez paddlewheel. I picked up my pace some more but barely felt it. I'd been increasing my distance every week, having to run back and forth along the trail to get in enough miles, but I still seemed to have a lot of energy left over. I made myself stop today. I could use the excess on the other things I had left on my agenda.

I saluted the twin cantilever bridges of the Crescent City Connection and turned back the way I'd come, using up a little more juice in a top speed dash to reach the beginning of the trail. Foregoing the wrought iron benches as was my habit, I dropped down onto the sandy slope just above the high grasses and wildflowers.

Slipping off my shoes and socks, I set my hot feet on the cool, fine like talcum sand, reminiscing about my mother performing a similar ritual. I exhaled the weight of the past, my current concerns and everything else, emptying my mind. I leaned back on my hands closing my eyes and lifting my face to absorb the renewing moisture from the river and the warmth of the mid-morning sun.

I liked to sit and take a moment to myself at this same spot every day. It was the simple pleasures in my life, my family and friends that brought me the most joy.

Love practically burst from the confines of my overly full heart. *Mamere*. Shane. Mr. Hill. And *Chantelle Glace*. My cup overflowed with blessings. But this, this time of solitude each morning, this I *needed*. It recharged me, made me feel whole, sane, balanced... right.

The steady lapping of the mighty Mississippi against the shore on its winding journey toward the Gulf of Mexico was music to my ears. The way my mother's voice had been. The way poetry was to me now. I heard a seagull's plaintive cry and reflected on a favorite poem, Langston Hughes' Negro Speaks of Rivers. I spoke the words aloud as a blessing upon my day.

I've known rivers:

I've known rivers ancient as the world and older than the flow of human blood in human veins.

My soul has grown deep like the rivers.

I bathed in the Euphrates when dawns were young.

I built my hut near the Congo and it lulled me to sleep.

I looked upon the Nile and raised the pyramids above it.

I heard the singing of the Mississippi when Abe Lincoln went down to New Orleans, and I've seen its muddy bosom turn all golden in the sunset.

I've known rivers:

Ancient, dusky rivers.

My soul has grown deep like the rivers.

I opened my eyes when I was through. The sun's rays reflected on the water. A thousand sparkling diamonds couldn't have been more beautiful to me than that sight, and I couldn't have felt any richer if I had owned all that the world contained.

Satisfaction settled deep inside my bones...into my very soul. New Orleans was my place. My home. I belonged here. Though there was a part of me that would always wonder where my mother had gone, I wouldn't dream of leaving. Jefferson Square with its iconic street performers. Café Du Monde with the flakey beignets that couldn't be duplicated. I'd tried. Music that flowed within the banks of the river and pulsated in the soil beneath my feet. And people who were warm and genuine, dedicated to preserving our unique history, art and culture.

I allowed myself a couple more lazy minutes since I didn't have to go back into work today. My lips curved into a dreamy smile as Shane's handsome face drifted into my mind. I felt like my future, maybe even our future together lay wide open and brimming with possibilities like the river before me.

I put my socks and shoes back on and brushed off my rear end after I stood. I walked at a brisk pace back toward the apartment. I couldn't have run anymore even if I had wanted to. It was too crowded now. The individual conversations of the people around me was almost deafening to my sensitive ears. There were squeaky wheeled trolleys, tons of delivery men and distracted tourists to dodge, too. So though I went back the same way I'd come, my progress was much slower.

When I neared The Hot Spot, an unadorned one story building painted black with red shutters that always remained closed even during its nighttime business hours, I went out of my way to avoid its nefarious owner, crossing to the other side of the street just on the off chance that he might emerge. I didn't want the aggravation of dealing with any of his high pressure pitches to purchase *Chantelle Glace.* Not when I was having such a relaxing day.

An unexpected shadow fell over me as I crossed beneath the columns of a gallery. I heard the sound of heavy breathing, but no footsteps. I whipped around heart thumping wildly inside my chest, fists up, preparing to defend myself if necessary while internally chastising myself for not having been more aware of my surroundings.

"Ty Boo." Leon Johnson in all his infamous creepy glory raised an auburn brow as he looked me over.

The Hot Spot owner wasn't a classically handsome man, though it was obvious he'd taken meticulous pains with his appearance. His pointed chin was smoothly shaven and his dark crimson hair was well-trimmed, but the planes of his face seemed too harshly drawn.

He wore a black fedora with a charcoal suit despite the sweltering heat. In fact, I'd never seen him without his hat or his jacket. He moved further into the shadows of the balcony that were out of place at this hour of the day and leaned his weight on his ebony cane, unsettling onyx eyes zeroing in on my startled face. His thick lips lifted. He seemed to be enjoying the fact that he unsettled me. "I do believe I've frightened you. Please accept my sincere apology. I thought you saw me crossing the street toward you." I didn't believe him for a minute. I often felt like his words were insincere and interlaced with ill intent.

"Of course you scared me. You can't just go sneaking up on people like that. And don't call me Boo." I don't know what I could possibly have done to give him the idea it would be ok to call me honey the way everyone else did. He wasn't my friend. I didn't want him to be. I didn't like him. He was overly familiar with *Mamere* and often leered at me when he thought she wasn't looking.

"Thyme, then." He reached out one of his gloved hands coming toward me. The hat, the cane and the gloves were his trademark accessories. He ran a finger against my cheek before I managed to avoid it.

I shuddered drawing in a shaky breath of air that was tainted like meat left in the refrigerator way beyond the sell date. I wondered not for the first time why no one else but me ever seemed to notice his rancid breath. "Did you reconsider my last proposal?"

He'd offered to pay ten times what *Chantelle Glace* was probably worth, but I wasn't interested in selling, not to him or anyone else. Another refusal was on the tip of my tongue but trepidation made me hesitate. There were scary rumors about what happened to people who made deals with Leon Johnson and even scarier ones about what happened to those who turned him down.

I glanced around suddenly feeling afraid and strangely vulnerable even though I was standing on a busy street full of people in the middle of the day.

"I told you no before and the answer still hasn't changed. We'll never sell."

"Very well." How was it possible for black eyes like his to get even darker? A muscle twitched in his tight jaw as he stared me down, pinning me in place by the disturbing power of his gaze.

There was something dark and twisted about him. He leeched the same creepy vibe as the time I had ventured into the old shop of voodoo on Bourbon. I went in, felt the oppressive evil within its walls and walked right back out, vowing never to enter it again. If only it would be as easy to be rid of him.

"The easy way is so boring, Thyme. I don't mind taking the harder route with you. Though you might not enjoy it as much," he hissed softly through teeth that suddenly appeared quite sharp, snaking out a gloved hand and snaring my left wrist.

I gasped. His gloved fingers were sharp and unyielding as if they were all bone without any flesh to soften them. His grip tightened, and I knew, even as I attempted to tug free, that there'd be no escaping him if he were determined to keep me there. A red haze clouded my eyes. I felt dizzy. My perspective suddenly changed, giving me an eerie vision of another place with me on my back full of fear and unable to move while Leon loomed over me with a gleaming triumphant gaze.

My sight cleared just as suddenly as it had clouded, but as I looked at Leon in the present moment, the expression beneath the brim of his hat was identical to the one I'd seen inside my mind, his eyes aglow with the same dark fire.

"Oh, my, my, my. What do we have here? How unexpected." He suddenly released my wrist, his gaze slithering its way up to my face. "A fennel staff. How very interesting." I stumbled back from him, rubbing the skin he'd touched, feeling sick to my stomach. "Chantelle's not your real *Mamere* is she?"

How could he possibly know that?

"Don't think badly of ole Leon. I know sometimes my tactics are a little...harsh. But surely you'll forgive me. I promise I won't pressure you to sell anymore. I can see that you have your mind all made up. I have other properties that will suit my needs just fine. Come over to the club. Let me buy you a drink. I want to make amends."

"No," I managed to rasp though my brain seemed to want me to say the opposite, and my vocal cords didn't want to work right.

He frowned and I knew that wasn't the answer he'd wanted or expected. "Another time then. I didn't mean to come on so strong. Bring your beau with you. No cover. Drinks, everything on the house. Anything you desire and it'll be yours. Let's be friends."

Chapter THREE

THYME

God's gift put man's best dreams to shame.
- Elizabeth Barrett Browning

I stayed under the shower a long while, feeling the need to wash off the taint of my encounter with Leon Johnson. The silver framed bathroom mirror was all fogged up, and my skin was raw and lobster red when I finally stepped out of the clawfoot tub. But though I held my wrist under the high intensity vanity lights to examine it, I couldn't see what had been so interesting to Johnson beyond a faint crisscross pattern on the inside of my left wrist that resembled a pinecone if I squinted just right.

I scooped my exercise things off the white hexagon tile floor, shuffled to my room across the hall wrapped in a towel and dropped the dirties into the hamper. Trying to hurry, I padded across the wide planked cypress floors, grabbed a pair of old shorts and a tank top from the dresser drawer and shimmied into them.

I had spent too much time down at the river. I'd have to forego the blow dryer and makeup for now. It was too hot for either anyway. I'd use the flat iron to smooth the waves from my hair and apply a little eye shadow and mascara later when I got dressed up to meet Shane and his parents. I'd have to skip the new dress and heels shopping, but that was ok. I'd just wear my white sundress and a broken in pair of shoes that would be easier on my toes. Mr. Hill was more important than any new outfit.

I quickly scarfed a granola bar for my lunch careful to toss the wrapper into the trash before I ducked into the shop to check on Gran and Tony. There was a line at the antique cash register and every single sweetheart chair around our café tables was occupied. They'd obviously been slammed. I bet they hadn't even had a break for lunch. I started to step in to help but Gran caught me. She shook her head and wagged a finger at me.

Knowing better than to insist, I blew her a kiss instead and went out the door. A blast of air like a sauna instantly coated my skin with moisture. I waded through the thick air on my way over to Mr. Hill's, scaling his front steps and knocking twice on his blue door for good luck before entering.

"Ty Boo," he said, shuffling around the chest high reception desk at the other end of his heavily antiqued parlor to greet me.

"Mr. Hill," I returned. On my twentieth birthday last year, he had tried to get me to switch to calling him Cornevius, but I'd refused. He was older than my gran. It didn't seem respectful to use his first name. Besides, I was now accustomed to the other, though I'd begun to think of him more casually as Mr. H in my mind.

He studied me for a moment with warm brown eyes a couple of shades lighter than his dark cocoa skin. "You ready to get to work?"

I nodded following him into a narrow hallway and down the back stairs to the lower level. He selected a key from a large silver ring attached to his belt and opened the door. The room was jam packed with furniture, knickknacks, stacks of books and boxes. I could barely see the parquet floor.

"It's a daunting task." His tone was apologetic but obviously he'd read the look of dismay on my face.

"Yeah," I agreed. It was a little more than I'd bargained for.

"But it probably won't be half as bad as we both think after we get started."

"Wisely spoken."

I thought back to my encounter with Leon and didn't feel so wise. In retrospect, I should have been more diplomatic. Creepy vibes aside, Leon Johnson was a powerful influential man. He sat on the city council. It wouldn't be smart to get on his bad side. I probably should take him up on his peace offering. What harm could come from visiting The Hot Spot with Shane at my side?

"What's wrong?" A small cardboard box in his hands, Mr. H took a step toward me.

"I ran into Mr. Johnson earlier." Mr. H knew all about his repeated attempts to buy our place.

His eyes narrowed deepening the furrows in his forehead. "When you were by yourself?" He made the sign of the cross over his chest. "I don't like that man."

"I don't either, Mr. Hill. I assure you. But he seemed to accept that my 'no' was final this time." I gestured to the large box I had filled with books. "These all going to be picked up by St. Annes?"

He nodded still looking concerned. "You run into him again, you walk the other way. Get your young man to talk to him if you need to, you hear?"

"Yes, Mr. Hill. I will." Normally, I would argue that I could take care of myself but in this instance I had to agree with him.

"Good girl." He ambled over to a stack of boxes about his height and started to reach for the top one before I stopped him.

"Let me do this. I don't want you to reinjure your back. I'm here to help, ok?" I added when he looked like he might be stubborn about it.

"You're as sweet as your *Mamere.*" He smiled fondly.

"No one's as sweet as her 'cept you," I countered. "I'll never forget all the times you took me with your boys to City Park and Storyland. All the suppers I ate over here when I was little. You and Helen treated me like I was part of your family." Sometimes I used to pretend that he was the real father I'd never known. In all the ways that counted he practically had been. Just like with Shane and his parents, I knew it was love and actions that bound people together to make a family unit even more than blood.

"You are family. Love you that way, sweet girl." His voice was deeper, heavy with emotion, his expression nostalgic. "Those were good times. I miss 'em. Miss the boys. Wish they would've stayed and gone to school around here. Miss my Helen, too." His brow dipped. His wife had died when I was twelve. They'd been such a devoted couple and such great parents to their four boys, a good example to me of what a loving marriage should look like. That's what I wanted, what I hoped to have someday with Shane if I was lucky.

"We all miss her." I crossed to him and gave him a hug. "She was the best." I cleared my throat. We didn't usually voice our feelings though they always ran deep and strong between us.

"You helped me move on after she passed. Gave me a reason to keep on living. Inviting me to all your school stuff. Asking after my advice and always listening to what I told you. You made an old man feel needed."

I looked away. He was going to make me cry.

"Troubles come and they pass, but life's easier when you have people around to remind you why it's all worth it. Know your heart, Thyme. Always follow it the way you do now. That's one last piece of advice I have to give you. You're all grown up now. There's not much I can tell you anymore that you haven't already learned for yourself."

"I will, Mr. Hill. I promise." I took a step back and put my hands on my hips. "Ok. We need to find you somewhere to sit. You can tell me how you want it done and keep me company, but you need to let me move the heavy stuff. Deal?"

"Deal," he countered, sliding a sheet cover off a wing back chair. After the dust cloud cleared, he settled in, and I got to work.

By the time I was ready to call it quits it was starting to get dark outside and my legs were trembling. I carried the last box upstairs and set it down alongside the stacks of others ready to be picked up the next morning.

"Thanks, Ty Boo." Mr. H came up the stairs leaning on the stair railing catching his breath. "You sure you won't let me pay you something?" he asked.

I shook my head. "You know I'm glad to do it. The joy is in the giving," I reminded him. "Someone very wise once told me that." I tapped my chin pretending not to remember who.

He chuckled knowing it had been him. "Heard you're going to Commander's Palace with Shane and his parents tonight."

I nodded.

"Is it a special occasion?" he asked.

"It's his last year of medical school at Tulane," I explained.

"That boy's over the moon for you."

"I feel exactly the same way about him. Truly," I admitted. "Hey, have you seen my sunglasses? I could have sworn I left them right here on your desk the other day." I drummed the surface while looking around.

"You should get a chain to keep them around your neck like I have," he teased. "So you don't lose them."

"Oh, there they are." I spotted them on top of the demilune table near the front door. "That's odd. I'm positive that's not where I put them."

"Wasn't me, either. Must've been Old Josephine helping out," he decided. Old Josephine was the B&B's resident ghost, a benevolent one according to Mr. H. Hauntings were a common theme in New Orleans. Practically every household had some sort of supernatural activity associated with it. Some liked to call our city a psychic seaport. It was fun to pretend, though I sometimes got the feeling that Mr. H really believed that Josephine truly existed.

Chapter FOUR

THYME

You were made perfectly to be loved - and surely
I have loved you, in the idea of you, my whole life long.
- Elizabeth Barrett Browning

Commander's Palace was in the Garden District, too far for me to walk. I was running late so I splurged on a taxi instead of taking the street car. It dropped me off in front of the famous restaurant with its turquoise turrets and white gingerbread columns. I quickly ducked under the striped awning, checked in with the hostess, discovering that I was the first to arrive.

Stomach grumbling I crossed over the tile welcome mat and stood off to the side next to a couple to wait. I smoothed a nervous palm over the eyelet fabric of my sundress. It wasn't long before strong hands suddenly slid around my waist. I leaned back into him inhaling his familiar evergreen scented cologne. His deep voice rumbled into my ear.

"Missed you, *bébé.*" Shane brushed his warm lips against the sensitive skin below my ear. As I turned around, he captured and kept my hands, arms outstretched as his gaze traveled the length of me. "You look beautiful."

"So do you." I threaded my smaller fingers together with his longer ones. His attire a step more formal than my own, he sported black tropic weight wool trousers and a light grey striped button down left open at the neck. His jet black hair was combed neatly back, accentuating his handsome face.

"I can't believe my good fortune," he said softly, his glittering gaze intense as it locked with mine. His eyes were so gorgeous. Mesmerizing as my river. The same shade of green as the Spanish moss that garlanded the old live oak trees in his Uptown neighborhood. "Prettiest girl in *Vieux Carre'*, and she's all mine."

I started to duck my head but he tipped up my chin. "Uh-uh. You always shy away when I compliment you. Don't you know how hungry I am to see your face after staring down all that mind numbing paperwork at the registrar's office?"

My lips lifted into a slow smile. "I missed you, too," I admitted.

"I wanna taste those sweet lips, honey, but my parents are right behind me."

"Thyme Bellerose!" Shane's father's voice boomed. Todd Lamar pressed between us hugging me hard as if he hadn't seen me in years. Actually it was only the past Sunday when Shane and I had hung out with them at their place.

"Good to see you Mr. Lamar," I said politely trying to disengage from the huge bear of a man. Demonstrative as always, he kissed both of my cheeks before letting me go. He almost stomped on Shane's mother's perfectly pedicured toes as he stepped backward.

"Careful, Todd. These are my Valentinos," Crystal Lamar cautioned before focusing her disapproving gaze on me. "How's your grandmother, Thyme?" she asked, disinterest unmistakable in her tone.

"Fine," I answered flatly.

"Good. Good." Crystal Lamar looked down her dainty royal nose at me. The queen of a recently renovated Mediterranean style mansion in Audubon Park, she hated me, and I didn't like her much, either. She was one of only two points of contention between Shane and me. She didn't think I was good enough for her precious only adopted son. Too much of the time I felt the same way, which made Shane furious, as much with me as with her.

Mr. Lamar checked in with the hostess who didn't try to disguise her interest in my beau. I didn't blame her. He was ogle worthy for sure, but he was mine. He never made me doubt it, either. He placed a comforting hand on my lower back, indifferent to the hostess as she escorted us to our table. Draped in a white table cloth, a delicate silver beaded lampshade in the center, it was nestled in a corner of the restaurant with floor to ceiling windows that overlooked the courtyard.

Shane pulled back a chair for me softly trailing his fingers across my bare shoulders before he took his own seat. I shivered. I wanted him so very badly. It was getting harder and harder to control my impulses when around him.

We ordered drinks. An iced tea for me. Sidecars for everyone else. As they arrived Crystal swiveled in my direction.

"You're getting so dark," she observed. "You should mind that better. Maybe try a higher SPF sunscreen. You look like a colored girl."

My spine stiffened. "I am," I replied tersely. At least I was on my mother's side. My father had been white, or so I was told. My mother had left him before I was born. "Though the term I prefer is black."

"Crystal," Mr. Lamar hissed. "You're being rude."

"And racist," Shane mumbled reaching for my hand and squeezing it under the table.

"I was just trying to help her, baby," she told her husband. "Shane's too sweet a boy to tell her the truth."

"The truth is, there's absolutely nothing wrong with the color of her skin. It's beautiful," he defended me. "And I don't know how it could be, but she just keeps getting prettier every single day."

He melted my heart this man. How had I gotten so lucky? I just knew that I was never ever going to let him go.

"Thyme created another new flavor this week," he bragged. "Muscadines, peaches and cream. It's delicious. It's been selling out every day."

My champion. I smiled at him.

"Congratulations, Thyme." Shane's father raised his tumbler to me.

"How delightful." Crystal's eyes nearly the same shade as Shane's met mine. "Still working at the ice cream shop then?"

"Yes, ma'am. I love it." My stomach tensed into an uncomfortable knot. This wasn't the first time she'd belittled my chosen occupation.

"Not much of a long term goal, is it?" She tsked. "Never going to try to better yourself?"

I looked away from her, ignoring her jibes, but I could feel the tension in Shane's fingers as they tightened around mine. This was the main source of my trepidation about our relationship. I was beneath him. He was going to be a doctor. I was always going to be what I was now, a high school educated girl who worked in an ice cream shop. Though I never felt as though I'd missed out not going to college. Not with all that I'd learned about business. I knew how to do the books. I knew all about our product. I even had a detailed business plan mapped out for the shop's future.

"How's your summer been, Thyme?" Mr. Lamar asked, not very subtle in his attempt to redirect the conversation. "How many miles you running now?"

"Ten, sir."

"Every day? That's fabulous. Good for you." He cast about for another neutral subject. "You and your gran been keeping an eye on the forecast?"

"No." I shook my head, wanting to smile. Was idle chit chat about the weather all that we had left to avoid having an argument at the table?

"Been an active season in the tropics," he continued. "There's a hurricane just crossing the Keys. Some think it might reform and get a good deal stronger out in warm water of the Gulf. The projected path shows it could hit anywhere from the Florida Panhandle to Louisiana. Governor Blanco issued a state of emergency just this afternoon."

"That sounds serious."

"Oh, Todd. You are so dramatic. Everyone knows they always oversell these things." Crystal finished her drink, eyes swiveling to me. "I hope you make enough at the store this summer to tide you over until Mardi Gras." There she went, right back at the financial crap again.

"Yes, ma'am," I said proudly. "In fact, we did better than last year."

"That's fantastic, Ty," Shane praised. "You didn't tell me that."

"I don't like to brag." I looked directly at Crystal. "But Hotel Monteleone is even interested in featuring some of my cocktail themed sorbets in their restaurant for next summer."

"Wonderful." Crystal smiled, but her eyes lacked any enthusiasm.

Shane cautioned me time and again not to let her get to me. He swore he didn't care about the things she did, or the differences between us that she so willingly highlighted. But when I saw how well he fit in with his parents and the well to do crowd that dined at places as expensive as the Commander's Palace, I worried.

As his parents gave their orders to the waiter, Shane leaned closer. "What's wrong, *bébé*? You look sad. You're eyes have lost their pretty sparkle."

"I'm not sad." I didn't want to let his mother ruin the evening for us. I needed to focus less on her pettiness and more on the joy he brought into my life.

I moved so I could place a soft kiss on his freshly shaven cheek. "I love you." I brazenly blew in his ear settling back in my chair. His eyes deepened to a more vivid green, and his focus dropped to my lips. He brought our joined hands to his upper thigh so I could feel what I'd done to him. And here was the second point of contention between us. While I wanted to take things to the next level physically, somehow we had yet to consummate our relationship.

He cast a quick glance at his parents before his gaze returned to me. "You mean more than anyone else in the world," he said leaning close, his voice vibrating with sincerity I could feel. My heart melted more for him.

After a divine dinner and dessert, Shane pushed back his chair and held out his hand.

"Come for a walk with me outside."

"Alright." I set my napkin in my chair.

As we stood, Shane's father gave him a meaningful look. Crystal glared.

"Are you sure about this, Shane?"

"Yeah, Mother. We talked about this. You know I am."

"What was she talking about?" I asked as soon as we were out of earshot.

"I'll show you outside." His mossy eyes were burning with an intensity that made my heart start skipping. Hand in hand, he led me across the concrete patio and into an enchanting romantically lit garden. When he dropped to one knee in front of me, my hand flew to my mouth.

"Shane!" I exclaimed.

"I talked to your *mamere*. She gave her blessing. As did my father. So then, Thyme Avens Bellerose..." He pulled a black velvet box out of his pocket and opened it. "Would you do me the very great honor of being my wife?"

Tears sprang to my eyes. "Nothing would please me more." I held out my trembling left hand, fingers spread wide as he slid on a lovely, no doubt wickedly expensive, multi carat princess-cut pink diamond solitaire.

Chapter FIVE

THYME

How do I love thee? Let me count the ways.
- Elizabeth Barrett Browning

"You like it, huh?" Shane's obvious pride made his deep voice even deeper.

"I absolutely love it!" His arm was draped over my shoulder, his strong hand resting warm on the bare skin above my knee. I held my own hand out in front of me turning it side to side letting the fire inside the stellar diamond catch the light as the taxi sped us back to my side of town. "I've never seen anything so beautiful."

"I have," Shane said before lowering his head to my upturned face and putting his mouth on mine. "Mmm." His heavy groan slipped between my parted lips just before his tongue did. Hot familiar need that was becoming harder and harder to contain pulsed through my veins. Shane's tongue rubbed against mine, and the kiss turned hotter and more carnal. Our mouths, lips and tongues moved in unison along the same heated path straining for the same pleasurable conclusion.

"Shane," I begged, tearing my mouth from his, my head falling back against the headrest of the taxi while he rained firm, warm, moist, tempting kisses along my exposed neck and above the swell of my cleavage. "Can't we please," I lowered my voice to a quiet, husky, for his ears only whisper. "Isn't it time that we were truly together?"

"No, Ty." He spoke the refusal against my skin, turning his head away so I couldn't see his face when he withdrew his arm and scooted to the other side of the taxi. "When we're married. It won't be long now." He maintained the distance between us until the cab pulled up in front of *Chantelle Glace.*

When we got out, the sultry sound of saxophone from a club up the street spilled into the humid night and lingered soulfully. Shane paid the driver while I stood on the banquette waiting and frustrated, getting angrier about the all too familiar rejection.

When he turned around and saw my face, he frowned. "*Bébé.*" He took a step my way arms reaching for me, but I took a backed away. "Don't be mad."

I turned my head crossing my arms over my chest, arms brushing over nipples that jutted against the cotton, my breasts heavy and achy, needy and revved up just like the rest of me. "I'm tired of this dance we keep doing, Shane. We've been a couple for eighteen months. I don't want to keep waiting. We love each other. That's what matters. So what if I get pregnant? I don't care." My voice rose louder than I probably should have let it. A couple of heads in a group of late night revelers turned our way as they stumbled drunkenly past us.

"*Bébé,* you know that waiting's hard on me, too." A sucker for his conciliatory tone, I turned back to him when he tried again, arms outstretched toward me. Closing the distance between us, he gently wrapped his fingers around my upper arms and pulled me into him. "You know how I feel."

"Do I, Shane? You say the words but then you push me away." Sometimes he'd even stay away for days after I'd pressed against the physical boundaries he set for us. It didn't seem right. He was my protector, but when he took off like that without explanation I felt abandoned instead.

He sighed, looking almost as frustrated as I felt. "This is my last year of medical school. After that I'll have a salary albeit an intern's one," he added wryly. "But I'll be completely on my own. Out of the dorm, making my own way, able to provide for you. Those things are important to me."

"As important as I am?" I pouted.

He brushed a soft apologetic kiss across my pursed lips. "It's all wrapped up together for me, Ty. I love you. I couldn't possibly love you more." His eyes searched mine under the flickering light from the gas lanterns. His heartfelt proclamation melted my anger. I fell back under the spell of his enchantingly familiar gaze. The way I always did.

He tucked a strand of loose hair behind my ear. I shivered as his fingers brushed against my ear. "I'll never forget the first time I saw you."

"I was just a kindergartener," I mumbled.

"Yeah." He grinned and his dimple winked at me. "Even then. You had these cute pig tails and such beautiful eyes. You never said a word but your eyes did. So expressive. So much pain. I just wanted to be the one to take it all away. To make you smile. To be your hero."

"You are. You always have been." I tipped my face up for another one of his sweet addictive kisses. "You always will be."

His hands were chaste, disappointingly still where they rested on my hips. He canted his head toward my door. "I'll see you tomorrow?" he queried.

"I guess."

"I've got stuff to do for my dad." He part timed some weekends at his father's law firm. He never took for granted the things he had. Never acted like a child of privilege. So unlike his mother.

"And I've got a double shift tomorrow." I had ice cream to make in the morning and I was working the counter till closing.

"Go out with me afterward? I'll ask Kip and Monica to go along. A double date. That sound good?"

I nodded, though inwardly I balked. His friends from Uptown weren't my favorite. They were nice enough but we came from completely different worlds. I didn't really have a lot in common with either of them.

Shane took my key opening the door for me, the white scar on the inside of his wrist flashing briefly as he handed it back. He was such a throwback. So old fashioned, such a gentleman. I mostly loved it, except as it applied to our romantic relationship, for obvious, extremely frustrating reasons.

I moved toward the door. I could feel him watching me so I added a seductive sway to my hips just to torture him a little. A year was a long time to keep waiting. If he thought I was just going to go along with that plan without trying everything I could to change his mind, he was sadly mistaken.

I peeked into the shop. The chairs were up on the tables, everything quiet and in order. I took the stairs up to the apartment unlocking the door and letting myself in. Slipping off my heels and tiptoeing on the old floorboards that creaked as I crossed them, I checked on Gran. She was snoring softly, a romance book with a racy cover across her chest, her lamp burned brightly.

I smiled. She'd been waiting up for me. My heart swelled with love for her. My mom might be gone, forever out of the picture, but I certainly had never missed out on unconditional love.

I transferred the book to her nightstand, careful to save her place, kissing her soft cheek. I switched off her light.

"*Je t'aime.* I love you, *Mamere,*" I whispered before heading down the hall to my bedroom.

I flipped on the switch inside. My skin prickled with awareness as if someone were watching. I moved to the French doors that opened onto my half balcony and peered out. There was no one there, but I frightened a black crow off its perch on the wrought iron railing as I closed the doors, latching them and drawing the inside curtains together for complete privacy.

Locating the remote, I flipped on the air conditioning unit and undressed quickly, tossing my dress and underthings in the hamper. I was tired. The run and working on Mr. H's basement had worn me out. As I pulled on an old Tulane t-shirt of Shane's, I stepped under the soft glow from the crystal chandelier, a fixture original to the apartment that had been in *Mamere's* family since her great great-grandfather, a French plantation owner purchased it.

I paused in front of the full length mirror next to bookshelves that were overstuffed with the poetry tomes that I loved. The mirror was really an old door that Mr. H had helped me reclaim. We'd worked on it together, gluing in the glass and painting the frame antique white with a crackle finish.

Neil Young's 'Love is a Rose' running through my head, I swiveled back and forth on my toes, posing in the reflection. Shane made me feel so cherished most of the time but I sometimes wondered what he saw when he looked at me. Love must have given him out of focus glasses. He definitely didn't fixate on the café au lait color of my skin the way his mother did.

I lifted my chin, my violet eyes flashing back at me in the mirror. I needed to stop letting her and my own insecurities regarding my appearance get to me. I turned off the overhead light and padded to my iron frame bed. I launched myself in switching on my lamp and holding out my hand so I could admire my ring one more time.

Shane Lamar had asked me to marry him. He thought that I was worthy. I wore the proof on my finger. He'd even thoughtfully chosen my favorite color for the center stone. I couldn't wait to tell Gran and Mr. H the good news in the morning.

Chapter SIX

THYME

Love is blind. - Geoffrey Chaucer

"I hope you enjoy it. The Muscadine Peach is one of my favorite flavors." I passed the double scoop across the counter to the teenager. I had just started to close out the register when my cell played Van Halen's "Can't Stop Loving You", a familiar ringtone. "Hello."

"Hey, *bébé*." I smiled delighted by the sound of his voice after the long work day. "Are you by chance wearing the ring of the most eligible fourth year medical student at Tulane?"

I laughed. "Yes I am, as a matter of fact."

"What'd your gran say when you showed it to her?"

"She said I'm a lucky girl." Gran's eyes met mine. I shuffled aside so she could take over the register for me.

"Tell her I'm the lucky one."

"She says she loves you, and I do, too, but I'd better get off the phone. Tony's had enough of our lovey dovey routine. He's making gagging noises. And we're really swamped here. With the storm forecast to come in soon everyone's decided to go out and have a little fun before the power inevitably goes out." The French Quarter was packed tonight. Though we were used to the threat of hurricanes, we didn't hunker down in fear of them like most cities did. We got out and celebrated them. Named a drink after them. "It's probably going to be a little bit longer before I can break free. I need to help Gran close up. Why don't I meet you instead?"

"No way. Not this late. Not with people acting all crazy. I'll borrow my dad's car. Mom's packed up the SUV with provisions just in case this thing intensifies and the voluntary evacuation of the low lying areas turns into a mandatory one for all of us."

"Alright. Where does everyone want to go?"

"Kip mentioned The Hot Spot." I nearly dropped the cone I'd just scooped. "That ok? I know the owner's the one who's been hassling you about selling your place."

"That's true." I handed the cone to the customer while continuing to balance my cell awkwardly between my ear and shoulder. "But it's ok. I forgot to tell you." I'd had much better things on my mind last night. "I ran into Leon Johnson yesterday. He apologized for being pushy. Said he wouldn't bother me about selling anymore. He invited us both to the club. Free drinks. Everything on the house. Says he doesn't want there to be any hard feelings, but..."

"But what?"

"Well, you know. He *is* kind of creepy." I washed my hands in the small sink behind the counter letting Tony serve the last group.

"Yeah, I'll give you that one. Always with the gloves and hat and all. But a lot of my dad's associates are just as eccentric. I think having all that money makes you kind of weird. I've heard that Leon is buying up real estate all over town, especially in the quarter, gambling that property values will go up soon. My dad thinks he might be right. If you wanted to sell, I bet Johnson would go a helluva a lot higher on his offering price."

"I don't. You know I don't."

"Whatever you want, I'll support you, *bébé*. I'll pick up Kip and Monica and then swing by and get you. We'll go to his club for a little bit. Stay for a while, if it feels cool. Play nice. Then head over to the Muses or something if you're not too tired."

***

We pulled up right in front of The Hot Spot. The valet had his podium beneath the club's purple neon sign. When I mentioned my name to the bored looking guy, he instantly perked up, taking the keys to the Volvo from Shane and refusing to let us pay the thirty dollar fee or even a tip.

Kip, an old football buddy of Shane's and his girlfriend Monica, a statuesque blond, showed their ID's to the bouncer and went on through the door ahead of us. Shane put his hand on my bare shoulder. "You look hot hot, bébé," he said in my ear. I'd paired a shiny silver halter and matching high heels with frayed cutoffs. He looked fine himself in an untucked long sleeved linen shirt and faded jeans. Then he said something else, but I couldn't understand him because once inside the music was too loud for normal conversation. The band I recognized as an extremely popular local funk group. Their trumpet player was Tony's brother, Nico.

My eyes widened to saucer size as I took in the decor. Dark and tawdry seemed to be the predominant theme. Risqué pictures lined black walls that had an iridescent sheen. A neon arrow pointed to a VIP rooms upstairs. There were moving works of art along the remaining wall even more lewd than the photographs. Dancers, male and female ones, behind glass, untouchable, but definitely on display, some singles, lots of pairs, even some trios. Their motions matched the rhythm of the song, but the things they were doing were blatantly sexual. Indecent. Sometimes just short of illegal. I looked away, cheeks burning hot.

I'm surprised Leon got away with that kind of thing. Even in NOLA there were rules. Seemed the rumor about him being above those might be dead on. I hoped none of the other ones were.

Hand on the small of my back, Shane guided me as we worked our way through the thick crowd to a free table Kip and Monica had spotted. The moment we took our seats, a waitress in a revealing devil costume with red velvet horns materialized. She informed us that drinks would be on the house. The valet must have called ahead. She didn't even card me when she took our order with her pitchfork pen.

After we tossed back a couple of Jell-O shots, Shane cautioned me to take it slower. I was no angel. I'd had a beer or two here and there even though I wasn't yet twenty-one. But the times I'd had alcohol, it had seemed to take a lot more of it to go to my head than it did anyone else. Shane liked to tease me. He said when I drank, I never got drunk, but that my eyes turned a deeper shade of purple.

Feeling really loose and having given up on trying to talk while the band was playing, I stood and held out my hand, leaning heavily on the table to steady myself with the other. "Dance with me," I told Shane.

He took my hand and led me to the dance floor. The place was so crowded there wasn't really any clear delineation as to where it started, so we just pressed into the center where everyone was bouncing. I lifted my hands over my head and shimmied down to a crouch while trailing my hands down his rock hard chest and abdomen. When I reached his thighs, he grabbed my hands and hauled me back up.

The shimmering lights from the disco ball overhead made his eyes look like they had been sprinkled with stardust. It was probably a good thing he'd stopped me even though I'd wanted to stay down lower a little longer and tease him. I still remembered my plan to seduce him but the alcohol was definitely hitting me. I was starting to feel really dizzy.

We danced through another song, giving up on trying out any moves. We just swayed together enjoying the feel of one another's bodies. I slid my hand under Shane's shirt. His skin was taut and slick with sweat and I felt his sudden swift intake of breath, his body responding as I skimmed a palm low across his waist.

"My baby knows what she wants and won't take no for an answer." His eyes were radiant, a moon sparkling off the bayou green, but he put an end to my fun, shaking his head and removing my hand. I noticed he swayed as he led me from the dance floor.

I wasn't the only one affected by the amount of alcohol we'd consumed.

When we got back to the table, there were more drinks we hadn't ordered. I swallowed mine but vowed that it would be my last of the night.

"Thyme Bellerose." Leon Johnson greeted, his voice seeming overly loud in the relative silence. The band had stopped. The crowd had thinned out. I hadn't even noticed. How long had we been here?

Definitely needed to stop drinking now.

Leon held out his hand. "And you must be Shane Lamar. You look a lot like your father."

Shane thickly introduced his friends while I studied The Hot Spot owner. He was attired in a black suit and hat combo tonight, wearing gloves that matched of course. He leaned on the silver handle of his cane while shaking hands with Kip and Monica. I wondered if anyone else had freaky hallucinations like me when he touched them.

He shifted his attention in my direction dark eyes narrowing. "I'd like to take you on a short tour," he offered. "What do you say?"

I wasn't so sure I was interested in a behind the scenes tour. And was it just me and too many Jell-O shots, or did anyone else notice that his eyes were doing that creepy glowy thing?

"That'd be fine, Sir," Shane answered for us, slurring the words.

Shit. This was going to be fun. Insert sarcasm. *Not.* I startled to scramble for a way to back out.

"Sounds interesting but we're gonna pass," Kip interjected, laying his hand on his girlfriend's shoulder. "Mon's not feeling well."

"I'm sorry, Monica." I touched her arm. Her skin was clammy and she looked a little green. Here was the excuse I needed. Crisis averted. I exhaled my relief before turning to Leon. "We need to get her home. We all drove in together. We'll have to take a rain check on that tour. Another time, maybe."

"You don't have to leave on our account," Kip insisted. "I already called us a cab. You guys go on ahead. It's your night to celebrate. We certainly don't want to put a damper on it just because Mon had one too many." He slapped Shane on the shoulder. "Congrats, bro." He leaned closer to me and very sweetly kissed my cheek. "You, too, Ty."

"Would you like another drink before we get started," Leon asked, noting our empty shot glasses.

"No. We've had enough," I admitted. "Though a ginger ale would be nice."

We followed Leon to the bar. He served us himself, slipping behind the counter and emerging a moment later sliding two tall glasses our way. I was so parched I chugged my soda dry, and noticed Shane doing the same. Leon looked pleased about this for some reason. I didn't realize until much later why, but by then, it would be too late.

After we set aside our glasses, Leon told us that he very much wanted us to meet his manager first. He led us to a door marked private behind the bar. Shane leaned on me heavily as we followed Leon down a dark staircase to a basement level. I found it odd that the bar owner was so agile on the steps. He didn't even seem to need his cane.

Leon pushed open the first door we came to. An elegant woman who looked vaguely familiar with skin the same color as mine rose from behind the desk in the dimly lit room. She wore a smart red business suit and her hair was concealed beneath a colorful African head wrap. She smiled at us, but it seemed more predatory than friendly.

"Hello. Thyme. What a pleasure to finally meet you." She studied me with eyes that seemed much older than her apparent age. They flickered beneath the overhead lighting as if they danced to some ancient tribal rhythm. I couldn't look away. I didn't even glance back when I heard a loud ominous thud behind me. "We've been waiting for you a long time." Canting her head, she slowly stepped further out of the shadows. I swayed, the ground feeling suddenly unsteady beneath my feet as if I were on a raft in my river rolling on the swells during a storm.

Through my haze, I suddenly realized why Leon's business manager looked so familiar. She was the spitting image of Marie Laveau, the famous New Orleans' voodoo queen from the eighteen hundreds.

But it couldn't be her, could it? That would be completely insane. Totally impossible.

I staggered backward, reaching for Shane, every instinct inside of me screaming that I should run. But my body wouldn't cooperate. It was already too late. The edges of the room started to blur, everything spinning around me. Then it all went black.

You can read the rest of the story on Amazon.
Free in kindleunlimited. Strange Magic is book 1
in a completed trilogy. Book 1 and 2 are available in audio.

Strange Magic
Dream Magic
Twisted Magic

Rock

F*CK CLUB

About the Book

• • •Complete Series Now Available• • •

10 cities in two weeks 10 famous rock stars
On my knees
Against the wall
On my tits
I don't care. As long as I get the evidence to prove it.
Why?
Because I caught my former prick of a boyfriend from Heavy Metal Enthusiasts doing a groupie doggie style backstage on the night we were supposed to be celebrating our 1 year anniversary.
He told me I was too uptight.
Too vanilla.
Too boring.
So I got drunk with my bestie, Marsha West, the aspiring videographer. I ranted. I raved. I came up with a crazy idea.
What I didn't know was that my best friend recorded me. Marsha put the video up on YouTube. It went viral with 10 million hits. Now I've got fans and sponsors offering me big bucks.
Rock stars are volunteering to be my f*ck buddy.
Hollywood is calling.
I get to choose which rock stars I want.
The stakes are high.
This sh*t just got real.
What could go wrong?

Know who you are before you step into the future.
– A Navajo saying

Chapter ONE

Tears curtained my eyes. My stomach churned. Raw emotion nearly doubled me over as I stumbled back out into the busy corridor at the Verizon Theatre, my arm thrown protectively across my waist.

Don't be sick. Walk away don't run. Exit the venue with your remaining dignity intact.

"Raven." I jerked upright at the sound of his voice. His lying cheating voice. No lead singer croon at the moment, just 'I got busted' conciliatory whine. "It's not what you think. Come back inside and we'll talk it out."

"It is exactly what I think." I threw a long length of my hair back over my shoulder pretending to be indifferent, amazed that I was able to string together coherent words while my mind kept replaying the scene of that two timing bastard doing another woman doggie style on the dressing room floor. I would never be able to Clorox wipe that image from my memory.

"It's over." My voice warbled. We had been through so much together. I had begun to nurture hopes of a future for the two of us, though I hadn't shared them with him. Thank God, I was spared that humiliation. "We're through." I threw a hand on my hip brandishing sass I didn't feel. "Don't bother calling. I sure won't."

"C'mon, baby. Don't be like that." Ivan Carl, the frontman of Heavy Metal Enthusiasts leaned his tattooed forearm against the dressing room door while holding up his unbuckled jeans. "Come join the fun. Expand your horizons. Try a little spontaneity for once, instead of planning every single thing you do down to the nth degree."

"I don't." I huffed.

"Oh yeah you do," he retorted. "It's that way with everything. Especially sex. It's the same position, the same two damn days every week when I'm home. Maybe I need more. Maybe I just wanted to shake things up a bit. Rattle your cage. Get back the girl I knew at the beginning, the one who knew how to relax and have a good time, the one I started out with a year ago."

That girl was gone. She wasn't ever coming back. I thought he understood. He had been so patient while I had regrouped and tried to put the shattered pieces of myself back together. I thought that he had loved me. I believed that he had been faithful. But who the hell knew after something like this? Maybe he had been cheating on me all along. My world careened on its axis. The blood drained from my face. Forget my mind. I suddenly wanted to sanitize my entire body.

"How many other women have there been?" My fingers clenched into fists, my nails biting into my palms.

"Only Clarissa. Honest to God."

I glared at him. So doggie had a name. The knife already lodged in my abdomen twisted in so deep that it seemed to sever my spine.

"I can't believe you're being like this." He sighed, his dark brown eyes shimmering with emotion. Regret, perhaps. Too freakin' late for that. He ran a hand that visibly trembled through the chestnut strands of his medium length hair. I think he was beginning to see how this was going to play out. The 'that's-all-folks' had been pretty clear to me from the moment I had caught him fucking someone else.

"So help me Ivan. If you gave me a venereal disease I'll lop off your dick with a pair of hedge trimmers."

He winced. "You've got nothing to worry about. I wore a condom. Besides, it was only this once."

"And it didn't mean anything." I cut him off, finishing his sentence for him.

"Exactly, baby." Biting down on his silver hoop lip ring, he stepped closer to me, his hips hitching with the cocky swagger I had once found so irresistibly sexy. But his hand holding up his pants reminded me yet again that his cock had just been inside someone else. That sobering fact negated the I'm-so-sorry pleading expression. It negated all the hopes and dreams I had built for us. I straightened my shoulders, not all that impressive, but it was the best show of strength I could manage at the moment. I would build stronger defenses later. For now, I stood up to his bullshit rock star charm. I recognized it for what it was. Cheap pyrotechnics and lyrical subterfuge. I should have known better. I should have listened to my father, my best friend, and even my brother. They had all seen through him. Why hadn't I?

"Don't touch me." I backed further away when he reached for me. His big brown eyes glistened like melted chocolate, but I ignored the temptation, spinning on my Steve Madden heels and running smack into a cart stacked with amplifiers.

"Sorry, Raven," Peter apologized. I knew all the roadies by name, even fashioning Navajo dreamcatchers for them as Christmas gifts. "I didn't see you." He moved toward me. "Hey, why are you crying?" He frowned. "Did I hurt you?"

"No." I shook my head.

"What's wrong then?" Peter pressed while Ivan's presence loomed behind me.

"It's nothing," I mumbled. "I gotta go." I slid my cell out of my bag to call my best friend. I had her number dialed before I hit the metal bar and opened the door to the blast of heat from the parking lot. "Marsha, it's me," I said as soon as she picked up. "You were right. Ivan is an asshole. I need you and tequila stat."

Chapter TWO

I squinted at the shot glass. Glasses. Plural. My vision had gone blurry about two hours into the marathon of tequila. My chapped lips burned with every bite of lime and shake of salt. But I wasn't through. I was on a quest for oblivion. I needed more to erase the memory of Ivan and Doggie Girl from my mind. I just needed to figure out which glass on the bar in front of me was the real one. I reached for the one on the right. It seemed the more solid of the two.

My hand went right through it. A mirage. Just like Ivan had been with his music, his thoughtful words and his mind blowing kisses.

Left, then. The only other choice I had. My fingers closed around the thick glass. I licked the salt from the back of my hand, plucked the lime from the rim and lifted the measure of tequila toward my mouth.

"I think maybe you've had enough." Marsha West, my bestie and partner in too many crimes to count, seized my wrist. Her grip only tightened when I turned to glare at her. Both of her. Duplicate gorgeous blue eyed blondes. Each with identical frowns. Lips pursed, I tried to mentally merge them into one person again.

"Just a more couple," I begged them, batting my lashes.

The two heads of Marsha shook their denial.

"Ok, maybe just this one."

"Maybe none. You're cross-eyed drunk. You can't even focus. You're gonna be sick."

"Please, Mars. It's already poured."

She sighed. "Ivan wasn't all that. You didn't even really notice him until I pointed him out to you. He's certainly not worth hurling over. Not after what he did."

I narrowed my gaze. "You're the one who said, and I quote, 'Ivan Carl is the hottest frontman I've ever seen. I want to have his babies.' End quote."

"So I exaggerated. But he does look good in jeans. And he does have that soulful singing voice."

My expression must have turned wistful or pained because she added, "But that was before I found out what a lying, cheating, arrogant prick he is. Now I say good riddance." She let out a weary breath. "Oh alright. Stop giving me that kicked puppy look. Have your one last shot. But don't say I didn't warn you." She released my wrist and twisted in her stool. "Bartender," she called, knocking annoyingly on the wood. Or maybe it was my pounding hangover headache kicking in early. "Pour me a double and fast. Can't you see I need to show some solidarity here?"

Through my alcohol induced haze, I saw a blur of movement and heard the slide of glass on polished wood.

"Here's to getting over Ivan." Marsha clicked her glass with mine, and I drained the double shot in a big gulp that washed down my throat like liquid fire. The room immediately started spinning in a dangerous way.

"Raven?"

"Yeah, Marsha?" I slurred.

"You're looking a little pale."

"I'm always pale."

"Paler than usual." She lifted my fringe of thick bangs feeling my forehead with the back of her hand as if she were checking for fever. "You gonna be ok bestie?" She searched my eyes.

“I’ve got you, haven’t I?”

“Always,” she said gently. “No more tequila, ok?

“Ok.” I would have nodded but I thought better of it. The less motion, the better. In addition to my buzz and blurry vision I was nauseated now. “But do you think maybe Ivan’s right? Am I too uptight? Am I boring?”

“Who cares,” a male chortled. “You get a pass because you’re smokin’ hot.”

“Shut up, Joey.” Marsha shot a glare toward the other end of the bar before she took and squeezed my hand reassuringly. “Don’t listen to that idiot. You’re alright. So you’ve had a couple of bad breaks recently. It’s understandable that you’re a tad OCD now.”

“She’s a walking talking *Rain Man*.”

“Joey, so help me if you don’t stay out of this, I’m not sleeping with you ever again, no matter how drunk I get.”

“Don’t baby her so much.” Joey tossed his bar towel over his broad shoulder and turned away from me and my drama to wait on another customer.

I dropped my head to the bar. The wood didn’t yield but the cool glossy surface soothed my tequila flushed skin. “I’m a mess,” I mumbled from beneath the black curtain of my hair. “I’ll never be right again.”

“You’ll figure it out, honey.” Marsha stroked my hair back from my face. “You’ve had a shock. Give yourself a little time to bounce back.”

“Maybe,” I allowed. “Or maybe I never will. I’m tired of being on the losing side. I’m tired of trying to do the right thing. It just doesn’t matter. I’m never going to be able to undo the mistakes I’ve made.”

“Raven, what happened to Hawk was an accident. It’s not your fault. You need to stop beating yourself up about it.”

I squeezed my eyes shut. A wave of soul crushing loss engulfed the pain of Ivan’s betrayal. My brother’s beloved face flashed inside my mind. The way his eyes crinkled when he smiled. His positive life force. His steadying influence. All gone forever because of how utterly I had failed him.

I had tried to atone. I had reordered my life. I had buried my wilder self alongside him. I had forced myself to go forward telling my reflection in the mirror each morning that everything would be ok somehow. But my tight grip on my life kept slipping. Bad things kept happening. I felt like an overwound spring, all that repressed energy begging to be released. This thing with Ivan was the catalyst for what was about to become a chain reaction.

"Why do guys like Ivan always get a pass?" I slapped my hand on the bar. "Why are women expected to be monogamous while guys get pats on the back for sleeping around?"

"Yeah," Marsha agreed. "Talk to me sister."

I lifted my head and managed to focus on her. The red light on her GoPro video camera flashed in my eyes. It was almost always on. She filmed most of the stupid shit I did. She submitted the more amusing stuff to film contests, even placing in a few of them. She might have settled on a career as a legal transcriptionist because a film degree had been too expensive for her father to afford on his cop's salary, but like me and my music her passion lay elsewhere.

"Keep going," she encouraged, making a rolling gesture with her finger. She wasn't the kind of friend who would talk me out of doing something crazy. She more often than not had a hand in helping me plan it. "Get it all out. You're speaking some major truth."

I obliged her, raging against the injustice of it all, ranting about the double standards for women. I had an outlet for my anger. A balm for my pain. I had lost too much. My mom. My brother. I couldn't get them back. But I could take back my pride. I could avenge the affront to my womanhood. I straightened in my seat. I'd paid my penance this past year. I was done with that. A heavy dose of insanity was what the present shitty reality demanded. "Why do chicks always have to be the ones to take whatever a guy wants to give us? Why can't I point out what looks good to me, crook my finger and get what I want for a change? Why can't I get some cute rock star ass without it having to mean anything? Why can't we fuck 'em then leave 'em? It's time to turn the tables on the guys with guitars who seduce us with their soulful lyrics and twist our hearts with their lying bedroom eyes." I lifted my shot glass and pointed to it for a refill, nodding my thanks to Joey as he sloshed in more golden elixir. "Tonight marks the end of boring Raven." Fresh pain gripped my heart as I recalled Ivan's accusations but I powered through it. "From this day I vow to be uptight no longer. I'm going to 'Kumbaya' and give into my wild side, and you're going to document it. It's time to shake things up. It's time for a new way of doing things. It's time for women to be the ones in control." I held up one finger. "We say when."

"When," she echo, echo, echoed as if she had shouted the word into an empty concert hall.

"We say how." I held up two fingers.

"I vote dirty." She grinned. "Filthy dirty."

I returned her grin, appreciating her enthusiasm but giving up on the finger counting thing. I was too drunk to go any higher anyway. "We'll hit the concert scene in ten different cities and rank the rock stars we fuck along the way for the betterment of all womankind so the sisters who follow us don't waste their time on losers."

Marsha guffawed. She was used to my drunken grandiosity. She put her fist up in the air, and I managed to bump mine to hers to seal the deal on the second try.

"We'll call ourselves the Rock Fuck Club."

Chapter THREE

People say that the burden of grief eases over time.

People are wrong.

A world without my mother or Hawk in it would never be right again.

"It doesn't have to be today, does it?" I posed the question to my father carefully. Though he sat right beside me on the bed in my brother's old room, he might as well have been a thousand miles away, my guilt the chasm that divided us. Devastated by loss, our close knit family of four had been reduced to a tenuous two.

"It's been over a year. It's past time, Raven."

But how could I manage it, the daunting task of sorting through a lifetime of his possessions, deciding in only a couple of hours what to give away and what to keep? At least with my mom and her diabetes we had been somewhat prepared, knowing the possibility existed for an early goodbye. But Hawk had been the pinnacle of health. My rock. The one I had clung to when our mother had passed during my senior year in high school. The solid foundation I had once believed would never be shaken.

"Ok, Dad." I nodded obediently, though the rebellious me that last night's tequila had roused wanted to argue. "Give me some time. I'll take care of it."

"Alright. I'll leave you to it." He patted my knee and rose slowly from the bed. He had aged decades after Hawk's death. "Did you bring enough boxes with you?" he asked as he shuffled toward the door.

"I think so." I glanced at my feet. I had one large one for the things I wanted to take back to my apartment. Several smaller ones awaited those destined for charitable donations.

"Raven." He sighed heavily. "I know it's been hard for you, too, with all of these changes." He paused in the doorway, knocking on the frame softly but melodically. My creative side flickered like a lightbulb about to burn out. At one time I might have been inspired to run for pen and paper to scribble down cathartic notes that captured the moment of melancholy, but no longer. Silence shrouded that part of me. "I'm just glad that you're being more careful and making better choices nowadays."

His departure left me alone in a room as bare as my emotions. No more family photos of Monument Valley vacations or woven Navajo blankets. Those things had already been relocated to the den along with Hawk's Native American flute collection. I rubbed my hand over my heart where the sting of my father's parting words lingered. If I had been more careful, if I had made better choices, Hawk might still be alive. Compliments that felt like allegations banded my chest, making it difficult to breathe. A sparkle near the dresser mirror caught my eye. Standing, I moved to investigate. The silver curb chain my brother had worn around his neck rested beside my mother's turquoise wedding ring. I knew Hawk had planned to offer that band to his intended one day. But that day had never come. All because of me. I scooped up both items, my fingers closing tight around the oblong stone framed by scalloped silver. "Mama," I breathed out, returning to the bed, dropping onto it and squeezing my eyes shut. I could have used one of her hugs right now. My father loved me, deep down I knew that, but she had been the affectionate one. She would have sensed my need. She would have drawn me into her arms. "Give me strength," I prayed.

"The strength of our ancestors." I imagined I could hear the haunting harmonies, the drums and the flutes of her Navajo heritage. The thought comforted me the way she once had. "I can't do this alone. I need help."

Opening my eyes, I unlinked the clasp of the chain, threaded the silver length through my mother's ring and refastened it along with its newly repurposed pendant around my neck. The invisible band around my chest immediately slackened. Before I could offer thanks for answered prayer, my cell rang. Marsha ringtone. "Don't Stop Believin'" the Glee version. We had chosen that one before high school graduation, in more innocent times. Before my mom had gotten sick. Before the accident that had taken my brother.

"Hey, Mars?" My spirit lightened just knowing she was on the other end of the line. We had been friends since childhood. She was always there for me, her love and exuberance giving hope to me in my darkest times.

"Are you sitting down?"

"At the moment, yes. I've been visiting my dad and finally sorting through Hawk's things."

"Oh, honey. I'm sorry. I thought you had convinced your dad to give you more time."

"It's ok. Putting it off wasn't going to make it any easier." And I had the pendant now. Part of Hawk. Part of my mom. The turquoise symbolized happiness, luck and protection to the Navajo. Maybe it would bring me some peace. I settled the phone between my shoulder and my ear and reached for a box, feeling more determined. "But why do I need to be sitting down? That sounds pretty ominous." Could I have done something even more embarrassing than all the impassioned nonsense I had spouted at the bar? Maybe regret was a six letter word, but it took seven to spell t.e.q.u.i.l.a.

"Well, I kinda put your tirade about Ivan and everything else up on YouTube last night before I went to bed."

"And..." I gulped, though it didn't exactly surprise me. She posted often and had a pretty impressive following on her YouTube channel that had grown substantially ever since she had uploaded the video of her flashing her tits down in Cancun during spring break. The line remained tellingly quiet as trepidation crawled up my spine. "Spit it out, Mars. Exactly how many people saw it?"

"It has ten million views and twenty thousand comments."

"What?" I screeched. My brows disappeared beneath my bangs. "You're joking, right?"

"No. I totally am not. Apparently a whole lot of women empathize with you."

"Ok, well, I guess I get that, but..."

"You can't back down now. I won't let you. You won't want to either after you see some of the rock guys who are volunteering to sleep with you."

I let that sink in, and as it did my lips lifted into a slow smile. It felt good to be desired after the blow to my confidence Ivan had dealt me. Even if it was only the internet. "But my job." As an elementary school music teacher, I had signed a code of conduct.

"When word gets back to them I'll get shit canned."

"Raven, stop. For once in your life stop doing what you *think* you should and do what you *want* to do instead."

"Which is?"

"I'm not sure exactly but you seemed to have a pretty good idea last night."

"I was hurt. Angry." I twirled a long lock of my hair around my finger. My father would flip if he had heard me. "What do the comments say?"

"That you're brave. That you should go for it. That it's about damn time."

I squeezed my eyes shut. The video that flashed onto the back of my eyelids was of Ivan with his bare ass and hips pumping while I stood there unable to feel anything but the pain of his betrayal.

Well, I wasn't going to be helpless any longer.

"We stick with the original plan." So we had some internet interest. Maybe it would wane. But I was committed to my path. Determined to be the opposite of boring. Dedicated to shake up the status quo. To hell with the risk.

Chapter FOUR

In the tiny living room of my efficiency apartment, Marsha and I sat cross legged on the carpet with a map of the United States spread out in front of us. "I can't see any way around it." She tipped her bottle of Shiner to her lips, took a long pull, then eyed the route we had highlighted. "We'll have to do some backtracking." She returned her beer to the coaster on my glass coffee table.

"But we should be able to do it all in two weeks."

"You mean do them all." Marsha grinned.

"Ha-ha!" I almost snorted my beer through my nose. I wasn't as drunk as the night before, but I was on my third bottle of Shiner. Even her corny comments seemed funny.

"Which guys will make the final cut with you?" She waggled a brow.

I groaned. "A little cavalier with the Pink Floyd reference, don't you think?"

"Good point." She nodded, assuming a somber visage. "No casual references to the icons of rock. Total respect and reverence at all times." She narrowed her gaze. "Speaking of icons, I noticed you eyeing the Google images of a certain someone who'll be here in Dallas when we kick off of our little adventure."

"Nothing little about Rayne Michaels." Six feet four inches to be exact. Sandy blonde hair. Green eyes. Talented as hell, on stage and in the bedroom, apparently. A prime choice to get over Ivan if I was bold enough to pursue him and lucky enough for the headliner to consent to being my fuck of the night. "The reports are so consistently glowing about him that I wonder…" I trailed off, losing my train of thought as I imagined being pushed up against the wall and fucked senseless by Rayne during the length of time it took his best friend and lead guitarist to perform a scintillating solo. My cheeks heated as I recalled the explicit online recounting of that very scenario. I made a mental note to reread it again later. "But I wouldn't have the nerve to be in the same room with him, let alone proposition him."

Marsha's private message notification on her cell sounded again. They had been pinging nonstop like raindrops on a tin roof since we'd commenced our planning a couple of beers ago. Her brow furrowed as she looked at the screen.

"Who is it?" I asked.

"You don't want to know." Her expression softened when her eyes met mine.

"Ivan?" My stomach plummeted.

She nodded.

"Ignore him," I whispered roughly, emotion swamping me as I remembered how supportive he had been after Hawk died. "I've got nothing left to say. It's over between us." I found the words slightly easier to speak today. At least saying them didn't slice as deeply. Dead silence greeted my admonition. I lifted my head to find her watching me.

"You sure?" she asked gently. I think she knew if we weren't here doing this, I would probably be in my bed curled into a ball with my face buried in his pillow.

"Absolutely." The lie was transparent to anyone who knew me as well as she did.

"So…Rayne Michaels from Sundown." She gave me a pass on the fib. "On the list? Yes or no."

"Yes." I held her gaze. I had fantasized about the guy plenty. He was one of the sexiest front men around. Older sure, but I think every woman had a mini orgasm when he sang 'Second Chances'. We all dreamed we could be the one to heal the heart his ex-wife had broken. "If you'll help me not look like an ass when I meet him." I had come this far. I couldn't back down now.

"Deal." She tapped a finger to her chin. "I'll try for the lead guitarist. He should be easier to snag than Rayne, though I'm sure there will be lots of competition for both of them. I don't think wearing corsets and leather minis will be good enough to get us backstage. Do you have a strategy?"

I didn't have much of one. I hadn't needed one for Ivan. He'd seen me in the audience and sent a roadie to fetch me. "I'm thinking of wearing my ice blue dress."

"That's a good one. Vintage flapper design. Spaghetti straps. Low décolletage. Shows just enough boob. The short hemline makes your legs look a million miles long." She tapped her lips. "You need to wear my Camuto heels. It'll be hard to stand in the pit for five hours through all the other acts, but when he spots you in those stilettos he's gonna imagine fucking you with them on."

"I hope you're right. If he even notices me. Hopefully I can score a backstage pass. He doesn't seem to give out many of them."

"Hold up." She made her hands into an NFL timeout signal. She'd been spending too much time with her dad and two older brothers who loved sports, especially the Dallas Cowboys. "Too much hoping. That's the old way of doing things. We're turning the tables, remember? We're in charge now. Make him interested. Make him come to you. And I have a spectacular idea how you can make that happen."

Chapter FIVE

In our hotel room at the Omni, I rolled up my silk stocking and fastened it to the garter. Marsha had gone down the hall to get ice. We were having whisky on the rocks when she returned. She thought I needed some liquid courage before we ubered to the outdoor concert venue in nearby Fair Park. She was right. I actually contemplated chugging it straight from the bottle like Slash. Her backstage scheme was brilliant, but just thinking about it had me quaking in my brand new crystal encrusted lace demi bra and borrowed stilettos.

A door creaked but not the one in front of me that Marsha had used to exit our room. My heart leapt to my throat remembering the connecting door behind me. Gasping as a blast of chilled air billowed out my silk robe, I whirled around. Unfortunately, I lost my balance and pitched forward. On my way down, I caught a glimpse of a compelling man standing within the doorframe of the adjoining room. Landing on my hands and knees on the plush carpet, I lifted my head, dragging my eyes from the masculine feet before me, then up and up and up over impossibly long legs to an unhooked belt and half unbuttoned jeans. I would have lingered longer at the dark happy trail the low slung denim revealed, but the hot fantasy of the body above it beckoned. Wondering whether the view could possibly get any better than that sculpted fantasyland, I rocked back on my heels and craned my neck to discover that yes indeed it could...if you liked ridiculously handsome men with tousled black hair and dreamy blue eyes. He crossed his arms and leaned backward against the doorframe, a half smile playing on his full lips as I continued to stare at him from my subservient position. It finally dawned that I should be frightened rather than intrigued to be alone in my hotel room with a total stranger, no matter how breathtakingly gorgeous he was.

"Who are you?" I stood, feeling a little stunned as his glacier blue eyes melded with mine, but I lifted my chin. "And how..."

"What the hell?" Marsha exclaimed. The door to the outer hallway slamming into the wall, she stomped directly to my side in her thigh high black velvet boots and lifted the ice bucket above her shoulder as if she might throw it at the stranger if need be.

"I'm ok. It's ok." My friend's more appropriate response to the intruder helped me regain my equilibrium. I pulled the edges of my robe together suddenly aware of every single inch of skin my lingerie revealed. Another glance at the sexy stranger revealed that he was aware of them too. His eyes darkened as they trailed over me.

"I'm sorry, Angel. I was looking for someone else." His deep voice and his British accent sent my senses into another tailspin. "Apparently, she's not here. Not that I'm complaining." He gave me a slow lazy smile. His eyes danced beneath the angled bangs that kissed them. He held my gaze seeming reluctant to relinquish it. "My apologies...to both of you."

"Lucky," a woman called from the other room.

He turned to glance over his shoulder giving me a glimpse of an exquisite tattoo. A Chinese dragon. Burnished gold and brilliant red, it started at his neck just under his ear, coiled artistically over one of his shoulders and spanned the width of his entire back, the flexing of his muscles animating the design.

"Give me a moment, Sky, my dearest." Lucky shifted his attention back to me, hooking his ringed thumbs into the front pockets of his jeans and gliding his gaze over me another time. Even though I had drawn the lapels of my robe together, my nipples tightened to points beneath his leisurely regard. A smug smile spread across his face. Arrogant bastard. He knew what he was doing to me with a look like that, and he had a woman in the other room. Yet here he lingered giving me a come-to-my-bed-I-promise-to-make-it-worth-your-while smile.

Bristling and uncomfortable with him making me feel things I didn't want to feel, I determined to ignore my body's reaction to him. I knew bad news when I saw it, and I was done with guys like him thinking they could gain the upper hand with me. "Get out of my room." My voice had a breathy quality to it that revealed too much.

"Why? Do you fancy coming to mine instead?"

"No, of course not," I huffed. "I just want you to leave."

"Is that what you truly desire, Angel?" Smile deepening, he cocked his head to the side.

"Yes." I planted my hands on my hips. "Don't make me call security."

"I'm sorry. I didn't catch your name." He ignored my threat. It didn't seem to faze him. "Shall I use the same door next time?" He arched a raven hued brow. "When you change your mind, that is?"

"It will be locked."

"Perhaps I'll knock then." He laughed, low and throaty. The sound of his amusement did crazy jumbly things to the inside of my chest.

"Who's this?" A pretty brunette poked her head through the connecting doorway. Her eyes widened when she saw me. My expression of surprise mirrored hers but for a different reason. Though fully dressed in jeans and a tee, she was young, at least two or three years younger than I was. She might not have been legal age, more evidence of the type of guy I was dealing with if I needed any extra incentive to get rid of him.

"Get out." I gestured to his room and moved to close the door on both him and his companion.

"Fine, Angel. I'll go." He chuckled as he walked backward. "Cheers and what not for now."

My fingers curling tightly around the cold metal handle, I slammed the door closed as soon as he was through it. I clicked the lock and exhaled a caged breath.

"I repeat, what...I mean who the hell was that?"

"I don't know." If not for Mars as my witness and the hyper-masculine scent of mandarin and rum that hung in the air, I might have been able to convince myself that I had conjured Lucky out of a men's fragrance insert in the UK edition of GQ magazine.

She let out a disbelieving breath though her nose. "I leave for two seconds to get ice and you already have a guy on the hook. A sexy English one."

"I didn't..." I swallowed to moisten my dry throat. "It wasn't like that."

"It was exactly like that." She put her hands on her hips and shook her head. "While you were in here playing let me drop to my knees and be your centerfold fantasy with our next door neighbor, I received a very interesting call from a rep at the Fringe. The radio station got wind of what we're doing. They're giving us VIP access with permission to film and everything. The only difficulty for us now is going to be narrowing down your list of potential fuck buddies once we get into the after-party."

About the Author

MICHELLE MANKIN is the *New York Times* bestselling author of over 40 romance novels.

Romance that rocks the heart

BRUTAL STRENGTH series:

Love Evolution
Love Revolution
Love Resolution
Love Rock'ollection Box Set

TEMPEST series (also- available in audio):

SOUTHSIDE HIGH
Irresistible Refrain
Enticing Interlude
Captivating Bridge
Relentless Rhythm
Tempting Tempo
Scandalous Beat
The Tempest World Box Set, books 1-7

The MAGIC series (also available in audio):

Strange Magic
Dream Magic
Twisted Magic

ROCK STARS, SURF AND SECOND CHANCES DIRT DOGS ROCKSTAR series (also available in audio):

Outside
Riptide
Oceanside

High Tide
Island Side
The Complete Rock Stars Surf and Second Chances Dirt Dogs
Rockstar Series, Books 1-5
STORM is a standalone spin-off from this series.

FINDING ME series (also available in audio):
Find Me
Remember Me
Keep Me

ROCK F*CK CLUB Girls Ranking the Rock Stars series (also available in audio):
ROCK F*CK CLUB, Girls Ranking the Rock Stars, Book 1
ROCK F*CK CLUB, Girls Ranking the Rock Stars, Book 2
ROCK F*CK CLUB, Girls Ranking the Rock Stars, Book 3
ROCK F*CK CLUB, Girls Ranking the Rock Stars, Book 4
ROCK F*CK CLUB, Girls Ranking the Rock Stars, Book 5
ROCK F*CK CLUB BOX SET, Books 1-5
ROCK F*CK CLUB, Girls Ranking the Rock Stars, Book 6
In His Eyes is a standalone spin-off from the RFC.

Once Upon A Rock Star:
The Right Man
The Right Wish
The Right Wrong
The Right Song

No Quarter
Hot Summer School Night
Breaking Her Bad

Addy's Rollercoaster Romance
Getting it Wrong
Getting it Right

Made in the USA
Monee, IL
23 March 2024

55003004R00164